I0583782

DAMNED IF YOU

DON'T

Hairann

A NineStar Press Publication

www.ninestarpress.com

Damned If You Don't

Copyright © 2020 by Hairann
Cover Art by Natasha Snow Copyright © 2020

Printed in the USA

Print ISBN: 978-1-64890-107-2

First Edition, October, 2020

Also available in eBook, ISBN: 978-1-64890-106-5

WARNING:
This book contains sexually explicit content, which may only be suitable for mature readers, depictions of war, minor gore, and the death of prominent characters.

All Erabus ever wanted was to stay out of his brother's way, to let him become king after their father and spend his life hunting in the forest outside the kingdom. That all changes when he uncovers the plot to kill his father. Erabus will do whatever it takes to save him, even forming an alliance with a strange ally named Xicuz—an incredibly gorgeous satyr he met in the forest.

If things weren't complicated enough, Erabus soon finds himself tangled up in a deal with a devil that puts the lives of the people closest to him in danger. He soon learns, sometimes you have to fight fire with fire and makes a deal of his own—one that will save the love of his life, but forfeit half of his own to do so. Xicuz accepts the fate that they are dealt, to live out their lives side by side, never being able to hold the other again—anything was worth the sacrifice if it meant that Erabus would live. But even cut off from his own clan, he could never turn his back on them. When he uncovers the plot to attack them, he will do whatever it takes to stop the human prince and save his people.

Damned If You Don't *is dedicated to anyone still searching for their soulmate. Have faith that they are out there somewhere, and you will find them one day. Sometimes, you'll find them in the most unexpected of places.*

Chapter One

The sun only just began to rise as Erabus made his way through the thick forest, his footfalls inaudible on the damp leaf-carpeted ground. He held his bow with an arrow notched and ready to fire as he navigated around one cluster of trees and then another. The sounds from the other hunters faded into the distance. They made far more noise than they should if they expected to catch anything.

Putting the far less skilled hunters from his mind, he paused to sniff the fresh forest air, filling his nose with the strong scents of pine and moss. He smiled at how the scents calmed him and continued in search of any deer that might have passed through the area recently. Though if the others continued to rustle around and break branches, he doubted they would remain in the vicinity for long. Erabus tuned them out once more as he crouched to the ground and removed debris from an indention in the dirt.

He traced the imperfect print with the pad of his index finger. *Deer or perhaps a goat down from the mountain.* The print didn't cause a deep enough indent to tell for sure which. The only thing he was confident about was the freshness of the print. With any luck, the animal would still be nearby, and Erabus was determined to catch it before the others could alert it to their presence. Careful to walk on the pads of his feet to reduce what little noise he made, he followed the prints farther into the forest until he heard the rustling of leaves coming from the other side of a cluster of trees that grew so close together he couldn't see through them.

He parted the branches as much as he dared, waiting only long enough to spot the horns before carefully releasing the branch and taking aim through the trees. Though his target wasn't visible from his current position, he knew roughly where the deer stood and took aim to the right and down a bit from where its horns should end. He inhaled as he pulled the string taut and released the arrow at the same time as his breath. The arrow pierced the air with an audible *whoosh*.

The gentle *thud* of the arrow striking wood came only a moment before a voice called out in alarm, startling Erabus. He barely caught his bow as he dropped it. *Had another hunter made it out farther than I realized?* But he'd seen the horns. Confused, he shouldered his bow to investigate when a voice called out, "Watch what you are doing!"

"I'm so sorry, sir. I swear I saw horns," Erabus insisted as he fell through the thicket. He took a moment to right himself before turning his eyes on the man he came inches from shooting. Only it wasn't a man standing before him. A foot away from where his arrow struck the tree stood a creature with the body and face of a man but the legs, hooves, tail, and ears of a goat. Most importantly, the horns of one too.

Staring at him in shock, Erabus gave him another once-over, noticing for the first time the loincloth that covered his lower bits from his view. He barely managed to squeak out a stuttered, "You're...you're a..." before snapping his lips closed once more when he realized his mind refused to supply him with the words he searched for.

The being before him smirked before offering in a deep, warm voice, "The word you are looking for is a satyr. It's a good thing you are as bad a shot as you are a speaker." Erabus glanced from the satyr to where the arrow stood embedded in the tree behind him. He realized just how wrong he was. It was true his arrow missed him, but he had not been the target.

"Look again, sir, my aim was true," Erabus said, his confidence returning. "If you were a deer, as I first thought, the arrow would have struck between your shoulder blades." He crossed his arms and gave him a smug look.

The satyr's silver eyes widened as he looked at the arrow. "It is a good thing I am not an animal then. Though how you ever confused these beauts with deer antlers, I will never know."

Erabus looked at the satyr's horns once more. The satyr was right.

Where a deer's antlers would have been large and branched out in every direction, he had two single arches on either side of his forehead, larger and thicker than a mountain goat's. There was no excuse for his mistake—he should have looked more carefully before he shot. However, he wasn't willing to admit it.

"You should be careful, sir. You shouldn't be wandering around in the human hunting area." It wasn't right to blame his mistake on his near victim, but in his embarrassment, Erabus couldn't stand the thought of shouldering all the blame himself.

"Actually, *sir*," the satyr countered, his sir sounding an octave higher than the rest, "you have crossed over into the land designated for the satyrs when our kings met ten years ago. It is you that should be careful."

It took him a moment to compose himself. Was the satyr threatening him? He doubted it but couldn't be sure. Erabus opened his mouth to insist he would have known if they crossed the border onto their land, but his words caught in his throat at the sound of the hunters' voices coming from the other side of the trees. Some bragged about the game they caught others complaining about, being unlucky in their hunt.

One called out for him, no doubt wanting his help to carry back their game as opposed to being worried about his absence. The hunters would soon overtake them, and they would not react well to finding a satyr on "their" land.

Erabus slapped a hand over the satyr's mouth and pushed him back against a tree, hiding the two of them in the shadows. He pressed his lips close to the satyr's pointed goat-like ear that twitched as Erabus's breath tickled it with each whispered word. "Do not make a sound unless you want the hunters to find you." Erabus glanced over his shoulder, barely able to make out the hunters as they made their way passed their hiding spot.

Erabus sighed in relief once the last of them disappeared back into the forest, heading toward home. He waited another moment to be sure before he turned back to the satyr and found his face an inch or two from his own. Erabus swallowed hard when he realized how close his lips were to his own, with only his hand separating them.

Before he could find the words to assure him it was safe now, something hot and wet dragged across his palm. He jumped back in shock. "You licked my hand!" he accused in disbelief, staring down at the moist spot on his palm.

The satyr smirked. "Would you prefer I licked something else instead?" He licked his lips and looked Erabus up and down.

Was he serious? Erabus began a stuttered reply, but he was saved from having to give an actual answer by a horn blowing in the distance.

The satyr sighed in disappointment before glancing off in the direction of the horn. "Alas, I shall not be able to hear your answer this time, sir." He gave him a slight yet exaggerated bow before smirking at him again. "Next time then."

Erabus didn't know if he said it as a parting or in reference to when he would be getting the answer from him. Before Erabus could respond, the satyr disappeared into the forest.

*

Xicuz sighed in disappointment as he made his way back toward his own village. He took his time. The sounding of the horn meant the king of the satyrs had called his people back for a reason. He already knew the cause, and he had no desire to get there quickly. No doubt others informed the king of the human trespassers, as they did each time they crossed the border from human to satyr land.

Only this time his king had decided to do something about it. "About time," he grumbled before hearing the horn go off again. Sighing once more, this time in annoyance, Xicuz picked up his pace and hurried along back to the village.

He joined the crowd gathered in the village square. He caught sight of his two closest confidants and nodded to them in greeting before turning his attention toward his king. As the king approached, every satyr took a knee as a show of respect. The king, though getting on in age, still stood as tall as he had the day he emerged victorious in their last royal combat.

That had been twenty years ago. Xicuz barely remembered it as he had only been five or six at the time, but even now he could still picture the way the tall, proud man looked when they placed the bear fur over his shoulders and crowned his head with the circlet of teeth and bone that every king of the satyrs before him had borne. Somehow, even after all these years, the king still looked as impossibly tall as he had when Xicuz saw him for the first time with the eyes of a child.

Running his fingers through his long, curly beard with one hand, the king gestured with his other hand for one of the satyrs to step forward. Xicuz recognized his confident Qom. The two of them, along with Xaaxex, spent their entire childhoods together. They had hunted their first deer together and slept under the stars every night together. They had even sought their first taste of a woman together.

She had been willing, but Xicuz had not. The only thing the three of them didn't have in common was their attraction to women. When he admitted his lack of attraction to women, they asked if he wanted them to find him a man that night. The human men had never hidden their disgust for their women bedding the satyrs, so he doubted any of them would have been willing to lie with him.

Or maybe that wasn't entirely true. Xicuz smiled to himself as he thought of his most recent human encounter.

"King Zhul," Qom greeted with a bow of his head before addressing the crowd. "The humans were hunting in our part of the forest again today. They are poaching all our game."

The crowd groaned and nodded their heads in agreement with his complaints.

Xaaxex added, "With as close as they were today, it will not be long before they invade our village if they are left unchecked."

"Today their voices could be heard from within Ebrein. They have allowed themselves to become too bold," Qom said. *So that is why the king was making a move now.* It was one thing to hunt the animals in the area designated for them, another thing entirely to dare to come so close to their village.

Where their elderly and children resided. Where the human women who chose to live with them instead of their own village lived. Where their king was. Coming that close could be seen as an act of war, though the humans' arrogance did not surprise him in the least. Ten years ago, when the satyr and human kings sat down to hammer out the deal, more than a few humans argued with their own king that they were entitled to more for merely being human.

That hadn't sat well with the satyrs who argued that humans were lesser beings and thus deserved less land. Though they had never been allies before, that was the first time Xicuz expected them to go to war with each other. Instead, both kings ordered their own to shut up and agreed to meet again in a few days with only two advisors and five guards each.

Xicuz didn't attend that meeting, but he was under the impression that the treaty had been a success. Though, judging by their continued behavior, the humans didn't agree. So much so they seemed unwilling to teach their young, like the man he met earlier, where the actual border lie. Instead, he legitimately thought he stood on human land.

He had been worried about Xicuz's safety. Such a strange human, yet Xicuz's attraction for him was evident, even if the young man remained blissfully unaware. He could not see Xicuz's manhood rising to greet him from beneath his loincloth.

He smiled at the memory as he tugged on the curly hairs of his beard before coming back to the present. "They are still roaring with jealousy after many of their women have chosen to come to us!" another satyr called out.

"Not that I can blame them, for I would be just as grumpy if I had such a tiny, unsatisfying stick between my thighs as they do. It's a wonder their women can even feel them!"

They met his words with laughter and shouts of agreement even though Xicuz doubted any of them had the slightest idea what a human's weapon looked like.

At that thought, he wondered what his own target's might resemble. Would it be as tiny as they claimed or large and thick like his own?

The king raised his hands, and a hush fell over the gathered satyrs.

"It is time then to meet with the humans once more and remind them what land belongs to who."

The crowd roared in agreement until he raised his hands to calm them once more. "Xicuz, step forward," his king called out, and he did without hesitation.

"Take two others and head to the human village and seek an audience with King Tribion. Tell him of my demand to meet where we have met before."

Xicuz nodded in agreement. He waved his hand at his two confidants even as his thoughts turned inward. Perhaps he would get an answer from his human yet.

As the crowd dispersed, Qom and Xaaxex made their way over toward him. "And what are you smiling about?" Qom teased.

He didn't want to tell them about his human yet, so instead he said, "I wonder if there would be any more defectors after this meeting."

The two of them howled with laughter, though whether it was at the thought of having more women to warm their beds or simply at the humans losing face again, he wasn't certain.

"Anyone in particular you have your eye on this time?" Xaaxex asked, his eyes dancing with mischief.

Xicuz threw a quick "maybe" over his shoulder before making his way out of the village as the two of them howled with laughter once more. He smirked. With the two of them by his side, his human didn't stand a chance.

*

Once Erabus arrived back in the village, he approached the leader of the hunt to speak with him once he while away from the others.

"Prince Jydral," he called out.

The prince's step halted for a moment, but he continued as though he had not heard him.

Erabus rolled his eyes—this wasn't the first time Jydral had ignored him. He picked up his pace to meet Jydral's larger strides. "By chance," he began as he fell in step beside him, "might we have strayed into the satyrs' territory? It felt, to me at least, as though we might have gone in too deeply during the hunt."

Though he chose his words wisely, careful not to sound as though he blamed him for the misstep, Jydral rounded on him with a far angrier expression than Erabus had expected. He practically bit off his head as he declared, "Animals cannot own land, Erabus. All the forest rightfully belongs to man and when I am king, I will see to it that all those animals are hunted down and wiped out before their perversion can corrupt anyone else!"

Erabus was taken aback by the threat. *Is he still bitter that his betrothed had run off with the satyrs?* Surely, he wouldn't let his personal feelings doom the peace between their peoples. That would be a threat not only to the satyrs' village of Ebrein but also to the human settlement, Edith.

Erabus prayed the king would live forever, preventing Jydral from ever ruling over anything more than his own anger and bitterness.

A cane clacked on the wooden floor of the hallway startling Erabus from his thoughts. The king strode toward them, two guards flanking him on each side.

Erabus knelt before the king. Jydral barely even tipped his head in acknowledgment of his presence. "Father," Jydral mumbled in lieu of an actual greeting.

Jydral's disrespect made Erabus's blood boil. He gritted his teeth to prevent from giving him the reprimand he deserved. Instead, he bowed his head and greeted the king. "Good day, my king. May this day bring you good health and fortune."

King Tribion instructed him to rise with a wave. He took Erabus's hand with a smile and led him down the long hallway toward the throne room; no doubt on his way to hear the grievances of his people as he did many times throughout the day. Jydral followed them.

"Tell me my child, is it not strange to refer to your own father as 'my king'? Would you not wish to call me father as Jydral does?" the king asked, and Erabus couldn't help but smile at his question. It was not the first, and probably not the last time he asked such a thing, though his answer always remained the same.

"I'm showing respect to those who have long since earned it, and that not strange, my king." Erabus returned the gentle squeeze his father gave his hand.

"How did the hunt fare?"

"Well enough," Erabus said. "But there is something you should know—"

"Do not bore my father with your failure," Jydral interrupted.

Erabus held his tongue. Better to speak with the king when his brother wasn't around to place the blame on him.

"As for me, only I managed to kill a deer," Jydral bragged.

Jydral's boasting didn't faze him.

While he was unable to kill an animal, his encounter with the satyr far outweighed the thrill of any hunt. The image of the satyr flashed through his mind—his back pressed against the tree, his own lips an inch away from Erabus's, his deep silver eyes locked with his. Erabus licked his dry lips.

No doubt he would never meet him again, which disappointed him more than he thought it would, but he'd always have the memory of the strange creature he met in the forest who had licked his hand. If Erabus didn't know any better, he could have sworn he even flirted with him. That short, confusing, enticing, strange encounter was far more action than he had ever seen in his twenty-three-years and probably more than he would ever see again.

*

It felt strange to Xicuz to leave the forest and approach the human village, even before the humans caught sight of him. Going somewhere you knew you would not be welcome was not a pleasant feeling, to say the least, and the fear and disgust in their eyes once they spotted him made his stomach turn. Deep within his mind, a voice cried out for him to turn back, that he would find nothing but hatred and violence there, but he pushed it down with a quick reminder that his king had ordered him there.

Welcome or not, he had a job to do, and he refused to go all the way back through the forest with his tail between his legs and explain to his king he turned back in fear before ever setting foot in the village. Drawing in a deep breath and regretting it a moment later when the overwhelming smells of the humans assaulted his nose, Xicuz crossed the threshold into the village with his head held high.

As soon as the humans saw them, shouts rang out for people to arm themselves. Xicuz raised an eyebrow at their fearful response. With their hands empty and nothing more than a loincloth to cover themselves, it should have been rather obvious they were in fact not armed.

"Lower your weapons! The satyrs are unarmed!" a voice of authority called out. His strong, confident tone caused a small shiver of excitement to course through him. Was that his human?

Before he had the chance to confirm his assumption to be correct, Qom called out, "The only weapon we need is the one between our thighs!" He turned his hungry eyes toward a beautiful woman as he wagged his eyebrows at her suggestively. Xicuz found the entire encounter comical, but the woman apparently didn't agree as she blushed prettily before glancing away when she could no longer meet his heated gaze.

The man who spoke before, who Xicuz couldn't see due to the crowd that gathered at their arrival, stepped forward to block Qom's view of the woman. "What is it you want, sirs?" His tone was hard, but not hostile.

Xicuz took in the sight of the man before him. It was his human after all.

His long, reddish hair draped over his shoulder in a single braid, though a few wisps had come undone to curl around the rest of it. His green eyes shone brightly, growing larger upon recognizing Xicuz. His buckskin pants and open vest were not unlike many of the other men who stood nearby, yet he opted to go shirtless while the others wore clothing underneath.

Xicuz licked his lips as his eyes trailed up his body, coming to rest on his rich, green eyes. It seemed his luck had changed. Not only was he able to meet the man from the forest again, but he was clearly someone with authority. Which meant his trip there might not be as pointless as he worried it would be. "We are here to speak to your king about your hunting parties breaking the treaty and hunting on our land."

*

Erabus nodded to the satyr who spoke, the same he'd met in the forest earlier that day. He could have told his brother this would happen, if only he listened. "I expected it might come to this," he admitted before glancing at each of the satyrs in turn, attempting to determine if they would prove to be a threat to the king. "I can bring you to

King Tribion for an audience. However, I will need to search you and bind your hands beforehand. I must ensure the king's safety above all else."

Though he spoke the truth, Erabus also wanted to test if they could be trusted. If they had a problem with either, they were more likely to be there to cause problems, perhaps even attack the king. Two of the satyrs complained, unwilling to comply. Before he could turn them away, the third satyr spoke.

"We consent to your search, sir," he said, using the same mocking tone as he had in the forest, before turning to his own people. "If we came for any nefarious reasons, they would have never seen us coming." The two other satyrs laughed, with one making some joke about "always see them coming", but Erabus missed most of it over the comedian's own laughter.

Erabus inclined his head in appreciation to him. He approached the quietest of the three and searched for any weapon, though he couldn't for the life of him figure out where they might have hidden one. He made sure to tap the inside of his thighs without any accidental slips. After he finished his search, he called out for rope and gently, but securely tied his hands in front of him.

"I hope it is not too tight," Erabus said, not wanting to cause discomfort to their guests even if he needed to restrain them.

In response, the satyr snapped his teeth at him, causing Erabus to jump back in surprise and the other satyrs to laugh at his expense. He shook his head at their strange behavior and moved over to the satyr who fancied himself a comedian. He patted him down before tying his hands as he had with the first.

"I prefer when your women tie me up," the satyr joked, or at least Erabus thought he was joking, as he turned his eyes back to the same woman he spoke to before. Erabus rolled his eyes and turned toward the third and final satyr as he made his way over to where he stood apart from the other two. While he remained proper and professional with the first two searches, images and thoughts appeared in his mind the moment he lay his hands on the satyr from the forest.

He could see himself running his fingers down the hard muscles that covered his arms and chest, reaching his hands under his loincloth... Realizing where his thoughts were turning, and the reaction in his body that they were creating, Erabus shook his head to clear the images before turning his full attention back to the satyr before him. Erabus bit the inside of his cheek to ensure he kept himself in line as he ran his fingers over the satyr's hips and waist to check for any hidden weapons.

As he searched, making sure not to do anything that might be inappropriate or unnecessary touching, the satyr leaned close to his ear, pressing Erabus's face against the taller male's chest. "Enjoy the feel of my body?" he asked, and for a moment Erabus worried his attraction made itself known by raising the front of his pants. Fortunately, he was not hard enough yet for that to have been the case.

He continued his search only to be interrupted once more when the satyr whispered, "The touch of your fingers on my heated skin is causing me to become hard."

Erabus froze midexamination with his hands on the satyr's inner thighs having almost completed his search. Erabus was at a loss for words. He had not expected this to happen when he climbed out of bed that morning.

Not even after their encounter in the forest.

"I am armed, you know. My weapon truly is beneath my loincloth. You should probably check with your hands to make sure it is safe," the satyr teased as he ran his tongue over his lips that were so close to Erabus's ear he swore he felt the moist appendage on his skin. Shivering at the thought of his licking him again, more intimately this time, or perhaps at the feel of his hot breath fanning over his ear, he could only stare at him in stunned silence for a moment before finally taking a step backward.

Erabus held his heated gaze. "I thought satyrs were only interested in women."

The satyr smirked at him in silence for a moment, and he worried he had only been teasing him. The thought of there being another like himself, when he had been alone for so long, gave him a glimmer of hope he'd long since given up on. If he took that hope away now, Erabus couldn't take it.

"I'm not like most satyrs," he admitted with a flirtatious smile, but anything either of them would have added to his words was forgotten when his brother arrived.

"What do you think you're doing?" Jydral demanded.

Erabus gave the satyr a soft smile. Perhaps they could continue their conversation later. He tied the satyr's hands in place, certain he felt his finger caress his own hand as he pulled away.

"I am taking them to see the king," Erabus explained as he turned back to find Jydral blocking the path to the door that would lead them to the throne room. It wasn't the only way to get to his father, but it was the easiest from their location. Not about to let his behavior intimidate him, he moved to walk past him only to have him step even more into his way.

"I forbid you from bringing those animals anywhere near my father," Jydral spat at him, leaving out the fact that they shared the same father, but as it wasn't the first time Jydral put himself above Erabus, he decided to let his brother's slight go for now. There were far more important things to deal with than to be sucked into his petty argument.

"When you are king, Prince Jydral, you can make demands such as this, but until then, I have only to answer to the actual king." Erabus brushed past him, gently pulling the ropes behind him. As he would either have to move or get run over by the three satyrs, his brother wisely stepped aside, though this would not be the last he heard about it.

Erabus stopped just before he would have passed his brother. "If you had not led us across the border today, this would never have been necessary," he said before continuing on into the dimly lit hallway he walked his father down only an hour or so before.

Chapter Two

As Xicuz followed along behind the human who led them to meet his king, he watched the strange exchange between the two men. Why did his human stand up for them against someone who obviously outranked him? Had he put himself in danger for their sake, and if so, why?

As much as Xicuz liked the idea he might be the reason for his behavior, he had seen enough human interactions to know their attraction for others was never as fast, or as strong, as a satyr's. He knew in the instant they met this man was someone who he would want beside him, though whether in his bed or in his life, only time and getting to know him would tell. However, he knew the same could not be said about his human.

Humans did not possess the more animalistic instincts his people were born with and would not connect so strongly upon their first meeting as a satyr would. But that knowledge made his behavior even more confusing for Xicuz. Whatever the cause, it would have to wait to be discovered, as there were far more pressing matters for him to attend to.

His arms were yanked by a tug on the rope as he watched this Prince Jydral carefully. They walked past, not in the least surprised when he spat at their feet once they were in range. Seeing Xaaxex had not taken the barbaric behavior well and had started to rise up on his haunches, a clear sign he planned to retaliate against the prince, Xicuz pulled on his tail to stop him in his tracks. As much as he hated to injure him for such an offense, he could reach nothing else with his hands bound as they were.

The yelp that resulted caused Xicuz to clench his teeth, silently promising to make it up to him later. "Do not give them a reason, Xaaxex. We are unarmed and still have our job to do," he whispered, his voice stern as he stroked his tail in an attempt to take away the sting. Either unaware or ignoring what went on behind him, his human guided them through a large doorway that led them into a sizable hallway with a strange wooden floor.

With wood both above their heads and below their feet, not to mention on both sides of them, the satyrs felt boxed in, none more so than Xicuz himself. He needed the open air, space to stretch his legs, and to run as fast as his legs could carry him. He needed the clear sky above him and the coolness of the dirt on his hooves. The air smelled of burnt wood and smoke. He scrunched his nose at the strange, overpowering scent.

"A lot of good this task of ours will do in the long run," Qom whispered. "If that man, and I use the term loosely as he must have been compensating for something with all that posturing, is to be the next king of the humans, he will undo everything we accomplish today and in the past." He said the last part loud enough that their host overheard.

Though his human pretended to not be listening, Xicuz knew if he were a satyr, his ears would have been twitching. Qom was right—how long would they have before that nightmare became their reality? But as the current king was the one he came to speak with today, he turned his attention back to his human as he led them through another doorway, this one open, and into an enormous room far bigger than anything he ever seen before.

The walls seemed to go on forever in each direction. Guards stood at attention along them, their hands resting on the hilt of the swords strapped at their waists. From the overwhelming number of wardens, and the odd wooden armor that covered their chest and hips, Xicuz barely saw any of the actual walls behind them. It unnerved him to be surrounded by so many armed men when he and his confidants were unarmed. Even more than that, he wondered what threat this king felt he faced in his daily life that required this many guards for what seemed to be a normal, everyday gathering.

Judging by the groups of people either speaking with the king, or waiting their turn on the sidelines, Xicuz figured the king listened to his peoples' grievances as Zhul often did. Only when his own king spoke with his people, he never had a single guard beside him unless they were there to air their own complaints. In fact, only his advisor, who kept track of each complaint and how he resolved them, ever helped him at all during these times.

Did King Tribion fear his own people, or did he expect an attack by outside forces at every waking moment? How sad an existence it must have been to constantly live in a state of panic.

"When this group is finished, we will walk down through the middle of the hall. Make no movements that might be perceived as a threat," their host instructed. "Keep silent unless called upon by the king to speak. Bow before the king and refer to him as 'Your Majesty' since I doubt you would want to call him 'my king'." As Xicuz nodded in agreement, Xaaxex protested at having to bow to a king not their own.

"We would expect no less respect if a human visited King Zhul. Show your respect, Xaaxex, not your teeth," Xicuz warned, pinning him with a warning glare before turning back to nod at his human. No one else would he rather have beside him in battle; diplomacy, however, was another story altogether. Qom held his tongue; after all, there weren't really any women present for him to flirt with.

*

Erabus prepared himself before making his way toward the long hallway once he realized the conversation had concluded, bringing the satyrs with him. As the problem was merely a petty squabble, Erabus was grateful they were going next. Things would be much harder if the satyrs had to speak with him after a difficult ruling. Erabus stopped to kneel a good, safe distance from the throne upon which his father sat.

On the opposite side of the room, Jydral stepped through the door to stand beside the throne. Had he run to beat them? Would he try to prevent their guests from speaking with the king? Erabus turned his attention from his brother to the satyrs behind him.

The leader bowed with more respect than Erabus had expected. The satyr glared at the other two who followed suit, though their bows weren't as deep. Erabus hid his smile behind his hand.

Erabus bowed his head to the king once more. "My king, if I may," Erabus requested, his voice booming throughout the room, so it echoed around them. Once the king nodded in approval, he continued, "Representatives from Ebrein have come to speak with you in regard to our trespassing on their land today."

He turned toward the satyrs once more. The leader stared at him in shock. Erabus paid his confusion little mind as he continued, "My king, may I introduce..." He trailed off when he realized he didn't know their names. Xaaxex was one, but which of the two it was, he didn't know. Only that it wasn't the leader's name.

Had he named the other? Erabus couldn't remember and his cheeks heated in embarrassment for not thinking to ask them before they were in the presence of the king. Being around the leader caused his brain to become fuzzy; it was a wonder he even remembered how to speak with him so close. He caught the leader's eye, silently asking for help.

"My companions are Qom and Xaaxex," he whispered. "And I am Xicuz."

Erabus flashed him an appreciative smile before turning back to the king. "Representatives Qom, Xaaxex and their leader, Xicuz."

His name tasted sweet on his tongue, and Erabus swallowed hard as the thought of him calling it out in the throes of passion flashed through his mind.

The king sat up straighter in his throne, looking even taller. "Rise, Erabus. Tell me, child, what is this trespassing you speak to me of? Do you refer to your own hunting party with Jydral this morning?"

Bowing his head in shame, Erabus admitted, "While we were hunting this morning, our party moved too far into the forest. I only realized my own trespassing once the damage was done." He glanced at Jydral. Should he inform his father of his brother's insistence that the entire forest belonged to the humans? No, he would only deny it, and he had no proof he crossed into the satyrs' territory intentionally.

His brother seethed. Whether angry that Erabus admitted their mistake or worried he would tell their father the entire truth, Erabus wasn't sure. He turned his gaze to Xicuz and gestured for him to step forward.

"Representative Xicuz, you may speak," the king allowed once he stood beside him.

*

Erabus. His sweet, kind, protective Erabus. He saw the way Prince Jydral glared at him, no doubt angered by Erabus's desire to tell his king the truth, and yet the hate and fury in his eyes had not caused Erabus to back down. The humans had done something wrong and not only did he own up to it, he also seemed to be trying to protect the others who were there with him, even Prince Jydral.

"Your majesty," Xicuz greeted with another respectful bow, "The hunting party indeed crossed into our land today—in fact, rather far onto it, not merely at the border. Unfortunately, this is not the first time your hunters have crossed the border. As such, King Zhul has sent us to request a meeting between our leaders once more."

Jydral scoffed. Xicuz half turned to confront him, but then he saw that Erabus clenched his fist at his side.

So, he was angry. Then why did he allow Jydral get away with it? Xicuz didn't share the desire to shield him. He wanted nothing more than to make sure the king knew how much his own son messed up.

He turned his burning eyes to Jydral, who continued to glare daggers at Erabus. Xicuz fought the urge to step in front of him. "In fact, Your Majesty, the hunters came far too close to Ebrein today. King Zhul worries for the safety of our young if even one inept hunter shoots so close to our village."

Prince Jydral stuttered a protest, but the king silenced him by raising his hand. King Tribion closed his eyes, collecting himself, then spoke again. "Tell King Zhul I agree to meet with him in the same place as our last meeting in three days' time. The same terms as before applying. Five guards and two advisors each may accompany."

Things were going far easier than he expected them to. Xicuz bowed again. "I believe King Zhul will find your terms satisfactory, Your Majesty." His task complete, he looked forward to having his hands unbound and returning home to inform his king of the agreement. Even though he would also like to spend more time with Erabus, there were far more important things than his own desires.

King Tribion, however, seemed to be on his side. "Now that this is settled, for the moment at least, you are all welcome to stay for supper and spend the night in one of our guest rooms so you may return home refreshed in the morning," the king offered, though Xicuz would not be wise to assume they had a choice in the matter. Not that he planned on fighting the chance to spend more time with Erabus.

"Your Majesty, we graciously accept your invitation but request one slight alteration if you do not object. We satyrs prefer to have not but stars over our heads as we sleep." Xicuz bowed once more in the hope he would not think they were ungrateful for his hospitality. He dreaded the thought of having to sleep surrounded by wood that was not still rooted in the ground.

Instead, the king chuckled before agreeing, "So be it. I shall send Erabus with you to see to any of your needs during the night." As the king turned toward his adviser to see who still waited to speak with him, Xicuz smirked at his human and raised his eyebrows suggestively. Erabus turned away to hide his blushing cheeks.

*

Jydral seethed, angrier than he could ever remember being before. Not only had his father entertained a conversation with those animals, but he allowed them to dine at the same table as his own men. Jydral pushed his nearly untouched plate of food away and turned angry eyes to the rest of the table, most of whom looked as uncomfortable with their "guests" as him.

Erabus, however, seemed in his element as he laughed at something the more arrogant of the satyrs said to him. *Of course, he does not have any issues sharing a table with animals*, Jydral thought bitterly as he glanced from his younger brother to the satyr who sat beside him, noticing his glaring eyes turned to him once more. Returning his gaze with a cold, hard stare of his own, he waited until his brother caught the satyr's attention once more before looking away.

Good, let him sleep outside with the animals tonight—it's better than he deserves. Jydral pushed his stool back and left the table without a word to the others, or more importantly, waiting for the king to dismiss him. He stepped out of the dining hall. The guards closed the door behind him, muffling the noise coming from within. He pushed aside all thoughts of his uneaten dinner and the horrible company that caused him to leave it untouched and made his way back to his own quarters.

Though his chambers were not as grand as the king's, Jydral knew no one else's came anywhere near the level of his own, not even Erabus's. Not that the finer things mattered much to his uncultured little brother. He was far more at home out in the forest, or under the stars, as the animals were. Turning his thoughts away from his brother, he pictured the smug satyr who dared to glare at him, not only in the throne room but in the dining hall too.

He would regret his disrespect one day, even if he had to wait until Jydral became king. He could be patient as he planned out the best way to get back at him for daring to think he was on the same level as the prince of the humans. He would put him in his place. That much was certain. Now only one question remained: how long did he have to wait?

*

Sitting down at the table beside Xicuz proved to be far harder than Erabus could have imagined, in more ways than one. No sooner had they taken their seats, Xicuz's hand slid up Erabus's leg, stopping as he hit the inner thigh before continuing back down the way it had come. Erabus bit his lip and turned away as his cheeks burned once more.

The more Xicuz teased, the riskier his movements became, the harder Erabus bit down until he risked drawing blood.

"If you want me to stop, you need but tell me," Xicuz whispered. The calm sincerity in his voice, in contrast to the heated desire in his eyes, threw Erabus off for a moment, and he could only stare at him dumbfounded. Apparently finding something in his expression he did not like, Xicuz snapped, "A satyr never forces anyone."

Even as Xicuz moved to pull his hand away, Erabus covered it with his own, squeezing it and holding it tight against his inner thigh. "I didn't mean it like that," he whispered, realizing he mistook his disbelief for an accusation. "You surprised me that you would give up so quickly. I have always heard you are relentless in your pursuits." He was a little ashamed of his words by the sad, silver eyes that greeted him when he held his gaze once more.

"That is just lies made up by humans to explain why their women left them for us. Satyrs do not pursue anyone; they come willingly and often," Xicuz said, the lust in his voice returning.

Erabus blushed once again and turned his head away. He moved to pull his hand back, having still been holding Xicuz's in place on his thigh, but Xicuz entwined their fingers so he could hold their hands in place.

When Erabus stopped trying to pull his hand back, Xicuz loosened his hold enough to flip Erabus's hand over and placed Xicuz's above it. The movement caused him to turn back to him, green eyes getting lost in endless silver.

Xicuz licked his lips. "If you desire the same," he whispered as he slid their entwined hands to Erabus's groin, so they could both feel how hard he had grown. "And you obviously do, you know where to find me tonight."

The moment he finished speaking, Xicuz released his hand and Erabus felt chilled from the lack of connection. The satyr turned his attention to his dinner for the first time since they sat down. Erabus did the same. The feeling of the satyr's larger hand gently squeezing his manhood throbbed between his thighs, as if his hand were still there—had always been there.

Chapter Three

Late that night, long after his confidants had fallen asleep beneath the open, star-filled sky, Xicuz lie awake, resting with his crossed arms under his head. Though it did not seem to affect the other two, the humans still wandered too close to where they made camp for him to risk trying anything. A few of them made more than one pass by them, either intrigued by their presence or wanting to make sure they weren't a threat.

While Qom and Xaaxex were awake, watching the humans scurry about had been a fun way to pass the time. Now it got on his nerves. He needed them to go into their strange walled in homes and go to sleep. Until they did, Xicuz knew Erabus wouldn't be making any moves. He rolled over on his side and propped himself up, resting his head in his hand, and watched his human in silence for a few moments.

Erabus hadn't moved since the four of them settled in for the night. Xicuz doubted he would until the other humans had gone inside. Erabus rested against a tree, maybe two or three yards away from him, his eyes glued to Xicuz. Even without looking at him, Xicuz felt his gaze on him, always following each and every movement he made, and if Erabus didn't do something about it soon, Xicuz worried he would lose it.

Taking his eyes off Erabus once more, he turned back to survey the village and found most of the humans had finally drifted indoors. Though one or two remained, they seemed to be guards tasked with keeping watch overnight, so Xicuz paid them little mind. Turning back to his human once more, certain he would make his move now, he was disappointed when one minute after another passed without Erabus making any attempt to approach him.

His lack of action could only mean one of two things: either he wasn't interested in him, but Xicuz already felt this to not the case, or he didn't have the courage to make the first move. Xicuz decided to give him a little push. He rose to his feet without a word and made his way into the darkened forest, making sure to walk close enough to Erabus that his tail brushed up against his arm.

Unhurried in his pace, Xicuz walked far enough away that the humans standing guard would be unable to hear or see them hidden within the dark forest. One thought echoed in his mind: *if he does not follow me, I will give him up.* He spoke the truth to Erabus earlier—satyrs did not pursue those they were interested in. They allowed them to come to them so there could be no doubt of their consent.

It hadn't always been this way, but after far too many women seemingly came willing only to take their own lives, a past king decreed the human had to be the one who pursued them. Technically, the king said, "human women," but Xicuz knew it would have applied to men as well had the king realized such an attraction was possible.

Not that he blamed him for not realizing it though, for as far as Xicuz knew, he was the first to crave the attention of other males. Certainly, the only one he ever knew about. Could the same be said for the humans? Was Erabus the only one? Were they destined to be together because they were the only ones of their kind, or did the fates see fit to make them the way they were because they were fated for each other?

It didn't matter why things worked out the way they had. All that mattered was Erabus became his, and if he didn't, if he chose not to follow after him, he knew he would spend his life alone. Not that he would tell his human though. No, he needed to make the choice entirely on his own, uninfluenced by him other than to know of his attraction to him as he could not risk making a mistake and having him take his own life to get away.

Xicuz shook the morbid thoughts from his mind. There was no point in thinking about the future before he figured out what move Erabus would make. He drew in a deep breath to further clear his thoughts. The scent of the forest filled his nose: the wet, earthy smell of the dirt. The strong, pine scent of the trees that surrounded him. The clean, crisp scent of the air. As if he was wrapped in a blanket made of the Earth itself. Xicuz's senses had never been more heightened, more entuned with the world around him. He'd never felt more connected, or more at peace. He inhaled deeply once more and caught another scent in the air that caused his heart to race, his palms to sweat, and his groin to stiffen beneath his loincloth.

Xicuz swallowed and licked his lips before ducking behind the nearest tree to hide in the shadows. Closing his eyes with a smile, he listened to the faint footsteps. Amazed at how little noise he made, as though he walked barefoot on a bed of soft moss. He shouldn't be surprised, Xicuz had been unable to hear him that morning when Erabus nearly struck him with an arrow.

He only heard his steps now because he actively listened for them. Realizing he was just on the other side of the tree he hid behind, Xicuz smirked to himself before stepping around the large tree enough to grab on to him as he passed by. Xicuz spun Erabus around and pinned him to the tree before he realized what happened. The sudden movement caused Erabus to gasp, causing Xicuz to smirk.

Xicuz leaned in close. "I told you I didn't need to pursue you," he said before crashing his lips onto Erabus's before he had the chance to respond to his taunt. Erabus froze beneath his touch for a moment, but as Xicuz started to back away to break the connection, Erabus pulled his head closer and returned the kiss with as much passion as Xicuz gave.

Moaning into the kiss, desperate to feel more of him against his own heated body, Xicuz wrapped his hands around Erabus's thighs and lifted him up onto his hips as he pushed him back against the tree even more. He pressed his manhood against Erabus's backside and felt more than heard him moan into the kiss. The vibrations the moan sent through Xicuz caused him to moan in response as his cock hardened painfully.

Xicuz needed to slow down unless he wanted to finish before he even tasted Erabus. He pulled back from the kiss, leaving Erabus panting as hard as him. Xicuz licked his lips, tasting Erabus on them, as he glanced down at the man in his arms. Bathed in the pale moonlight, the sweat on his brow glistened. Xicuz turned his hungry eyes to the pulse that beat in his neck.

Xicuz ran his tongue along Erabus's neck and felt his pulse beat harder beneath his touch. He stomped his hoof in ecstasy, not just from the way he tasted but from how he responded to him. He leaned over so his lips grazed past his ear and whispered, "You taste delicious."

"Xicuz," Erabus panted.

Xicuz growled with lust before crashing their lips together once more.

*

Late into the night, Jydral was confident no one else would still be awake, other than the men he posted to guard over the animals that were trespassing on his land. He stayed up thinking about what he could do to stop his idiot father and brother's plan from coming to fruition. He refused to give up his hunting ground to those animals.

He would much rather hunt them in the forest instead. As he made his way from his room, having decided now was the perfect time to stop them before they had the opportunity make it back to their own village, Jydral wondered if they might be worth his time to actually hunt. Could their horns be turned into something useful? A dagger? The ones that came to see his father had rather small, useless horns, but perhaps the older ones would fetch a better price.

If he remembered correctly, the older one whom he refused to call a king, who met his father, had much larger horns than those currently trespassing on his land. The tails he figured could be sold for such things as horsetails, though he couldn't for the life of him remember what one might use horsehair for at that moment. The rest of them would no doubt be a complete waste, but he would be perfectly happy to stack their bodies and light them on fire if it meant he could rid the world of their perverse existence.

Jydral picked up his pace as he made his way toward where they slept. He gave his two guards a look of warning to ensure they would remain silent and turned his attention to their little camp only to realize only half the beasts he expected to find were there.

His brother and the leader of the group were nowhere to be found. Glancing toward Aothorn, the closer of the two guards he posted, he gestured toward the half-empty camp in silent question. The guard pointed toward the forest. *What are they doing in the forest?* Certainly, they would not be out hunting; that would be difficult enough even on a full moon, and currently it waned above him.

Perhaps one of them needed to relieve themselves, but even so, why would it take two? Perhaps my brother is smarter than I have given him credit for and realized the animals shouldn't be allowed to wander around on their own. Whatever the reason for their late-night walk, it worked to his advantage. He could easily sneak up on his brother and kill him, blaming it on the satyr who had been foolish enough to wander away from his own guards.

*

Startled by the sudden sound of footsteps heading toward them, Erabus pulled back from the kiss, breathless both from the physical exertion as well as from the risk of being caught. Even more so as he knew exactly who was currently on a course heading straight for them. He learned his brother's unique footsteps while growing up, rather quickly in fact, as knowing when he needed to hide from his warpath was sometimes the only way to protect himself.

Though he was able to defend himself against one or two attackers, his brother never did know how to fight fair. He would always have his four friends with him whenever he came to take out some imaginary slight on him. Usually, their father had refused consent for something he wanted or wanted to do, and somehow it became Erabus's fault.

His heavy footfalls in the forest told him all he needed to know; Jydral was angry and things would not end well for whoever he encountered. It would not be long before he stumbled upon them in their hiding place. He untangled himself before pulling Xicuz deeper into the low-hanging branches. "If you wanted to be closer to me, you need only tell me," he joked as he nuzzled Erabus's neck.

"Keep quiet if you value your life," Erabus warned him as he placed his hand over Xicuz's mouth to ensure his compliance. Though complete darkness swallowed them, the tree overhead blocking out the moon, Xicuz's silver eyes glowed enough that Erabus saw the worry in them. Erabus held his gaze, partially from fear that if he looked away he would see Jydral standing beside them and also from a strong desire to get lost in his beautiful eyes.

A *snap* sounded beside him. Erabus forgot how to breathe as he glanced to his right just enough to see his brother's boots mere inches away from his own. He forced himself to hold still. He felt a newfound strength when Xicuz rested his forehead against his in comfort. Reminding himself he wasn't alone this time, he smiled in appreciation before turning his eyes back when he realized his brother's boots were moving away.

Once Jydral left hearing range, Erabus finally released the breath he held and let the hand that covered Xicuz's mouth drop to his side before turning back and finding Xicuz's face only an inch from his own. "You fear him," Xicuz said.

"If you knew the type of man he truly is, you would too, Xicuz. Jydral is not in any way a good man, and he has been leading our hunting parties onto your land intentionally. He told me himself when I called him on it today. He does not see the satyrs as anything more than animals," Erabus admitted to him, not for the first time finding himself ashamed to be related to such a man as his brother.

"And how do you see us?" Xicuz inquired as he reached down and held Erabus's hand, forcing him to unclench it.

"I see you as satyrs," Erabus said.

Apparently not getting an answer that satisfied him, Xicuz wondered, "And how do you see me, Erabus?"

A sudden sadness came over him at the thought of admitting the words out loud, but he knew he had to be honest. He owed him that much at least.

"As a regret," he whispered, able to feel the instant Xicuz moved to pull away from him, and not wanting him to walk away without hearing his reason why, Erabus held him in place. Grabbing Xicuz's chin, he gently but firmly forced Xicuz to look him in the eyes as he continued, "Regret that this cannot be, Xicuz. I regret this can never happen again, no matter how much I may want it to, or how much I may want you. We already came far too close to being found by Jydral, and I will not risk your life."

"I disagree," Xicuz decided with a smirk as he pulled Erabus's body against his once more, his hand tracing gentle circles on Erabus's lower back. "We can't be together out in the open. We need to be better hidden next time." He pressed his lips against Erabus's again before he could voice an objection. For a moment, Erabus tried to push his body back, to convince him he was not worth putting himself in danger for, but Xicuz's soft, wet tongue caressing his lips forced every thought and objection from his mind and instead he pulled Xicuz closer as he returned the kiss with the same fervor.

*

Regretfully, Xicuz pulled back from the kiss and rested his head against Erabus's forehead as he tried to get his heavy breathing under control. "We need to get back before anyone else notices we are missing. I will find you the next time you are hunting in the forest," he assured him, his words coming out in pants before pulling back to look into his deep green eyes once more.

Erabus objected, insisting there were always others around whenever he hunted, but Xicuz placed his finger across his lips to silence his protests. "The added danger will only make our encounters that much more exciting," he promised with a lustful smirk that caused Erabus to swallow hard before starting to stammer out an objection once again. "Fear not, my sweet Erabus, there is no danger too great it could ever keep me away from you and those soft, delicious lips of yours."

Xicuz didn't give him the chance to respond. He turned and made his way back through the dark forest toward the camp where he had left Qom and Xaaxex sleeping. Behind him, he heard Erabus following him, not putting anywhere near the same effort to be silent as he had when he first arrived, but his attention was mostly elsewhere. Xicuz kept his eyes and ears on the surrounding forest, watching for any sign the human prince had returned.

Fortunately, they made it back to the village without any issues. Xicuz found his two confidants still asleep and blissfully unaware of what might have transpired. He lay back down and glanced at the two guards; they were too busy playing a game with dice to realize he had returned, if the guards even knew they were gone in the first place.

He turned his gaze back in the direction he came from. A moment later, he spotted Erabus crossing the threshold into the village; he sat back down at the base of his tree. For a moment, Xicuz watched him in silence, soon catching his gaze. He licked his lips as the memory of their kisses flashed through his mind with such clarity, he could swear he was currently engaged in them. He smiled to himself when Erabus turned away, his rosy cheeks visible even in the pale moonlight.

*

The next morning, as the bright sun rose on the eastern horizon, Erabus led the satyrs into the throne room to meet with the king once more. This time, however, the guard who summoned them informed him King Tribion instructed him not to bind their hands. The two other satyrs, Qom and Xaaxex—Erabus still hadn't learned which was which—sighed in relief at the news while Xicuz only smirked at him.

That smirk probably had more to do with their encounter the night before, rather than the king's newfound trust in them. Erabus blushed bright red once more but the dimly lit hallway hid his rosy cheeks before the others could notice. Xicuz's, who he was certain knew he would react thusly, smirk widened. Erabus knew he would keep himself in check while around the others and was grateful for the distraction the meeting with the king would give him. He stepped into the throne room and led them toward the throne once more.

Erabus knelt before the king. "Good morning, my king. I pray this day brings you good health and fortune," he said as he bowed his head as low as he could. Beside him, he saw the satyrs bowing too, repeating their own greetings, before stepping back so only Xicuz stayed beside him. King Tribion greeted them both with a nod before gesturing for them to rise to their feet once more.

"Erabus, my child, I task you with guiding the satyr representatives back to the border of our lands." Once he nodded in agreement, the king turned his attention to Xicuz. "Please inform King Zhul I will see him in two days' time at sunrise," the king assured him before gesturing they were dismissed. Erabus bowed to his father once more; Xicuz did the same behind him. Erabus rose and made his way back out of the throne room.

Glancing behind him to check on his brother's whereabouts, he realized gratefully that while he glared daggers at them, he was too occupied with his father's next appointment to do anything about his anger for now. The satyrs, at least, he could keep out of reach of his wrath. Leading them through the long hallway and outside to a land bathed in the light of the rising sun, Erabus followed much of the same path Xicuz took the night before as he made his way out into the forest.

In the shadows of the trees, the air grew cooler once they left the village. Erabus shivered. As they walked in silence, Qom and Xaaxex soon overtook him and began leading the way back toward their village. Realizing it meant he could spend a few more minutes alone with Xicuz, he smiled even as he grew curious; had they done it intentionally?

Did they know of his attraction to males? To me? he wondered before all thoughts left his mind as Xicuz entwined their fingers, holding his hand as he fell in step beside him. "When are you going hunting again?" he inquired softly as he ran the pad of his thumb over the back of Erabus's hand, causing gooseflesh to pop up wherever they touched. Loving his soft caress, he could only stare at him dumbfounded for a moment as he tried to remember what he asked.

"Not until after the meeting between our kings, unfortunately. I must stay close to home and prepare for it," Erabus explained, gently squeezing Xicuz's hand to assure him he wasn't making excuses.

"Will you be going as one of King Tribion's guards?" Xicuz asked.

Erabus smiled at the thought that Xicuz believed him strong enough to be one. "Advisor, actually," he admitted before adding, "I can't risk not being there in case Jydral tries something."

"I will see you there then," Xicuz promised before giving him a chaste kiss on the lips and hurrying to catch up with the other two who were nearly out of sight now. Pausing his step, Erabus watched them in silence as they crossed the border into satyrs' land before touching his fingers to his lips. At the same moment, Xicuz turned back to wave good-bye, smirking at him when he saw what he did. Laughing for the first time in what seemed like forever, Erabus shook his head and began making his way back home.

Chapter Four

On the morning the two kings were set to meet, Xicuz walked beside King Zhul as he, along with Qom and Xaaxex, acted as part of his royal guards. The other two, along with his two advisors, walked in front while his own confidants walked behind, leaving Xicuz and the king in the middle. It was still dark as they set out, though they knew the sun would be rising soon; already the first streaks of light could be seen on the horizon.

As they walked, Xicuz held on tightly to his spear and prayed he would find no need for it today. Keeping his eyes and ears on the forest that surrounded them, for the first time finding himself concerned to be wandering through the forest without the rest of his people, he kept enough attention on the king to answer his questions and pose a few of his own.

"I do not trust him, my king," he said. "There is something about this Jydral that doesn't sit well, even with his own people. I fear he might try something at the meeting."

Xicuz remembered how afraid of him Erabus had been that night in the forest. He trembled against him, terror so prevalent in his eyes. *What had he done to make one of his own people so utterly afraid of him? Was only Erabus terrified of him, or did he affect the other humans the same? How would he react to "animals" confronting*

his behavior when we are far away from the endless line
of guards who were there to protect his father?

"Keep an eye on this Jydral, so they can't catch us unaware," the king said. "I know we can trust King Tribion. Unfortunately, the same cannot be said about this son of his."

They continued to walk through the forest in silence. With each minute that passed, another scenario flashed through his mind of what could go wrong at the meeting. Jydral might have an ambush lying in wait for their arrival, attacking before they even made it to the table. Or poison the food that would be served, though it would be rather difficult to attack King Zhul this way as he would only be eating the food the satyrs themselves brought.

Would he risk poisoning his own king to make it look as though the satyrs did it? Not knowing the answer to that did not sit well with Xicuz. He decided that, if by some chance Jydral did not make a move, he would ask Erabus if this was a possibility. By then, it would be too late for the knowledge to do him any good for today, but perhaps such information should be known for future reference.

They passed through the thick trees that encased the meeting place. Xicuz stepped into a quiet meadow with a crudely carved stone table in the middle and continued his musings. If Jydral attacked during the meeting, how many other humans would follow suit? Would the king, or was he as trustworthy as Zhul believed? The only thing Xicuz knew for sure was that he could, and did, trust Erabus.

If he possessed any ill will toward the satyrs, he would not have been able to meet his kisses with such fire and passion as he had. His body would not have reacted as it did to Xicuz's passionate kisses and heated touches. No, Erabus was the one ally he knew for certain the satyrs had in the human village and as he glanced around the mostly empty clearing, he couldn't help but pray something didn't go wrong and Erabus ended up being forced to stay back at the village.

*

About the same time the satyrs were leaving their village with their own king, Erabus left the human village with his. He worried about what his brother might be planning to do that day. Nothing about the entire trip sat well with him. An unrelenting fear gnawed at the back of his mind since he woke, and he knew it would not leave him in peace until everyone was safely back within their villages with this entire day behind them.

They needed this meeting so the two sides could work things out before his brother had the chance to destroy their alliance, but he knew it wasn't safe to have Jydral there with them. But leaving him back in the village to gather an army didn't sit well with him either. At least this way, he could keep an eye on his brother and hopefully head off any plan he might have.

Though he might not have known what it was, Erabus knew Jydral plotted against them. Just the way he walked with two of the other guards, Aothorn and Elovonos, whispering amongst themselves and glancing back at the king every so often, confirmed his nefarious plans. "My king," Erabus began, keeping his voice low so the three "guards" in front of him and the two behind couldn't overhear.

"I believe Jydral is up to something. He has been behaving strangely since we left the village, for a long while before that in fact, and I think he might be planning something for the meeting today," Erabus admitted, causing his father's other adviser, Odinel to glance over at him in question for a moment before turning his attention back to the scroll in his hand. Knowing his unquestionable loyalty to his father, Erabus wasn't the least bit concerned about him listening in.

"Erabus, my child, you need to have more faith in your brother. Fear not, Jydral's true character will make itself known in time, but until then you should give your own blood the benefit of the doubt." He placed his hand on his shoulder before turning his eyes back to the road ahead a moment later as though he had not said anything at all. His father's assurances did little to abate the gnawing fear, and Erabus prayed it was not too late when Jydral did finally show his true self.

*

Jydral stomped through the forest, wheels turning over on themselves in his head. He glanced back toward his father and brother once more, not surprised to find them whispering between each other. Erabus was always trying to turn their father against him—why should today be any different? It didn't matter to him what his brother whispered in his father's ear as none of it would matter soon anyway.

As long as they did not overhear his own plans, they could mumble to each other as much as they pleased. He turned his attention back to Aothorn and Elovonos, who he managed to get assigned to guard duty for the meeting. It perturbed him that he couldn't get Dlivion and Azemar signed up in addition—the four of them were the only people in the entire world he knew were trustworthy.

"Position yourselves on either side of him at the table," Jydral instructed.

"The plan will be set in motion as soon as they raise their cups in a toast." Glancing back once more, he found Erabus staring straight at him, accusation, and distrust in his eyes. He hardened his gaze before turning back to his men.

"What of your brother?" Aothorn asked.

"I will see to it the blame falls on his shoulders, along with the animals," Jydral swore as he pushed his way through a thick wall of trees and stepped into the meadow.

*

He helped the king cross the threshold out of the forest and into the clearing. He spotted the stone table and the six satyrs who were already waiting. Erabus's gaze landed upon Xicuz, who locked eyes with him and smiled in greeting. The images of their night in the forest played in Erabus's mind. He shook his head, clearing his thoughts, and turned his attention back to the two kings.

His father was unable to use his cane in the grassy clearing, so Erabus allowed him to rest his hand on his arm for support. He guided him over toward the others, releasing him only to bow respectfully to the satyr king. While the other guards on both sides had at least nodded their heads if not outright bowed, Jydral didn't give a single indication he even noticed the presence of royalty.

"Let us sit." King Zhul gestured toward the table with a smile. King Zhul fell into step to the right of King Tribion so Erabus could continue to guide his father to the table. Seating King Tribion on the left side of the table, Erabus moved to stand next to his father only to find Elovonos already stood to his immediate right, positioning himself in the time it took him to get the king settled in his spot.

Annoyed, but not wanting to make a scene, Erabus took his position to the right of the guard, vowing to keep an eye on him as well. Glancing to his left, far passed two of the guards, the king, and Odinel, he found Jydral standing at the end of the table. He turned his gaze to the satyrs' side of the table, recognizing two of the guards as Qom and Xaaxex. If he remembered right, the latter was the one who snapped his teeth at him, as he had done when he bound his hands.

Rolling his eyes at his antics, Erabus finally allowed himself to look at Xicuz once more; he'd been avoiding him for fear he would get distracted and miss a movement by his brother. He noticed Xicuz's ears twitching, and his silver eyes had a far-off look in them. He didn't seem to notice Erabus's attention.

Time froze for him in that moment, all sounds faded away in the clearing other than that of his own pounding heart, echoing inside his ears. The faces of those who stood around him became blurred masses just outside his vision. All except for Xicuz. His face seemed to become impossibly sharper as though his entire mind was concentrated on him, bringing him more to life.

As his silver eyes finally found his, they widened a fraction in the same moment Erabus heard the *swooshing* of an arrow as it raced toward its target. "Get down!" Erabus shouted as the arrow came flying over the table on a path for his father. Faster than he was aware he could move, he wrenched the shield off the guard to his right and spun around just in time to hear the arrow *ping* as it struck the wood.

Barely giving himself the chance to register he caught the arrow before it could strike the king, Erabus tossed the shield back to its owner and leapt onto the table with a shout of, "Protect the kings!" before jumping off on the other side and rushing into the forest in the direction the arrow came from. Squeezing through the thick trees, he drew his bow even as he pulled an arrow from his quiver and notched it on the string.

Erabus spun around and searched in vain for the archer who was nowhere in sight. Knowing he couldn't have gotten away without leaving some sort of trail in his wake, he searched the ground for his footprints but soon found that search to be as fruitful as his first. Hearing a sound behind him, Erabus spun around as he pulled his arrow taut and found Xicuz standing with his arms raised.

He lowered his bow but kept it at the ready in case the archer returned. "Do you see any signs of the archer? I can't find a single footprint even though the mud is more than soft enough to leave an impression."

Xicuz knelt closer to the ground and searched the area. Though he managed to find a few shallow impressions, Erabus confirmed they were his own markings.

"How did he escape without leaving a trace? And why did he only fire a single shot? Surely, he could have notched two or three arrows in the time it took me to find which direction he came from," Erabus insisted, though neither he nor Xicuz was certain who he spoke to, himself or the satyr. As he glanced around the area once more, again wondering why an attacker would only fire one shot before running away, a thought sprang to mind.

"To draw us away!" he realized even as he turned to push his way back through the thicket, rushing back to the stone table as he prayed he wasn't too late. Yet, when the others were in sight, Erabus found them, other than the guards who moved into protective formations around the two kings, to be undisturbed by what happened. Apparently, the attacker had not returned after drawing them into the forest.

Had he been expecting more guards to follow after Erabus, leaving the two kings more exposed? Had he given up on his attempts when he realized this failed? Had he ever planned on shooting more than one arrow? And if not, what was the point? Had he been so confident in his skills that he assumed he would only need one?

Too many questions filled Erabus's head without any sign of answers in sight. "Something isn't right. Be on guard," he warned Xicuz as he heard him fall in step beside him. Though he didn't answer verbally, Xicuz's hand brushed against Erabus's as he passed by to make his way over to the satyr's side of the stone table. How he wished he could have reached out for his hand and held on to it tightly as the worry continued to gnaw away at him.

"What happened, Erabus?" King Tribion called out as he approached the table and bowed to the two kings.

Erabus bowed his head in shame. "There is no sign of him. I am deeply sorry I failed in finding him."

"Worry not, my child," his father said. "Few can compare to your tracking skills. If you did not find signs of him, they were not there to be found. Of this I am certain. For now, keep a close eye on the trees in case he returns, as I will not end this much-needed meeting of our two people because of some coward," the king insisted.

"It is better to reschedule," Erabus pleaded. "It is not safe, my king."

The king ignored his warning. Instead, he turned back to the satyr king and raised his glass. "A toast to King Zhul and our continued alliances."

*

Xicuz remained alert for danger, but the rest of the meeting went on without further interruption. Both sides came to the same conclusion they had ten years before, but with an added stipulation. Anyone caught hunting on the others' land would be subjected to a week of manual labor at the village of the landowner. Of course, none of the satyrs had any problem with the newest stipulation as they were not the ones trespassing in the first place.

A few of the humans, however, had objections to it—mainly the prince. Realizing his king planned to walk the human king back to the edge of the meadow, signaling the end of the meeting and his last chance to speak to Erabus, he fell in step beside him. Lowering his voice so only he could hear, Xicuz wondered, "Is it possible the archer acted alone? And his attack was the entirety of the plot?"

Erabus sighed beside him and, without ever taking his eyes off Jydral who walked beside his king, he admitted, "I doubt it, but there is no way for me to prove it. Or to confirm Jydral was behind it even though I know in my bones he was." He turned toward Xicuz; his deep green eyes held sorrow and pain. "The arrow was meant for my king, that much is obvious, but guard yours well just in case."

Xicuz nodded, having already planned to keep a closer eye on his king. "When can I see you again?" Their short, minimal interactions during the meeting had been nowhere enough to satisfy his craving for Erabus. Though, judging by his sad expression, it would have to hold him over for some time. He opened his mouth to question him when one of the human guards walked past, giving him a dirty look when he noticed his gaze.

Once the guard stepped out of earshot, Erabus drew his attention back. "I am sorry, Xicuz, as much as I want to meet you, how I dream about your touch every time I close my eyes, I cannot chance leaving King Tribion alone for the foreseeable future. Jydral will strike again; of this I am certain." Seeing the others were stepping back through the thicket, apparently planning to separate once they were on the other side, he moved to follow suit when Erabus grabbed his hand.

He gave it a gentle squeeze, meeting his gaze with his own for a moment before sighing and releasing his hand. He disappeared into the thicket as the others had done. Quickly making his way through himself, Xicuz glanced around at the others and found the humans had already started away while his own group waited for him. Erabus bowed before King Zhul before running to catch up to his own king.

As Xicuz watched, he turned back to look at him once more with sorrowful eyes before vanishing into the forest. Sighing softly to himself, ignoring the look Qom gave him, he followed his king, all the while keeping his ears trained on the forest in case there were any other attacks.

Chapter Five

Only a few days after the meeting of the two kings, King Tribion grew ill. Two days after that he was confined to his bed by order of the royal healer, Jeqor. As worry continued to take its hold on him, Erabus sat at the foot of his father's bed all day, every day. He refused to leave his side unless he absolutely had to, terrified he would take a turn for the worse when he wasn't there.

Jydral kept himself busy elsewhere and had yet to visit the king after the healer informed the two of them he fell sick. When Erabus confronted him about his absence on the night the king was confined to his bed, his brother claimed to be busy dealing with the affairs their father usually dealt with day to day. If Erabus hadn't already known the king's advisor Odinel took care of all that, he might have believed him.

No, Jydral never visited their father because he was the one responsible for making him sick, even if he had no way of proving it or even figuring out how he managed to do so. His brother made his move at the meeting, but how he had done something in front of both kings, three advisors, and nine guards without being seen, Erabus doubted he would ever know. Even accounting for the two guards who he knew were on his brother's side, there were still seven men who were trained to spot and prevent an attack, and yet it was the only possibility.

For the briefest of moments, he wondered if Jydral didn't, in fact, avoid their father due to his guilty conscious, but his brother's actions reminded him he didn't have one. As King Tribion lie on his bed, his skin ghastly pale and his breathing labored, Erabus heard reports from Odinel that his brother was already trying to undo everything the leaders of Edith and Ebrein accomplished only a week before.

He had been planning for the abolishment of the alliance the moment their father took his last breath, claiming any treaty the king agreed to would die with him. He authorized a large hunting raid in celebration of his future coronation that would hunt the whole forest through for two days and nights. When Odinel got to the point where Jydral bragged about wearing the antlers of the deer they hunted when they hunted down the animals who paraded around like men, Erabus had heard enough and dismissed him from the room.

At best his brother planned to bring them to war, all for the sake of more hunting land. At worst, he would wipe out an entire race of an ancient clan simply because he did not like them. As much as Erabus wanted to march into the throne room to put an end to all his brother's evil plans, he knew the best way to stop him was for their father to live. And as long as he remained in the room to guard him, the king stood the chance of a recovery.

Much to his delight, he awoke one afternoon from a midday nap, two weeks to the day since the meeting of the two kings, to the smiling face of the healer who looked up at him after checking his father's pulse. "Rejoice, young prince. King Tribion is growing stronger. I daresay he should awaken soon. Alas, I am in need of more herbs for his tonic and these old bones cannot walk through the forest as they once did to collect them.

"I trust only you to this task as the guards are as liable to mistakenly bring me back poisonous weeds as they are healing herbs. I know you fear for the king's life, so I will remain here until you return and adviser Odinel has seen to it that only men entirely loyal to King Tribion guard his door." Jeqor spoke in a calm, but unrelenting tone, undoubtedly knowing Erabus would reject his suggestion to leave his father's side.

Sure enough, the moment the healer finished speaking, Erabus protested, "Jeqor, you know I can't leave my father's side."

The healer turned back and gave him an understanding smile. "Young prince, you cannot greet the king in the state you are in. You have hardly bathed in two weeks, and forgive me for saying, you reek. Gather the herbs, bathe, change your clothing and return here. By then, the king may very well be awake."

Holding the healer's old, tired eyes for a moment, he finally relented and made his way toward the door. Before opening it, he turned back to demand, "Neither he nor any other man than you is to be left alone with the king, for even a moment." He didn't have to explain who he meant. He already admitted to him, around a week after the king became sick and nothing the healer did seemed to make any difference, that he believed his brother poisoned him. The healer agreed it was possibly poison and changed his healing tactics accordingly. It was only after this that King Tribion regained some of his color and recovered from what ailed him.

On his way out of the room, he glanced at each of the guards posted at the door. Alyster and Garion were loyal to his father. He whispered, "If anyone, *at all*, attempts to see the king, you are to be present in the room at all times." They nodded in understanding.

Erabus stepped out into the fresh, crisp air. He breathed in deeply, relieved to be out of his father's stuffy room.

When was the last time he saw the sunlight other than from between the cracks of the curtains pulled over his father's window? How long had it been since he felt the dirt crunch beneath his soft-soled boots or the breeze upon his pale, tired face? How many nightmare-riddled, sleep-deprived nights had it been since he laid eyes upon Xicuz? Just the thought of him brought a smile to his lips, but Erabus quickly pushed him from his mind.

As much as he wished desperately to see him again, he knew he had to keep his focus on his father for now. If he daydreamed about the satyr who fully captured his attention, he knew he would be lost in his silver eyes and he might make a mistake that could take everything from him. No, he needed to keep Xicuz as far from his mind as possible, even if it was next to impossible as he began making his way into the forest.

Everything reminded him of the satyr. The trees which surrounded him reminded him of the one he had been pushed up against and the fiery kissing session that ensued. The cool breeze blowing across his skin reminded him of his gentle touches. The scent of pine and moss, heavy in the air, brought to mind the woodsy scent of Xicuz himself. It seemed the more he tried not to think about him, the more he sprang to mind.

Erabus stopped trying to fight the images of Xicuz that floated through his mind—nothing he could do would banish them. He knelt to search for the herb the healer sent him to find in the shadow of a tree. As they tended to grow in cool, damp areas, he wasn't surprised to find a three-leaf plant in between two of the tree's roots. Picking them, and knowing they wouldn't be enough, he continued his search at the next tree.

*

Jydral clenched his fists and glared daggers at his brother's back as he left the village. He'd had enough of his interfering in his plans. He had gotten in his way for far too long and would soon pay for his meddling. First, he caught the arrow that should have taken their father's life two weeks ago and then he refused to leave the king's side since he fell ill.

He hadn't had the opportunity to give King Tribion a high enough dose to be fatal and needed access to him before he had the chance to heal. Now, Jydral would have to start poisoning his father all over again and his guard would be up even more after getting so close to death this time. If he were unable to get to him before he recovered, he would have to scrap his entire plan and start over from scratch.

Jydral would not accept defeat.. But as long as Erabus hung around he would never be able to get uninhibited access to his father. He'd already overheard him telling the guards to not let anyone be alone with the king and he couldn't exactly poison him with witnesses—at least not unless they were loyal only to him. Erabus would need to be dealt with before he could ever hope to finish off his father.

And the fool gave him the perfect opportunity. He wandered around in the forest alone and left himself wide open to an attack. Jydral would be happy to show him the folly in such a decision. Even better, he could blame his brother's death on the satyrs and kill two birds with one stone. Glancing around and spotting those he knew were loyal to himself, he gestured for Aothorn, Elovonos, Dlivion, and Azemar to follow before heading into the forest.

As the four of them fell in step around him, he explained softly, "We are going to deal with Erabus, once and for all." Pulling the hood of his cape over his head, bathing his face in shadows, Jydral knew the others followed suit without having to look back at them. Weaving his way in between the trees, it did not take long before they found him kneeling beside a large tree as he gathered an herb from its shadow. "Attack!"

*

Jumping in surprise at the sudden shout that came from behind him, Erabus managed to get out of the way just in time to avoid a sword that came down where he had been a moment ago. Before he even had the chance to register someone attacked him, a second sword nearly took off his head and would have if he hadn't ducked at the last moment. "Hey!" he cried out as he tried to back away as another sword and then another—or was it the first one again? —came within inches of drawing blood.

Erabus tripped over one of the larger tree roots protruding from the ground and scrambled backward, each crab crawl barely taking him out of reach from the swinging swords that struck dirt instead of flesh. He tried to count how many attackers there were, but they moved too quickly and randomly for him to get an accurate count. The one thing he knew for sure, there were more than two.

He tossed a big a handful of dirt into their faces buying himself some time. He scrambled to his feet and dodged out of the way of another swing before ducking under a large branch and moved deeper into the forest. He would not last long against so many attackers without a weapon of his own to defend himself, but he might stand a chance if he could render their weapons useless.

The only way he knew to do that was to pull them so deep into the branches they couldn't possibly swing their swords without them getting caught in said boughs. It seemed to be working as he heard a couple of them cussing before sheathing their swords, but soon enough they were chasing him again.

Erabus ducked under one branch and then another, crouching so low in some places he practically crawled on his hands and knees. He thought he might have lost them in the darkness when he felt his braid being yanked back behind him. Crying out in pain, he fell back against a thick tree branch roughly. His attacker wailed on his face.

One punch after another came without giving him the chance to breathe, let alone defend himself. Erabus's lip split and his eye began to swell. He tried to pull away, but one attacker still held his hair, holding him in place. Hearing others getting closer and knowing it wouldn't be long before he would be entirely defenseless and at their mercy, he did the only thing he could at that moment.

He broke a smaller branch off the one they pinned him down on, wrenched his arm painfully over his head and stabbed the hand that held his hair. His attacker screamed out in pain and rage as he released his grip. Erabus rolled out of the way as they aimed another punch at his head. Judging by the howl of pain that followed, his attacker instead struck the branch.

Taking full advantage of their disorientation, he continued on his original path through the low-hanging branches. He weaved in between countless trees as his pursuers followed. One moment they were on his heels, trying in vain to grab him, and the next moment the sky opened and began to pour rain down on them, causing the ground to instantly become a slippery mess.

Nearly losing his footing more than once, Erabus's determination to live was the only thing that kept him moving, even after he could no longer hear his attackers following. Somewhere behind him, sounding far away over the roar of the rain, he heard a voice call out, "Leave him! Let the wild animals finish him off!" Though he had been pretty certain from the beginning, the voice confirmed his suspicions of his attackers was correct.

Jydral. And no doubt his loyal goons. Knowing his brother followed him out into the darkened forest and tried to kill him in cold blood didn't affect Erabus as he thought it might. Erabus always knew his brother was capable of horrible things; this proved him right. He glanced behind himself once more to check to see if it was a trick and they were still following. He didn't dare slow down for even a moment in his escape. He had only begun to turn back when he crashed into something hard and unrelenting. *Jydral!*

*

Xicuz wrapped his arms around Erabus's waist the moment he ran into him. Which turned out to be a good idea as the force would have knocked his human down if he hadn't. "If you were so desperate to see me, you should have come sooner," he said with a chuckle.

His laughter died on his lips as a flash of lightning lit the sky above and he got his first real look at the man, who stopped struggling in his arms once he heard his voice. Streaks of blood ran down his face, although the rain washed it away as soon as it appeared. Xicuz released Erabus's still-shivering form to gently cup his cheeks to survey the damage.

"What happened?!" he demanded. His ears twitched, searching for any sign his attackers were still pursuing him. Even though he found none, Xicuz didn't dare take his full attention off the surrounding forest in case they decided to return after all.

"I was searching for herbs when at least three men attacked me. Jydral led the attack, but I never got a good look at any of them to be absolutely sure of the others," Erabus admitted.

Xicuz saw red. *That coward dared to attack him outnumbered and from behind?*! He clenched his hands into fists at his side and moved to go after the cowardly humans when Erabus stopped him.

"Stay away from them, Xicuz, you would only get yourself hurt."

"As if that would matter." Xicuz tried to pass him once more only to meet the same resistance. "I do not care if I get hurt, Erabus. I will not let them get away with attacking you like this. They will pay for hurting you."

"Why are you so willing to risk your own safety for someone you barely know?" Erabus asked so softly Xicuz froze in place. He turned back toward him, confused. *Could he really not know?*

"You truly know nothing of satyrs, do you?" Xicuz wondered softly before gently pulling him out of the rain and under another tree.

"What do you mean?" Erabus asked, his voice barely heard over the rumble of thunder.

Xicuz smiled softly at Erabus as he pushed him against the tree and covered his body with his own, sharing a bit of his body heat with Erabus who was shivering.

"Other than rejection, a satyr will stop at nothing to have his desire once they are attracted to another. We are driven by our animalistic instincts to take what we want, and as is the case with us, when it goes beyond basic attraction, when there is a desire for more than just the physical, there is nothing we wouldn't do to protect our chosen." Xicuz gently caressed his cheek, able to see his wounds were still bleeding when lightning lit up the sky once more.

"But you barely know me," Erabus insisted.

Xicuz laughed at his innocence and rested his forehead against his. "Attraction is instantaneous. We are not held back by the limitations of what you humans think of as love. I only know desire and the uncontrollable yearning to get what I want—what is mine." Xicuz pressed his lips against Erabus's near frozen ones, careful not to further injure his split lip.

Erabus returned the kiss. After a moment or two had passed, Xicuz pulled back and looked into his deep green eyes. "If, my dear Erabus, you do not desire me the same, push me away now. I am about to let myself go and would prefer the rejection now than risk asking something of you that you do not wish to give."

*

Erabus grabbed Xicuz's beard as lightning flashed across the sky once more and illuminated them both in the golden light and smirked at the startled expression in Xicuz's eyes before the light faded once more. Erabus pulled him close by his beard and pressed his lips against his with as much heat and passion as he could.

Xicuz moaned into his mouth. Erabus released his beard so he could wrap his arms around him and pulled him close. Their embrace heated up even more, their tongues and lips fighting as though it were a competition of their passion until at last Erabus hissed in pain when their movement caused his split lip to hurt.

Breaking the kiss, Xicuz pulled back, but Erabus was having none of it. "Don't stop, Xicuz. I will not let those bastards take anything else from me," he swore as he pulled him back toward him for another kiss. This time their embrace ended mutually when they both pulled back for need of air.

Panting, Xicuz rested his head against Erabus's and said breathlessly, "I love the fire burning within you, my dear Erabus, but we need to see to your wounds and not get lost in each other's touch and taste." Xicuz smirked as Erabus felt the heat rush to his cheeks.

"Not much we can do about them in the darkness, especially since the rain shows no sign of letting up," Erabus insisted, even though he knew he was right. Instead of answering him, Xicuz grabbed hold of his hand and led him through the near pitch-black forest. He wondered how the satyr managed to see so well in the darkness, especially with the rain still pouring down, but kept the question to himself as he allowed himself to be led to wherever they were going.

The minutes ticked by slowly, but Erabus didn't mind as it meant he could spend even more time with Xicuz, his warm, strong hand holding his so tightly it amazed him it didn't hurt. Finally, but also much too soon for Erabus, they reached the mouth of a dark cave, only able to make it out as the trees thinned overhead and allowed for more of the moonlight to penetrate. Before he could even think to ask him why they were there, Xicuz pulled him inside.

Chapter Six

Pulling Erabus into the cave just enough they were both out of the rain, Xicuz squeezed his hand in reassurance. After he released it, he felt along the damp, mossy wall for the nook he knew would be there. After only a few moments of searching, his hand slipped into a hole eroded into the wall by countless years of weather.

He grabbed the flint and tinder and lit the torch above the hole. The entire entrance was instantly bathed in the warm, orange glow of the flame. Xicuz removed it from its sconce and made his way around the cave to light the others. Soon enough, they saw every crack and crevice in the cave, including the steam rising from the hot springs at the far end of the cavern.

Xicuz replaced the torch and turned back to Erabus, who looked around the cave in amazement. Xicuz had felt the same way the first time he saw the secret cave. "We will be safe here for now," he said. "Only King Zhul is allowed to use the hot springs. Most don't even know of its existence, and he only uses it when he is ill."

Xicuz took Erabus's hand again and led him over to sit on the edge of the springs, where the naturally heated rock would warm him. Once he was settled, Xicuz took a closer look at his wounds now that he could see them properly. His split lip didn't appear to be as bad as he first thought. He had a few scrapes and scratches along his face and at least one of his eyes would be swollen by morning, but it seemed he managed to protect himself well enough that there were no serious injuries.

Xicuz gently ran his finger beneath one of the larger cuts, grateful when even his slight pulling on the skin did not cause it to bleed again. Anger rose within him at the thought of Erabus's own people doing this to him. Apparently realizing where his thoughts had turned, Erabus squeezed his hand gently and brought his attention back to the present. Smiling at him, he pulled him to his feet once more as he shivered despite the warm rock beneath him.

Xicuz tugged Erabus's soaked vest down over his shoulders and placed it over one of the higher rocks before turning his attention to his buckskin pants. As he moved to pull those down, Erabus stammered, his cheeks blushing bright red when he realized what he intended.

Xicuz smirked. "You have a dirty mind and I love it, Erabus, but I am only removing your clothes so you can soak in the hot water before you get sick."

Once Erabus wore nothing but his loincloth, Xicuz stepped into the steaming water before helping him to step over the large rocks that surrounded it. Gently sitting him down on a rock protruding from the wall, he moved to sit directly across from him, giving him plenty of space to himself. Even with the distance between them, Xicuz could see Erabus intentionally looked anywhere but at him.

"Why so shy now, dear Erabus? I am wearing the same amount of clothes I always am," he teased, smirking when his cheeks flushed yet again. Barely catching his mumbled "I'm not", Xicuz laughed before standing once more and making his way back toward him. Erabus refused to look at him, so he gently grabbed his chin so he would have to.

Licking his lips, Xicuz ran his eyes over every inch of exposed skin, which was quite a bit with the water. "You do look better this way. And you should look upon my own naked flesh as much as you want." Xicuz expected him to blush in response. He didn't expect him to stand up, despite his embarrassment, and place his hands on his chest.

"They're so hard," he whispered, though Xicuz wasn't sure if he spoke to him or to himself, as he gently ran his fingers across the muscles on his well-toned chest. The feel of his still cool fingers on his heated flesh caused Xicuz to suck in a breath, biting his lip to stop himself from moaning out loud.

"They're not the only thing that's hard," Xicuz teased, hardening even further at his own words and from the innocent, shy expression that went well with Erabus's nearly constant rosy cheeks. Though he glanced away to avoid his heated gaze, Xicuz took hold of his chin once more, careful not to apply enough pressure to hurt him or aggravate the injuries on his face.

Turning him back to look into the beautiful green eyes that threatened to entrance him, Xicuz licked his lips once more before leaning down to kiss Erabus. As much as he wanted to, his body practically begging him to, he knew he would not be learning the taste and feel of Erabus's body tonight. It wasn't exactly a good time, and he refused to let the earlier incident put a dark shadow over their first time.

Especially not when it would literally be his first time. "I will not take you tonight, my dear Erabus, no matter how much my body might crave your touch. You must heal and I am quite certain the rather strenuous activities I have planned would be counterintuitive," Xicuz admitted, certain the disappointed look that marred Erabus's face mirrored his own.

"I am not afraid to be with you," Erabus insisted as he stepped toward him. Before he could say a word, Erabus pressed even closer to him so he felt all that his loincloth hid.

Biting his lip against the moan that threatened to spill out once more, Xicuz drew a deep breath to hold back his ever-growing desire and explained, "It is not about fear or courage, though I have never doubted which you possess, but I cannot bear the thought of hurting you further. Your body is not ready, no matter how you try to convince me otherwise. Perhaps the next time it rains, and we can meet without being seen, you will be healed and ready."

*

Even from within the darkness of the cave, Erabus knew dawn was near. The air smelled heavy of dew instead of the rain from the night before, and he heard the early rising birds already beginning to sing to one another. Though he could not see much of him, as the one remaining torch was so far back it cast most of them in shadow, Erabus couldn't help but smile down at Xicuz and at how much he loved being able to awaken in his strong, comforting arms.

His hard, muscular chest made him a much finer pillow than Erabus expected, and the heat he gave off kept him warm throughout the night. So much so he barely noticed the cold, unyielding ground beneath the rest of him. No matter how much he loved the feel of being in his arms, he knew he needed to get back to the village and check on his father.

Though he doubted he would have done anything during the night, as a rain soaked Jydral demanding to be left alone with a king would raise some questions, there was no telling how long he might wait once the sun rose. Especially since Erabus wasn't there to watch every move he made. Turning back to the still sleeping Xicuz, Erabus realized in that moment how much he hated the thought of leaving him.

He kissed him gently on the forehead before untangling himself, careful not to wake him. There was no reason both had to be awake so early. He silently made his way toward the back of the cave, his footfalls inaudible on the mossy ground, and gathered up his clothing from where Xicuz left them the night before.

Once dressed, Erabus glanced back at the still sleeping Xicuz to make sure he hadn't accidentally awoken him. Certain he would continue to slumber on and finding himself missing the warmth of his body once more, Erabus quickly took off in the forest before his desire to stay could get the better of him. As he ran, Erabus wondered how his brother would react to him returning, the wild animals not having finished him off as he hoped.

*

Only when he could no longer hear his retreating footsteps did Xicuz finally open his eyes. He couldn't help but smile, confident that had he revealed he was awake, Erabus would have been unable to leave his side. But Xicuz knew Erabus's king needed him, and he would regret it for the rest of his life if something happened in his absence. So, he had kept quiet.

Gently touching his forehead where Erabus kissed him only a few minutes before, Xicuz smirked to himself as he lay back down. An image of him standing in the hot springs, wearing not but a loincloth, flashed through his mind with crystal clarity. Licking his lips at the tantalizing memory, he was about to go back to sleep when he heard footsteps approaching.

As there was more than one pair of feet, it couldn't be Erabus. Xicuz quickly jumped up and searched the dark cave, to make sure no sign remained of their presence. Certain none remained, he quickly made his way out of the cave.

As the footsteps grew closer, Xicuz dove into the thick, low-hanging branches of the nearest tree. Not even a moment after he hid away, he caught sight of the King Zhul with his two guards.

Xicuz silently pleaded for him to go unnoticed by the group and worried about the king's health. If he came to visit the springs, he was either sick or injured, and he was neither the day before when he saw him last. Had something happened to his own king when he was distracted by Erabus the night before? He didn't blame himself, and he trusted that his own people would not hurt their king. So, what could've happened?

*

Jydral spotted Erabus the moment he stepped foot back into the village. He seethed with anger. How had he managed to survive in the horrid elements of the night before? At the mercy of the wild beasts that roamed the forest throughout the night and without a single weapon to defend himself with? He should have been dead, or at least holed up somewhere slowly freezing to death while scavengers picked apart his flesh, not waltzing back into the village like nothing happened the night before.

Jydral gritted his teeth as he held back his desire to go after his brother and finish what the wild animals hadn't. It might do more harm than good to attack him in the middle of the village in full view of the others. There was no telling who might be treacherously loyal to Erabus. It was far better to use his death as an advantage to his plans than risk him becoming a martyr.

And anyway, the soon-to-be-late king has already been given his "medicine."

Watching in simmering silence as Erabus made his way to their father's room, he realized his early morning visit would work to his favor. If King Tribion's symptoms only returned after being visited by his younger son, it would give him the perfect scapegoat.

The only thing that remained now was finding a way to connect the half goats themselves to the assassination so he would have the perfect excuse to attack them. And if not for the death of his father, then he would have to come up with another plan to validate their aggression when his people were still reeling from the king's death and his brother's execution for being behind it. With many things left to plan, Jydral headed toward his own chambers.

*

Erabus stopped before the door and asked the guards, "Did anyone attempt a private audience with the king last night?"

At first, both guards shook their heads no, but something in the look they gave each other made him wonder if there wasn't something that needed to be said.

"Tell me," he instructed as he turned to face Alyster, hoping his full attention would loosen his lips.

"No one tried to see King Tribion alone last night. However, Prince Jydral did stop by with a few of his guards late last night. He never even asked us to leave the room. He sat down beside him for a few minutes, speaking about how he hoped he would get well soon and then left. His own guards never said a word."

"Did he feed the king anything? Give him something to drink? Did his guards stand in the way of your view of the king at any time?" Erabus demanded, his worry growing once more now that he knew for a fact his brother took advantage of him being away to get close to their father. Even with the guards there, men he knew without a doubt were loyal to his father, Jydral had far better access to the king than he should have ever again.

Alyster looked at him strangely. Was he shocked he would think his brother capable of attempting something on the king, or that he would say so out loud? Erabus didn't know. Alyster shook his head in response to his odd line of questioning. "No, Prince Erabus. He didn't even touch the king other than to hold his hand. Not so much as a drop of water or crumb of bread passed between them."

After a moment of searching his eyes and finding nothing but the truth, and perhaps a bit of confusion, Erabus nodded to both Alyster and Garion before continuing into his father's room. What he saw when he opened the door caused his heart to skip a beat and his breath to catch in his throat. There he was, King Tribion, who lay on his deathbed for two weeks, who was pale and clammy the last time he saw him, who had not regained consciousness in so long he could barely remember what color his eyes were, sitting up in bed with his pillows propped up behind him.

In his lap lay a tray of soft bread, the crust removed to make it easier for him to chew, and on his nightstand sat a glass of water, both of which he alternated bringing to his lips. In such complete and utter shock at the extreme change that happened overnight, Erabus could only stand in the doorway, his feet refusing to move and carry him any closer in fear any movement might shatter the illusion before him.

"There you are my son." His father beamed as he glanced up and noticed his presence. His father's voice sounded strange to him, as if he'd forgot what it sounded like in the two weeks since he heard it. "Come to me, my child," he called out softly. Erabus approached, more willing to obey his king's commands than his own.

Sitting down beside him as he had countless times since his father fell ill, Erabus took his hand in his own, holding on to it as though it were a lifeline to keep him from becoming sick once more. "What has happened, my son?" his father asked softly as he reached his free hand up to gesture at the wounds on his face. Smiling at him despite the split lip, he decided what he would say, and it would not be the truth.

"I lost the fight with a few trees last night. I got caught in a sudden downpour, and ran into a rather dense thicket when I could no longer see mere inches in front of me," Erabus said, making sure to end his words with a truth so his father would be less likely to read the lie on his face.

Though half of him wanted nothing more than to tell his father the truth about his other son, the other half couldn't help but wonder if he knew the truth or not. Here their father was, getting better and even sitting up in bed.

Surely Jydral would have used the opportunity the night before to poison him again as he was already getting better if he had done so in the first place, would he not? Even his appetite has returned. Perhaps he'd only sick after all and his fears of his brother poisoning him were unwarranted.

Had the arrow been unconnected to him too? Was it even Jydral that attacked him the night before as he first thought, or did someone else have a grudge against him? And if so, what had he done to make them hate him so? And perhaps more importantly, would they attack again?

Chapter Seven

Xicuz had been waiting for this day to arrive for what seemed like weeks, although it had only been three days. When the grey clouds filled the sky, casting most of the land in half shadows, and he felt the moisture in the air, Xicuz made his way through the forest with little more than a quick word to Qom and Xaaxex about when he would be back.

He was so desperate to have Erabus in his arms again, he didn't even wait long enough to confirm they even heard him. Images of him filled his mind, and the memory of the taste of his lips caused his mouth to water. He found his legs gaining speed on their own and couldn't help but smile at the realization that his body wanted Erabus as much as his mind. Xicuz found his way to the tree they had met beneath before in no time at all and sat on the lowest branch.

As he waited impatiently, the rain soon arrived, but Erabus did not. Though it did not pour as it had the last time, it still came down heavy enough that Xicuz was confident it would keep others inside. The other satyrs would be using this time to clean what few tools they used such as their knives and arrows. If the rain got too bad, they would hide under the cover of the trees inside the forest, but otherwise, they would go about their day in the village.

The humans, on the other hand, would scurry inside their strange dwellings at the first sign of rain, other than those who would be forced to keep working for as long as they were able. Every one of them would remain within Edith's borders until the rain let up and they were certain it was safe again.

Though Xicuz didn't know what they thought was so unsafe about the forest since all the animals would be hidden away until the weather cleared, and knowing this, not even the satyrs would be out there hunting or exploring the forest. They were as safe inside the trees as they would be within their own border, perhaps even more so with the way some of them treated their own kind.

Although satyrs weren't exactly peaceful, and their tolerance of the humans was now far greater than it had been for most of their history, they would never stoop so low as to fight amongst themselves as he saw the humans do the other night. If an issue arose between them, they would have requested a combat trial instead to settle their differences. And if by chance, the combat ended in a draw or if one opponent far outmatched the other in combat preventing a fair fight, they left up to the king to settle the matter.

And none of them would ever even think to attack the king in such a cowardly manner as the human prince seemed to be. If anyone ever coveted the crown, they only needed to challenge him for it. An upset like this one happened a time or two in the long history of the satyrs, but no one ever attempted to assassinate the king. So much so that, in fact, they didn't even have a word for the act themselves.

Time dragged on without any sign of Erabus. Xicuz worried he might not get away to see him as they had planned. Had he forgotten his promise to meet at the next rainfall? Or changed his mind about wanting to? Did something happen to him when he returned home that morning? Were the others somehow aware he spent the night in his arms wearing nothing more than a loincloth?

Had the men finished what they started the moment he returned? With this last thought, fear and panic coursed through his veins before his rational brain pointed out the flaw in that idea. He would have known. Had anything happened to Erabus, if the men who attacked him killed him, Xicuz would have sensed the moment he perished; of this he was certain.

Though a rare occurrence amongst the satyrs, there had been those throughout the years who had felt the moment their chosen was hurt or killed. Even though he had not experienced his pain when the men attacked him, Xicuz could swear it echoed through him as he lay beside Erabus throughout the night. That feeling assured him he would bear a pain much stronger than what his shallow wounds caused.

Even as he talked himself out of panic, it set in once more as the minutes continued to tick by without any sign of Erabus. Just as he moved to head toward Edith, he could make out soft footballs over the noise of the rain. Recognizing the skillfully placed steps as belonging to Erabus, all the worry and panic and unanswered questions that filled his mind a moment ago were washed away as though they never existed in the first place.

Xicuz smirked at the thought he would bear the cold and uncaring weather to be with him. It was one thing for Xicuz, who managed to get to the cover of the tree before the rain started, but another thing entirely for Erabus who, judging by the time it took him to arrive, left his village after the rain had already started.

Certain he would be in desperate need of some warming up, which Xicuz was more than happy to provide, he hid within the shadows of the tree, listening as Erabus's footsteps drew him closer with each passing moment. Once he was just around the tree Xicuz hid behind, he reached out and grabbed a hold of Erabus, spinning them around until he had him pinned to a tree.

He squeaked in surprise, and before Erabus could question who he was or Xicuz could assure him of his presence, a flash of lightning lit the sky ablaze, illuminating the area under the tree where they were cast in shadows.

A moment later, the area dimmed once more as the lightning faded away and the sky returned to dark and overcast. At the same instant they were bathed in shadows once more, Xicuz leaned forward and pressed his lips against Erabus's.

*

Their embrace quickly became heated and after a few minutes, Erabus finally had to pull back. "Wouldn't it be better," he panted, "to go back inside the cave where we can see what we are doing and could start to dry off?"

At first, Xicuz responded with a quick, "Can't," before his lips were on Erabus's once more and they returned to the same passion as a minute ago. Moaning into the kiss, he gave back everything Xicuz put into it, barely noticing the way his back scraped up against the rough tree bark. This time Xicuz pulled back panting, resting his head on

Erabus's shoulder as he tried to get his breathing under control.

After a moment or two passed, he explained without lifting his head, "King Zhul has been sick the last few days and has been spending more of his time in the cave." Erabus couldn't help but grow worried at the thought of a second king being ill. Though his own king had begun to recover, what if the satyr king didn't have access to the same level of medicine?

Was he right all along and Jydral somehow managed to poison both kings without anyone else noticing? Conscious his thoughts were going to a dark place, Erabus decided it would be best to confirm his suspicions before getting too wrapped up in worst case scenarios. "Is there any chance Jydral is responsible for making your king sick as well?" Even as the words came out of his mouth, he knew it was a ridiculous thing to ask.

Even if he managed to corrupt all the guards with his father and his advisor Odinel, he wouldn't have been able to reach all the way across the table to the satyr king and poison him also without drawing attention to himself.

And even if Jydral could force himself to talk to one of the satyrs himself, instead of just glaring at them from the other side of the table, he would have never been able to turn them against their own king to his side.

"No, my king has been ill, off and on, for a long time, since far before the meeting," Xicuz said. "King Zhul is getting on in age and it will not be long for him now."

Erabus nodded in understanding, knowing it would not be long for his own father even with him recovering from his illness, and he pushed both kings from his mind once more.

After a moment of silence passed between them, Erabus admitted, "It's going to be a bit difficult to do this in the shadows under this tree in the middle of a thunderstorm." He tried to figure out the mechanics of how they would accomplish things when they most certainly would be unable to lie down. Perhaps they could rest upon one of the larger branches, but they ran the risk of it breaking.

"We can wait..." Xicuz began, the disappointment audible in his tone, but Erabus interrupted him by pulling off his vest and tossing it in his face in one smooth motion.

Smirking, Erabus looked him up and down as a flash of lightning lit the sky above them and laughed. "If you want to wait, you'll be waiting alone."

Xicuz tilted his head to the side, undoubtedly wondering if he realized how ridiculous his statement was, but Erabus smirked. "That makes no sense," Xicuz insisted even as he reached down to help Erabus pull his buckskin pants down over his hips. Tilting his head back to moan as Xicuz's hands traveled down his legs, causing goosebumps to appear anywhere he touched, Erabus barely noticed how dark the sky became before he had to close his eyes against the sensation.

Desperate to have Xicuz's body against his, Erabus reached out in the dark and pulled Xicuz close even as he pushed him back, trapping Erabus against the tree. Moaning once more as his hands traveled up his thighs and hips, Erabus leaned forward to run his fingers through his dark hair and brushed his fingers against one of his pointed ears. Smiling devilishly, he brought his lips to his ear and breathed over the sensitive bundle of nerves, loving how it twitch in his fingers.

Hearing Xicuz groan beneath him, he was emboldened by the sound and nibbled on his ear. In a much huskier voice than usual, Xicuz could barely pant out, "You have no idea what you do to me," before a flash of lightning lit the sky once more and Erabus saw his heated silver eyes, the passion in them stronger than he had ever seen before. He sucked in his breath at the sight as the sky faded to black once more. A moment later, Xicuz dropped to his knees before him.

*

Xicuz clenched his teeth against his desire to take him that moment, his painfully erect manhood begging him for release as it throbbed against his thigh. Ignoring it for the moment, Xicuz ran his hands up the inside of Erabus's thighs, smirking in the dark when he moaned above him from such a simple touch.

Pulling up his loincloth and tucking it into the waistband over his hip, Xicuz blew his hot breath over the already hardening member, causing it to jerk and bob against his chin. Smirking as Erabus shivered above him, he took hold of his manhood and gently stroked him from base to tip, causing him to shudder.

Giving him no time to adjust to the new sensation, Xicuz pulled him toward his mouth and licked the tip. As Erabus groaned above him, he took him in his mouth, gliding his lips as far down the shaft as they could go. As he pulled back, dragging his lips and tongue along his member, Erabus moaned an animalistic sound. Smirking as best he could around the shaft, he pulled his lips off far enough that he could lick the tip once more before creating suction with his mouth as he drew him back in.

The more Erabus moaned, the faster Xicuz moved, applying more pressure with each pass. Soon he had the perfect rhythm and Erabus's heavy panting assured him it would not be long. Xicuz growled softly beneath his breath, causing the sound to vibrate through his length. He wasn't surprised when Erabus found his ecstasy moments later, releasing into his mouth. Once his member stopped quivering, he pulled it from his mouth and licked up any remaining trace of his essence.

Licking his lips to ensure they were clean, Xicuz rose to his feet just in time to catch Erabus as he leaned forward, panting against his chest. "I-I-I," Erabus stuttered as Xicuz kept him on his feet, his legs too shaky from their encounter to fully support himself.

"I know," Xicuz assured him with a smirk.

*

Resting his head against Xicuz's naked, well-toned chest, Erabus panted for breath. Never in his wildest dreams had he imagined anything could feel so earth-shatteringly good. It certainly hadn't whenever he found release with his own hand. Was it always so intense or just that this was his first time? As much as he enjoyed every moment of it, Erabus wasn't convinced he would be able to handle such a feeling every time they got together.

However, he couldn't wait to find out. Resting against his chest, feeling more than hearing his heartbeat pounding nearly as loud as his must have been, Erabus's breathing slowly came back to normal when he felt Xicuz shaking beneath him as he laughed. Annoyed, but only a little, he gently bit Xicuz's shoulder in retaliation, causing him to groan in a way that caused his resting member to throb once more.

Erabus licked the mark he made in Xicuz's skin, and then he kissed it before spinning them around and pinning Xicuz to the tree. "Erabus, you don't have to—" Erabus cut him off in the same way Xicuz had earlier, by dropping to his knees before him.

Grabbing a hold of his heated, hard member with his chilly fingers, he smirked in satisfaction as Xicuz sucked in air above him, loud enough he heard him over the storm. Using his free hand to tuck in the loincloth as Xicuz did with his own, he tried to remember exactly what he felt so he could duplicate the sensations in him. The first touch on his member was certainly not something he could ever forget.

With less confidence than Xicuz had shown, Erabus gingerly licked the tip of his shaft. Emboldened by the long, drawn-out moan that came from Xicuz, he did it again, applying more pressure. Again, he moaned and Erabus felt his member jerk in his hand at the sensation he caused. He bit his bottom lip—would he be able to make Xicuz feel as he made him feel? Erabus decided to make a move before he lost his nerve.

Slipping his parted lips over the length of his shaft, amazed by how warm it felt in his mouth, he applied a bit more pressure and came back up to the tip once more, pulling a feral growl from Xicuz's lips. For a moment, he worried he had hurt him, but his fears were put to rest when Xicuz ran his fingers through his hair and pulled him closer to his manhood.

Erabus grew more confident in himself with Xicuz's unspoken request to continue. Repeating his earlier movement, he waited until his lips were at the tip once more before running his tongue across it, causing Xicuz to growl out, "Erabus," in a husky voice that caused Erabus's own member to throb. "Faster," he panted and Erabus realized he must have been close to his own completion.

Picking up the pace as instructed, Erabus moved at the same speed Xicuz used toward the end, feeling him buck into his mouth. He fought the urge to smirk, lest he break the suction he created, at the thought he made the strong satyr before him tremble and lose control. A moment later, Erabus was startled when something hot and wet shot to the back of his throat, instinctively swallowing before he could realize what had happened.

As it dawned on him the somehow earthy, musky taste in his mouth was Xicuz's seed, he decided it was not like what he expected, but still very Xicuz. Before he could dwell on it further, Xicuz yanked him to his feet and spun them around, so Erabus was once again the one pinned to the tree. At first, instead of saying anything, Xicuz rested his head on his shoulder as he panted for breath.

After a minute, Xicuz asked, "Was that your first?"

Erabus wondered what gave it away. Had he not done as good a job as he originally thought, allowing Xicuz to figure out his lack of experience? Erabus looked away, realizing for the first time the storm finally started to die down, but it had grown dark for another reason.

Xicuz grabbed a hold of his chin, forcing his face back to him and kissed Erabus before he could realize what he intended to do. His feelings of inadequacy forgotten in an instant, he returned the kiss, tasting both of their essences. When Xicuz finally pulled back, Erabus could practically hear the smirk in his voice. "Good. I want to have all your firsts."

*

The sun would still not rise for another hour yet, leaving the forest pitch black, the canopy of leaves overhead blocking out most of the pale moonlight, as Xicuz led the way back toward the human village. Once the two of them had gotten control of their breathing, Xicuz climbed onto a strong branch a little way off the ground and helped Erabus to pull himself up.

Situated on the branch, Xicuz pulled Erabus onto his lap, and the two slept in each other's arms well off the rain-soaked ground. The chill from the rain hung in the air long after the storm passed, but their shared body heat kept them warm. Now, knowing the others would be rising soon, they hurried back to the village before anyone could realize Erabus had gone.

Xicuz continued along an unseen trail as he led Erabus home, their fingers intertwined the entire way back. Realizing they were now as far as he would dare go, Xicuz stopped as he spun Erabus around to him. Bringing their intertwined fingers to his lips, he gently kissed his hand before releasing him.

Cupping his cheeks with both hands, Xicuz gazed into his eyes for a moment, wanting to remember every speck of color to be found within, before leaning down to kiss his lips. The kiss didn't have the same passion as the night before, but there was something else in his embrace that he hoped to convey with his touch. More than he knew how to put into words at that moment.

Erabus seemed to understand the new emotion behind the kiss as he returned it as gently, smiling against his lips. Their moment over. Xicuz pulled back with a promise of, "Until next time," before turning and disappearing back into the forest the way they came, already knowing he would not be going far. Had he told

Erabus he planned on waiting just within the forest until he was safe, he knew he would object, worried about Xicuz's own safety.

To prevent the argument that would ensue, as he had no desire to back down from his decision, Xicuz felt it best to keep his plan to himself. It felt more than just strange to keep things from Erabus—in fact, it caused him pain to lie to Erabus, but Xicuz reminded himself that keeping him safe was worth the little white lie and the discomfort it caused him. Once he knew Erabus would be unable to spot him no matter how hard he tried, he hid behind a tree and glanced back to find Erabus still staring after him.

He held his fingers to his lips with a soft smile on his face, and for a moment, Xicuz wanted to move toward him, but Erabus waited for only a breath more before turning and walking away. He climbed the tree, his hooves slipping on the smaller branches still damp from the rain the night before and made his way up as high as he could go before jumping to the next tree.

Though his sudden weight caused the branches to sway, the leaves rustling and betraying his presence, Erabus was too far away to hear it as anything more than the wind. Jumping onto the next tree, and then the next, Xicuz paused for a moment to determine where Erabus had gone. He caught sight of him a little way off and waited until Erabus put some more distance between them before continuing to jump from one tree to another.

Once Xicuz was a few yards out, he climbed high enough he could get a good view without giving himself away. Down below, he watched in silence as Erabus nodded to a few men he passed, their expressions showing no sign they found it odd for him to be outside already, before disappearing into the building he knew the throne room lie.

It was the strangest, largest building he had ever seen with tall spires raising toward the sky, like long, dark fingers reaching toward the universe itself. Its walls were made of stone instead of the wood used on the other dwellings that were littered around it. Tall, glass windows painted in an array of colors reflected the light of the sun, showing pictures of birds in flight and flowers in bloom, splitting up the seemingly endless stone walls at even intervals.

He had only been inside it twice, but it seemed to him then that its halls stretched on forever and the grand throne room could fit two of the other dwellings inside. As he glanced around the village once more before turning to head back the way he came, he wondered which dwelling Erabus lived in.

Erabus seemed rather close to the king. Was it close enough to warrant a room within the largest building or did he, like most of the other humans, reside in one of the one or two room homes that took up much of the rest of the village? Shaking his head, as Xicuz had no way of getting an answer at that moment, he made his way through the forest once more, heading toward the cave instead of his own village.

If he weren't already there, King Zhul certainly would be soon. In little more than a few minutes, Xicuz nodded to the two satyrs who were standing guard at the entrance to the cave before making his way inside. Xicuz knelt before the king who rested in the hot springs, his eyes closed and a painful expression on his face. Xicuz wondered if he had just arrived or if he had been soaking the entire night.

Without opening his eyes, the king asked, "Where have you been, Xicuz?" before calling him to rise and sit on the edge of the springs.

Doing as instructed, Xicuz took another look at his king once he drew near. The deep pruning of his skin was impossible to miss, even from the distance of a few feet, and it confirmed his earlier suspicions that he had been there all night.

Was he now so unwell he'd been unable to leave the springs, or had he wanted to ward off the cold from the rain? Realizing he had yet to answer his question, Xicuz quipped, "Enjoying the beautiful weather," as the scene from the night before flashed through his mind. He heard every moan, every sudden intake of breath, every gasp of ecstasy that escaped Erabus's lips.

He could still feel the way Erabus trembled beneath his touch and the way it felt to have his warm hands and lips around his manhood. Just the thought of Erabus sprung him to life once more. Xicuz wondered how he could make it to the next storm without his touch. A touch that he craved more than the air in his lungs and the beat in his own heart.

The king's sudden laughter shattered the images in his mind, bringing him back to the present, and Xicuz found himself equally grateful for the distraction and disappointed by the loss. "Have there been any issues from the human village lately?" the king asked. "Anymore trespassing on our land?"

Xicuz hadn't been paying attention to their side of the forest, always searching the human side for a sign of Erabus. But he knew if there had been any problems lately, he would have heard about it from the other satyrs. "No, my king, but to be honest, I have been keeping an eye on the human prince. I still do not trust him, and I fear what he might be capable of once he is crowned the new king."

King Zhul nodded. "In truth, I was not rather fond of him myself when we met. He had the eye of a man waiting for another to die so he might take their place. Keep watch on him as you have been and if there are any developments, report them to me." Though Xicuz nodded in understanding, Zhul had closed his eyes once more causing him to miss the gesture, the look of pain returning to his face.

Xicuz wished he could help end the suffering of his own king. He made his way back out of the cave, deciding to let him rest. He nodded once more to the two guards as he passed them. It would not be long now before the king called for a succession melee, giving any who wished the chance to fight to be the next king.

As the king had fallen far too ill to fight himself, those who wanted their chance would have to fight one another. Though he knew with confidence he could beat the majority of those who might be interested in fighting for the crown, Xicuz wasn't interested. The king would fight by their side if they were ever to go to battle again. However, he spent the majority of his time stuck within the borders of Ebrein, constantly dealing with squabbles and disagreements that cropped up, delegating all the fun things to the others around him.

Xicuz had no interested in being king or anything that went with it. He would gladly lead the charge into battle, but he would never sit around and play diplomat. But that was all right. There were plenty of other great, wise, just, satyrs whom he would fall in line behind and give his life to protect if it came to that. Confident that, no matter who became the next king, they would be far better off than the humans with their next leader, Xicuz thought of Erabus once more, worried about what would happen to him the moment Jydral became the next king.

Chapter Eight

It happened all over again, and this time Erabus wasn't even able to be near his father to comfort him or make sure Jydral didn't do anything to make him worse. It seemed, as King Tribion once again grew sicker and sicker, he hadn't prevented his brother's treachery. How did he manage to poison their father again without being left alone with their father?

He knew the men who stood guard during his visit had not lied to him; they were loyal to his father. Had Jydral managed to poison him even under their watchful eye? If it hadn't been for the way his brother acted, he might have believed the king had simply fallen ill. He had been on the mend, but relapses were always possible, especially with his father's advanced age.

Instead, through Jydral's suspicious actions, Erabus became even more convinced he had not only poisoned their father when he realized he regained his health, but that he poisoned him at the meeting of the two kings as he believed in the first place. When he returned to the village, after Xicuz dropped him off, he met with his father and sat with him without any issue.

The next day passed much the same. Although Jeqor assured him the king would be well enough to move around again, his father had taken a turn for the worse. Faster than he had before, King Tribion became weak and pale, barely able to open his eyes, let alone sit up in bed.

His heart raced, and his breathing became labored once more. As if the few days his father was getting better had only been in Erabus's imagination.

Still, until then, he was able to stay by his father's side and try to nurse him back to health. Then one day, three days after he returned from his night with Xicuz, the guards who he knew were loyal to his father, Alyster and Garion, mysteriously grew ill themselves.

Before Erabus could even question what happened, he spotted the new arrivals, Dlivion and Azemar, men he knew to be loyal to his brother, relieving the others of their duty. The men were on their feet the entire night, guarding the king's door without a break to eat or sleep and yet they tried to refuse, insisting they would stay there until the other two were well enough to relieve them of their duty as scheduled.

Jydral arrived at that moment and had Alyster and Garion arrested for failing to comply with a royal order. "You can't do that!" Erabus insisted, trying to step in front of the guards who were beginning to draw their swords in confusion, only to be shoved to the floor by the closer of Jydral's two guards. Erabus scrambled to his feet and shot Dlivion an angry look, but he already turned back to helping Azemar arrest the other two.

Before he could come to their defense again, his brother stepped in between them. "Effective immediately, I am restricting all access to the king, other than by Jeqor. My father needs to get his rest if he is going to get better," Jydral said, making it sound as though they did not share the same father. In any other situation, Erabus would have laughed at that.

Now though, he felt the anger rising within him at the thought that a man like Jydral would have the audacity to think himself more deserving to be called their father's son than Erabus. "You cannot forbid me from seeing my own father, Jydral," Erabus insisted. Even though he was slated to become the next king, Jydral wielded as little power as he did until his coronation.

One of his ancestors did away with the idea of crown princes and all the power they wielded after his own son abused said power to kill all but one of his eleven siblings in fear they might one day rise against him. Once their ancestral king imprisoned his eldest son and rescued the youngest, who had been incarcerated, he passed a law that even though the firstborn son would continue to be next in line for the throne, he would wield no more power than any other prince or princess.

It was another thing he worried Jydral would change the moment he became king. He already tried to claim more power than he had their entire time growing up. Erabus would not be surprised if his brother ordered his death the moment they laid the crown upon his head. Of course, that was assuming he didn't find a way to kill him while their father still lived.

Refusing to let his brother think he could intimidate him, Erabus moved to push past him, only to find himself thrown to the floor once more with Dlivion's sword at his throat. Glaring up at them from where he landed, he spat at them, "You're both traitors, just like Jydral."

Dlivion seemed about to step forward, undoubtedly planning to draw blood with the movement, when Jydral raised his arm to stop him. In a calmer voice than he remembered him ever having before, he said, "You are not to go anywhere near the king, Erabus. Father was doing better until you returned and visited him again."

For a moment, Erabus could only stare at him in stunned silence, but a sound coming from behind him explained everything.

He's playing for an audience. Though he wasn't sure who stood behind him, he knew it didn't matter. He couldn't let anyone believe his brother's vicious lies about him. "No one would ever believe I had anything to do with making the king sick. They know what type of man I am, and what type you are," Erabus insisted as he shot to his feet and stared defiantly at his brother.

"Do not be so sure, Erabus," Jydral said coldly, lowering his voice enough that those behind him were unable to hear his threat. "Now I suggest you leave or I will have the guards lock you in the dungeon to ensure our king can recover," he said, raising his voice back to his usual, hard tone and if Erabus thought for even a second his brother might let the king recover while he rotted in the dungeon, just to prove Erabus made him sick, he would have allowed himself to be arrested in a heartbeat.

But he knew he would never let the king get better when he was so close to having the crown on his head already. Pinning Jydral with cold, hateful eyes, he warned, "You will pay for what you are doing to Father. Of that, you can be sure," before taking off down the hallway. He needed to get away before his brother could follow through on his threat to lock him up. As long as Erabus remained free, he still had the chance to come up with a way to get back into the king's room and figure out a way to save him.

*

Try as he might, Erabus couldn't come up with any plan to get in to see his father. If he didn't act quickly, it might be too late to save him. With no other options left to him, he turned to the only person he could: Xicuz. Though it was not raining, he hoped he would find him anyway.

Grabbing his bow and quiver of arrows, he glanced around to make sure his brother didn't have eyes on him and stepped into the near darkness of the forest. Where the sun shone brightly in Edith, the thick canopy of leaves overhead blocked nearly all the cheerful light out. The dimmed, gloomy light that did penetrate the canopy matched how Erabus felt perfectly.

He hurried to their usual meeting spot, but Xicuz wasn't there. *Of course, he's not here*, Erabus pointed out to himself with disappointment. *It's not raining.* He would not risk being so close to their borders when the skies were this clear and there might be hunters roaming about.

Erabus sighed and leaned back against their tree. Should he head back home or stay in the complete off chance Xicuz happened to travel that way? But even as he tried to make up his mind, he realized his feet had no intention of obeying him if he decided to go back home.

Confidence in his decision to stay slipped away with each minute that passed. Erabus just gave up when he felt a presence nearby. Glancing up expectantly, he couldn't help but smile when he saw Xicuz standing a few feet before him. "What are you doing here, Erabus?" Xicuz asked. "It's not raining."

"How did you know I was here?" Erabus asked.

"I could sense you were near." Xicuz glanced around, and apparently deciding it was safe, he closed the distance between them and pulled Erabus into his arms. At any other time, Erabus might have worried about others seeing them, but at that moment, he had far more pressing matters to worry about.

"I know I should not be here when it is not raining, but I needed to talk to you, Xicuz." Erabus rested his head against Xicuz's shoulder and listened to the mesmerizing sound of his heart beating. "It's happening again. King Tribion is sick once more, but now Jydral is blocking all access to him, and I feel if I do not get in to see him soon, it will be too late to save him from the poison."

Xicuz mulled over his words in silence before finally asking, "Would a distraction be able to pull the guards off him?"

"That means a lot to me, but I can't risk endangering you," Erabus said. "You are one of the people I care about most in the world."

"Rest assured, Erabus," Xicuz insisted as he kissed his forehead, "I will be fine. I will simply take a page out of Jydral's book."

"We still don't know how he pulled that off," Erabus said as his own thoughts turned back to the day of the meeting of the two kings. The archer his brother sent to either kill the king or distract them so he could poison him, managed to get off a single arrow and get away without ever leaving a trace.

"I haven't had the time to tell you, but I have figured it out. The archer used the trees. I went back and checked. I found at least three paths starting from the tree the arrow came from that you can take jumping from branch to branch without ever leaving the trees. The paths lead far enough away no one would ever search where they would drop down for tracks."

Unable to process the information for a moment, Erabus could only stare at him.

*

Seeing his stunned expression, Xicuz cupped his face with his hands and waited until he turned his eyes to him before placing a chaste kiss on his lips. "Head back into your village and get into a position that would allow you to get to the king's side quickly but would keep you out of sight. I will distract them and get away long before they can reach me."

Even with his assurances, he sensed Erabus starting to object and silenced him with another kiss. "Meet back here at midnight tonight, with or without the rain." After a moment, Erabus's eyes searching his, he nodded before reluctantly pulling back from his embrace. Xicuz caressed his cheek before relieving him of his bow and arrows.

After slinging them over his own shoulder, he took Erabus's hand in his and led the way back toward the human village. Once he walked as close as he dared, he glanced around to make sure there was no one else around before placing one last gentle kiss on Erabus's lips. Though his lips moved against his own, showing his desire to put more heat behind it, Xicuz pulled back before they could get worked up.

As much as he wanted to, he knew if he allowed himself to get lost in Erabus's touch this close to Edith, they would risk getting caught. The last thing they needed was for Jydral to be able to use Erabus's relationship with a satyr against him. "Be safe," Erabus whispered before touching his cheek, much as he had done to Erabus only a few minutes earlier. He turned and made his way back toward Edith alone.

Waiting until he was out of sight, Xicuz climbed as high as he could into the largest tree nearby, situating himself on the largest branch. For a few moments, he held his breath, wondering why he couldn't see Erabus yet.

A moment later he spotted him crossing the threshold into the village, giving one last longing look over his shoulder. Apparently, he was as reluctant to leave as Xicuz was for him to go. Smiling softly to himself as he finally released his breath, he watched Erabus make his way back toward the door leading to the throne room.

He withdrew the bow and grabbed one of the arrows from the quiver. He glanced around for an opening.

Finding a big enough area, Xicuz notched the arrow and let it fly. Even as the arrow hit its mark, he heard shouts coming from those who were nearest and watched as some called out, they were under attack while others searched the tree line with their frightened eyes.

Xicuz notched another arrow and released it as soon as he acquired a new target. The arrow landed exactly where he wanted it to. The humans were lucky he wasn't aiming for any of them. They were making it far too easy.

Glancing back to where Erabus hid, Xicuz saw no sign of the door opening or the men coming out. He chose another target and let loose a third arrow. "To arms!" he heard someone calling out as guards rushed toward the speaker. In the same moment he figured out the voice belonged to Jydral, he realized none of the guards came from the door.

Knowing he pushed his luck, he shot one last arrow toward his fourth and final target. This one happened to be close to where Jydral stood, though far enough away that he was never in any danger. The shriek that came from the human prince when the arrow landed a few feet away was well worth the effort.

"Arm yourselves, men!" he called out before leading a large group of humans toward the edge of the forest. Shouldering the bow so he would be ready to go the moment he could, Xicuz glanced back toward the door and sighed in relief when he spotted the guards coming through it. He noticed Erabus sneaking in just before the door could close behind them.

Confident his plan worked, Xicuz turned and leapt toward the nearest tree in the opposite direction from where the humans were coming. He heard them closing in on the tree he had been shooting from but paid them little mind as he knew he would be far out of their sight before they thought to look up.

*

"Search carefully! They are here somewhere!" Jydral called out, certain they traced the arrows back to their source. And yet, as they searched the forest floor for any sign of the attackers, he soon found there were none. Not a single footprint or hoofprint could be found in the area. There was no wind to push the arrows off course so their tracks should have been there, exactly where his men were searching and coming up empty.

Unless the animals shot from the trees. Looking up into the thick canopy of leaves, he searched for any sign of the archers, though he already knew it would be in vain. They'd had more than enough time for them to escape since the final arrow landed a few feet away from where he stood.

Had he been their intended target all along and they gave up when they realized their aim hadn't been as true as they first thought or...? As another thing dawned on him, Jydral paused his search as he turned back toward the village. *Could it be merely a distraction?* Much as the lone arrow he aimed at his father had been. His was so he could keep Erabus and the guards on both sides of the table busy, allowing him to slip poison into his father's cup.

What could be the reason for this one? *Erabus*, he realized as only his pitiful brother would ever dare to do something behind his back. And if he wanted to distract him, there was only one place he would go. Glancing around as he called out, "Search for tracks further out. They were in the trees!" He spotted Azemar and Dlivion who he knew were supposed to be guarding the door to the king's room.

They left it unattended, just as Erabus wanted them to and gave him the perfect opportunity to get in to see their father. He had to stop him before he could do anything to undo all his hard work. He was so close now, close enough he could feel the weight of the crown upon his head, and he would not let anyone take away what was rightfully his. He would sooner slaughter his brother where he stood and lose him as a scapegoat for the death of the king than risk their father getting well enough to mess with the line of succession.

*

From the shadows, Erabus watched in nerve-wracking silence as Xicuz shot one arrow after another into the middle of the village. Though he knew Xicuz would not hit anyone, it did not stop him from worrying about the satyr himself. Would he be able to get away before they could get to him? Would his brother, who called for men to arms themselves, realize he hid in the trees quicker than they were expecting?

And were the guards going to fall for the distraction and leave their posts? Hearing the ping of the fourth arrow hit the ground, rather near to his brother judging by the sound of fear it wrenched from him, Erabus realized Xicuz still hadn't left yet. Why was he still in the trees? Even as the door beside him opened, he realized Xicuz had no intention of leaving before the guards did.

As he stepped out of the shadows to wave him away and risk the whole thing failing in order to protect him, Erabus noticed their plan worked as Azemar and Dlivion ran past him. The moment they were far enough passed the shadowed area he hid in, Erabus snuck through the door before it could close behind them.

Silently hoping Xicuz was already long gone and out of the reach of the guards, he rushed down the hall toward his father's room. The moment he pushed open the door Erabus noticed two things.

First there was no sign of Jeqor, the royal healer, and as he doubted the elderly man would be rushing out to join the crowd who were undoubtedly searching the forest by now, it could only mean his brother lied about continuing to allow him access. Did his father have anyone by his side in his absence? The second thing he noticed was his father's prone form sweating profusely with the rise of his chest barely discernible.

Gasping at the sight of his once proud and strong father, Erabus crossed the room in only a few steps before sitting down on the bed beside him. He reached his hand up to touch his cheek and nearly pulled it back as though it had been burnt. His skin burned hot as fire. Undoubtedly awoken by Erabus's cool touch, his father opened his tired eyes, focusing on his after a few moments of looking disoriented.

Erabus smiled at him sweetly. "I do not know what to do, Father," Erabus admitted, calling him by the title he had long given up in respect to him as a king. At that moment, he wasn't the king of Edith or a great leader who saw his people through turmoil and peace, but purely the father he loved. The only true family he had left.

Even though his father had been able to save Erabus's mother from a traitor's execution by hiding the fact she bore a son from another man, nothing could be done to prevent her death when an illness swept through the village when he was only a few years old. "I know Jydral has been poisoning you, and I thought I stopped him; you were getting better. Somehow, he managed to poison you again even though I had him watched, but I do not know what he used to make you sick.

"I do not know how to make you well again, but I will not let him get away with this. I will make sure everyone knows what he has done. They will know him for the monster he is, and they will learn the truth of his birth," Erabus swore, burning with hatred for his brother like he never felt before. The intense emotion that welled up inside him frightened him for a moment, but he soon found it to be a strength as it breathed new life into his desire to fight back.

"No, my child," his father began in a raspy voice. "Do not go against him. You will put yourself in grave danger. If he is willing to do this to me, there is no telling what evil might befall you at his hand. Live this day so you may help protect our people when they need you," the king pleaded, his voice echoing the same concern for his only true son that shown in his eyes.

"It doesn't matter, Father. Any danger I might put myself in is worth it if I can do something to save you," Erabus insisted as he squeezed his father's hand, his eyes pleading with him to not only let him fight but to continue the fight himself. If his father gave up, Erabus would not be able to stop Jydral on his own. The few men who were loyal to his father might follow him if he revolted against Jydral, but as he had no men loyal to himself, he knew they would be outnumbered.

"There is no saving me," the king whispered, startling Erabus to the point he could only gape at him in silence for a moment, convincing himself he misheard him. Though, judging by the resigned, regretful expression on his father's face, he had not.

"What do you mean?" His voice came out at a far higher octave than it usual.

"The poison has spread too far now for me to be saved. Jeqor already confirmed this last night. I assume it to be the only reason why Jydral let him in to see me, to confirm for himself that my time was running out. My time is short, my child, and there is nothing that can be done to save me now."

His father's words were like a slap to the face, even though he knew without having to ask that his father hadn't blamed him for even a moment for the fate that befell him. Jydral was the only one responsible for their father's impending death, but that didn't stop Erabus from feeling the blame land on his shoulders too. His brother had gotten into the room because he left to go gather herbs for his father.

The king had gotten better, and Erabus let his guard down long enough for his brother to poison him again. He failed to stop him at the meeting of the two kings and he failed again within the walls of his own home. He left guards at his door, gave them explicit instructions that Jydral was not to be left alone with the king, to watch him like a hawk when in the king's presence and yet Jydral managed to poison him right under their noses anyway.

Would Erabus have seen what he was up to if he stayed in the room to watch him personally? Would he have been able to see what the men, who swore to give their lives in defense of their king, missed completely? Would he have been able to stop his brother even if he had seen proof of his betrayal? His doubts did little more than affirm his suspicions that he should have banned all visitors to his father, himself included, other than the healer as it would have been the only way to keep his brother out.

Of course, realizing that now did no one any good, and it made Erabus hate himself even more for his failure to protect his father. Not about to give up and admit defeat, Erabus insisted, "I refuse to believe we are past the point of no return. There must be something we can do to save you." Whatever his father would have said next was cut off by voices coming from outside.

Though they were too far off to hear what they were saying or confirm his brother's voice in the mix, the worried expression on his father's face assured him he knew the implications of him being found in the room. "The only thing you can do now, my sweet child, is live. Do not give your brother a reason to want you dead. Go now, before they return and find you here with me," his father pleaded. "As your father and your king, I order you to leave my room at once. Obey my last command as king as you have obeyed every other in your life."

Seeing the unshed tears in his father's eyes, Erabus held back his refusal as he leaned forward to kiss his brow, even as his heart broke at the thought of leaving and never seeing him again. It went against everything he believed in, everything he stood for to leave his king's side in order to save himself, but he couldn't imagine his last interaction with his father to be his disobeying his dying wish.

The guards' footsteps were getting closer. "Carry my love with you, Father, and know one day he will pay for his betrayal," Erabus vowed before bowing to him for the last time and making his way back out of the room. He ducked into the king's sitting room and closed the door behind him.

His brother's muffled voice called out by the closed door. Erabus hid within the giant wardrobe that held the king's winter clothes. He scooted as far back as he could to hide beneath the thickest clothes he could find and prayed his brother wouldn't find him.

Chapter Nine

Jydral burst into the room. "Good morning, my king," he called out mockingly as he glanced around, expecting to find his brother weeping at their father's bedside. Instead, he found the room empty other than the pale, sweating king who stared at him coldly from where he lay.

He turned back to Dlivion and whispered, "Search the sitting room," knowing it to be the only place his brother could have gone if he left just before they arrived. The window stood far too small for even Erabus to fit through and if he tried to take the hallway, he would have run straight into Jydral.

Dlivion took longer to return than he would have expected. Jydral wondered if his suspicions in the forest were incorrect.

Had it not been a distraction like he originally thought? Had it been Erabus, himself, in the tree shooting the bow instead of satyrs as he assumed?

Dlivion returned a few moments later—sans Erabus. "He's not there, Your Majesty."

Jydral turned back to his father in confusion. The king could barely keep his eyes open, his icy glare looking less daunting with each passing second; Jydral smirked.

"It will not be long now, my king." He stood beside his bed, towering above him. "Worry not, Father. I will be a far better king than you ever were. I will take my people to greater heights than your feeble mind could have ever even fathomed."

"You will never be a king, Jydral," the king spat. "You will merely be a *usurper*." He fell into a coughing fit that had him fighting to breathe before it ended. Instead of being wounded by his father's words, Jydral's arrogant smirk grew even larger.

"Poor, ignorant King Tribion. All kings are the usurpers of their fathers. For once in your life, do something with my best interest at heart and die quickly. I do not wish to have to help you along any more than I already have." Jydral turned his back and made his way toward the door.

Behind him, the king called out, "A father will always put the best interests of his son ahead of a bastard's," but Jydral paid him little mind as he closed the door.

"Do not move from your post," he instructed the guards. "Not even if the entire village catches on fire." Though it was far too late for Erabus to do anything for the king now, Jydral wouldn't give either of them the satisfaction of being able to say good-bye.

*

Erabus's arms and legs had long since cramped, every inch of his body protesting being in such a confined space for so long, but he couldn't risk leaving his hiding place until there would be no one walking around to catch him trying to escape. Especially not after one of his brother's goons came into the room not long after he hid and brushed past the wardrobe.

He came so close, in fact, that the sword he jabbed into the pile of clothes Erabus hid in barely managed to pierce between where his arms and legs were curled up on one another. An inch higher or lower and he would have been stabbed. It took every ounce of willpower he had to not call out when he realized how close he was to being caught.

He waited until long past dark out before emerging.

Crawling out from underneath the clothing his father would never wear again, the realization breaking his heart for the second time that day, Erabus held his breath as he listened for any sound coming from outside the sitting room, unable to hear anything else other than the guards occasionally speaking to one another. He made his way over to the window and opened the shutters enough to see the darkened sky. He waited with bated breath for a sign of anyone passing by.

Finding none, Erabus climbed as quietly as he could out the window, pulling the shutters closed behind him after jumping the short distance to the ground. He took off into the closest entrance to the forest before anyone could spot him.

Once hidden inside the darkened forest, he took off as fast as his legs could go, heading straight for where he promised to meet Xicuz. Even in the near pitch darkness, guided only by the small amount of moonlight that could penetrate the canopy overhead, Erabus skillfully avoided the exposed roots and fallen branches that littered the forest floor.

Too many days of his life were spent exploring the forest, learning every inch of the area that surrounded Edith in attempts to keep out of his brother's way. Erabus wanted to leave him alone, to give him no reason to become his enemy once he realized Jydral was jealous of him even without any cause for him to be, but as he ran from the soon-to-be deathbed of his father, he knew now no matter what he might have done it would never have changed the way things would end up.

Jydral was an evil man, capable of killing their father as though he were a stranger and not the man who raised him to be a just and honest man as he had with Erabus. His father never showed him partiality, even after he learned the truth of his mother's betrayal, and in fact had shown more favoritism to Jydral, no doubt wanting to make up for the fact he would never get to know his true father.

If he knew then everything he knew now, Erabus would have outed his brother for the bastard he was the moment he learned the truth, ensuring he would never grow to be a man with power that would corrupt him into an evil, despicable man. Would that have changed the outcome? Was it truly his taste for power as a prince that led him to be the man he became, or would he still be as corrupted if raised by his birth father?

Erabus knew he would never have the answer to that question as he never learned who or what type of man Jydral's true father was. Their mother took the secret to the grave, and as far as he knew, even his father remained in the dark all these years. Did he look at all like his father? Or enough like their mother that it didn't help his father narrow down the suspects?

Shaking his head against questions long unanswerable, Erabus realized he stood before their tree, his feet instinctively bringing him to his destination when his thoughts were focused elsewhere. Reaching up to touch the cold, rough bark as though it somehow connected him to Xicuz himself, Erabus drew a deep breath before glancing around. He was alone.

Sighing softly to himself, he leaned back against their tree, staring into the dark forest in the direction he knew Xicuz would be coming from. He shut his eyes. With them closed, he saw his father lying in his bed once more, weak, and helpless to stop the fate that would soon befall him. He saw his father's lips moving, repeating the last command he gave him but was unable to hear his voice no matter how much he tried to concentrate on it.

"I'm here," a voice called out, startling him back to the present. For a moment, Erabus thought his father spoke in his memory, but realized it was the other voice he longed to hear. Opening his eyes, he spotted Xicuz standing a few feet before him and jumped up, rushing forward to wrap his arms around him, as if he feared he would disappear the moment he let him go.

"I was too late," Erabus said before Xicuz could speak. "The poison has already spread too far, and he cannot be saved. I have failed him." He buried his face in Xicuz's naked chest, finally allowing the tears he held back since he left his father's side to flow unchecked. His body was racked with uncontrollable sobs. Xicuz wrapped his arms around him.

"I am so sorry, my dear Erabus, that you cannot save your king. I truly wish I could do something to help," Xicuz whispered above him, and Erabus knew Xicuz would do anything he asked him to. As much as he loved the thought of having someone who he knew to be completely on his side, he realized at that moment he had never been totally honest with him before.

"Father," he said, his voice cracking. Xicuz stared down at him in confusion. "King Tribion is my father," Erabus explained, finding the weight on his shoulders a bit lighter at the announcement as though speaking their relation out loud gave him a newfound strength.

For a moment, Xicuz's only reaction was to tighten his hold. Erabus scanned his eyes for any sign he angered him by withholding such important information, but he found nothing but sympathy and kindness. "You are a prince of man," he confirmed after a moment, his tone soft and without a hint of judgment as he caressed his cheek with the back of his fingers.

"I am sorry I never told you before, Xicuz. I hadn't meant to hide it from you, it's just that I simply stopped referring to myself as a prince long ago. As a child, I saw how much it made Jydral jealous for me to refer to him as Father, or myself as his equal by using my rightful title, and I did not want to cause any unnecessary conflict between us. Though," Erabus paused as he turned his eyes back toward the village, "if I knew how things would turn out with him even with my attempts to placate him, I would have referred to myself as Prince Erabus more just to spite him.

"Hell, I might even have spoken in the third person." Thinking of ways he could have gotten back at his brother in preparation for the cruel man he would become now, long after the fact, did little more than cause Erabus to feel as if he failed his father even more. What if Jydral had the audacity to behave as he did because he didn't stand up to him while they were growing up? Realizing where his thoughts were turning, Erabus shook his head and buried it in Xicuz's shoulder once more. "What am I supposed to do when there is nothing I can do to save my father?"

*

"I am afraid I do not know, Erabus," Xicuz admitted, holding Erabus close as he sat down against the tree and pulled him onto his lap. He felt the change in Erabus's body, his tensing vibrating through Xicuz's fingers and he knew what was coming long before Erabus broke down in tears. Holding on to him as tightly as he dared, he stroked his hair as Erabus burrowed in his arms and released what little control he still had.

Sobs rocked his body once more, unchecked by Erabus as he seemed to allow all his defenses to fall in Xicuz's embrace. Covering Erabus's face with his free hand, Xicuz hid him away from the empty forest, his own pathetic attempt to protect him from the rest of the world. He could not save his king and father. He could not undo everything his brother did against him. He could not save the humans from the fate they were dealt, but at that moment, at least, he could guard him against the prying eyes of the world and allow him to mourn in peace.

Though it was not much, it seemed to be enough that he managed to cry himself to sleep, soon settling down until only an occasional shudder interrupted his even breathing. Watching him in the pale moonlight, Xicuz wished he could do something to save him from his pain.

Xicuz wondered how he hadn't seen it before. *How could I have missed he was a prince?* The young man in his arms acted far more like a prince than he ever saw, or heard of, Jydral acting. He was diplomatic, respectful, and honest—all the things he saw in his own king.

*

Jydral awoke in the middle of the night to someone pounding on his door. He expected it, yet it still caused him to growl out in annoyance at having his sleep interrupted. He already knew what words would spill from the lips of his guard, knowing they would not dare disturb him for anything else. Yet, he still wanted to hear them. He needed to have them spoken out loud as though that would make them even truer.

He needed to hear the announcement he had been waiting to receive for as long as he could remember. "Come in," he called out as he smirked to himself in the darkness, his hands wringing the sheets in anticipation. His door opened, revealing the silhouette of one of his guards, his face hidden in shadows by the candles that lined the hallway behind him. "Say it," he said, a dark excitement rising in him.

"Prince Jydral," Aothorn said, "the king has passed away. Long live King Jydral." He dropped to his knees and bowed before him. The first of countless others who would address Jydral by his new and rightful title before the day ended. He decided at that moment Aothorn would be the one who would get the honor of being the commander of his royal guard.

The perfect reward for his most loyal subject. Jydral rose from the bed he lay down in as a prince and allowed his feet to touch the cold floor as a king for the first time. The realization that everything he ever wanted was now in his grasp caused a peaceful calm to come over him, the likes he had never felt before. "Forgive me, my king," a second voice called out, and he glanced up to find Elovonos kneeling outside the doorway. "I tried to inform Erabus of the king's passing, but he isn't in his room. None of the guards in the area have seen him all night."

Standing there in silence for a moment, his foot halfway inside the soft, slip-on shoes he kept by his bed in anticipation of the cold stone floor, he thought back to earlier that night before he went to bed. He hadn't seen his brother either and he couldn't remember the last time he had. Erabus had not been in their father's room as he assumed.

He hadn't been outside where the arrows were shot into the village, nor did he join the group who went in search of the archers. If he did, Jydral would never have needed to hurry back to ensure he hadn't snuck into the late king's room while the archer kept him distracted. Was he the archer after all and remained in the forest even after Jydral and the others all returned to the village?

Confused by his absence, Jydral threw his cloak over his shoulders as he made his way out of his room, his guards parting for him to pass before falling in step behind him. He wound down the halls until he reached his brother's door. He reached up to open it as a sudden thought struck him; he could not remember the last time he stepped foot into Erabus's far inferior room. *Have I ever?*

He could remember going into Erabus's previous room, which had been much closer to Jydral's own when they were children, but he had no memory of stepping into his current room after he switched. Though he would never admit it to him, Jydral knew Erabus made the switch because he feared being so close to him while he slept. It made him far too vulnerable, and they both knew it was only a matter of time before he took advantage of that.

As he crossed the threshold into the cold room and glanced around, Jydral soon realized he had not been there since his brother moved. He had only been to that particular room once in his entire life, the night he got his first taste of a woman's touch. She was one of his father's serving girls, only a few years older than Jydral. He couldn't even remember what she looked like.

In fact, he couldn't even recall her name, but at the same time, he wasn't entirely sure he ever learned it in the first place. Dismissing her memory, he glanced around the room once more before shutting the door behind him and making his way outside. Though it crossed his mind for a moment to stop by his father's room, if for no other reason than to confirm his death for himself, Jydral decided against it as he had no desire to look upon his lifeless form.

The only thing that mattered at that moment was to announce his death and officially begin his life as king, fulfilling the destiny he worked toward his entire life. He stepped out into the cold, dark night and breathed in the icy predawn air for the first time as a king. Jydral smiled at the thought of how many firsts he would experience that night and in the countless days to come.

The first time he would eat a meal as king. The first time he would lay down in bed and go to sleep as king. The first time he would greet his wretched brother as his king. And a seemingly endless number of other firsts that he could never dream of counting at that moment. Stepping farther out into the village, noticing no one other than a few scattered guards on patrol who were currently walking about, he made his way over toward one.

"Ring the bells to alert the village to my father's passing," he instructed, and continued on his way, wanting to be in the throne room as soon as the announcement was made, when the guard's words stopped him.

"Shouldn't we inform Prince Erabus first, so he does not find out from the bells?" he asked.

Anger flared in him. "I said ring the bells!" he roared. He spun away without waiting to make sure he would follow his orders this time.

Making a note to demote the guard first thing in the morning, Jydral began making his way toward the side entrance of the throne room before stopping to stare out at the dark forest. Erabus was out there somewhere.

He didn't know where he hid within the darkened forest or why he was there, why he spent countless hours there, but he knew it would not matter soon. Once he heard the ringing of the bell, he knew his brother would come running back to Edith, putting him exactly where he wanted him.

*

The instant the bells echoed through the surrounding forest, Erabus shot to his feet as a heartbreaking, ear-piercing wail was wrenched from his lips, sounding foreign and inhuman even to himself. "Father!" he cried out, barely noticing when Xicuz leapt to his feet beside him and put his arms around him. The sudden warmth and pressure around his waist were enough to cause him to collapse in his arms, an inhuman "No!" escaping his lips even as he lost the strength to remain standing.

"Erabus, my love, what is it?" Xicuz asked as his hold tightened around him and he turned to sob in his chest once more. For a long time, Erabus could do little more than wail through his tears as he shook against Xicuz's strong hold. His mind was incapable of realizing it at that moment, but later when he had the chance to calm down and think coherent thoughts once again, Erabus would be certain Xicuz's embrace kept him breathing at that moment as he felt his heart breaking.

"My father," he sobbed when he finally regained the ability to speak. "The bells are only rung to herald a death in the royal family." As the tears began anew, Xicuz pulled him into a tight embrace, whispering soft words of sympathy and concern that seemed like nothing more than mumbled nonsense to his emotionally exhausted brain.

A few minutes later when his foggy mind finally cleared, and he realized Xicuz was whispering he was sorry over and over, Erabus shot up when he realized how much time passed since the bells had been rung. The memory of the sound that hadn't echoed through Edith since his mother died all those years ago brought a new wave of tears and despair upon him, but Erabus pushed it down as deep as he could, knowing he could not afford to get lost in his sorrow again.

At least not until he returned to the village and his brother could not use his absence against him. "I need to go home," Erabus explained when he realized Xicuz, who jumped to his feet moments after Erabus did, still had a hold of him and showed no sign of letting him go so he could. For a few moments, he stared at him in silence, wondering if he ever planned on letting him go, but Erabus soon realized the answer was written plainly on his face.

Not only did Xicuz have no intention of letting him go, his concern for the outcome of his return to the village was practically readable in his expression even before he asked, "Wouldn't Jydral blame the king's death on you the moment you returned?"

Realizing Xicuz had the same concern he had thought about a few moments before, Erabus couldn't help but smile before taking a hold of his hands and squeezing them reassuringly. "That is exactly the reason though. If I do not return, Jydral will use that as proof I am behind our father's death, and I will not be there to defend myself. It is far easier to convince the rest of Edith if there is no one there to speak for me. And besides," Erabus said as he squeezed his hands once more, swearing he felt more confidence the longer he held on to him, "If I am there, there is the chance it will be enough to cause him to back down."

It took a few moments but Xicuz finally nodded his approval and released his grip on Erabus's hands. "I do not know when I will be able to see you again, Xicuz," Erabus continued. "And I would tell you to stay as far away from Edith as you can, but somehow I know you would not listen," Erabus smiled when Xicuz smirked at his playful accusation before caressing his cheek. If it didn't mean he would never be able to return to his village again, Erabus would have stayed right there with him.

"Each night, to assure you that I am all right, I will leave a sign for you to see. I will hang a small scrap of fabric on the tree just inside the forest; you should have no problems seeing it from where you shot the arrows," Erabus assured him before reaching up to kiss his cheek. Apparently refusing to allow that to be their parting, Xicuz took hold of his chin and tilted his head up before placing a less than chaste kiss on his lips.

Erabus returned the kiss with passion before pulling back; he would never leave if he didn't stop things from heating up more. Holding on to the memory of that moment, Erabus turned and started back toward the village only to find himself stopping when Xicuz grabbed a hold of his hand. "Be careful, my dear Erabus. I cannot stand the thought of anything happening to you."

"I will be safe, Xicuz. That I promise," Erabus assured him with a smile before disappearing back into the forest before Xicuz could stop him again. As he made his way back toward his village, Erabus wondered if his assurance would turn out to be correct. Would he be okay or was he walking right into a trap?

Chapter Ten

Jydral held his breath as Erabus passed beneath him unaware, not daring to release it until Erabus grew too far away to hear. The idiots made it far too easy for him. They handed him the perfect ammunition to use against his brother and he didn't even need to work for it. He saw the heated kiss they exchanged. At least now he understood why his brother was always gone and what he was doing.

Taking his eyes off Erabus, he turned his attention back to the satyr whom he recognized from when he came to the village and accused him of hunting on the satyrs' land. Of course, his accusations were accurate, but that was beside the point. Jydral heard his name that day, but he couldn't be bothered to try to remember it. Besides, his name wasn't important at that moment, as he would find out soon enough. His connection to Erabus was.

As he watched the satyr watching his brother, his eyes lingering on the direction Erabus disappeared in long after he was out of sight, he couldn't help but notice the look of longing in his eyes. A moment or two later, he turned and made his way back toward his own village. Even with how his feet were itching to move, Jydral held himself still until the satyr was too far away to hear him.

He dropped from the tree and glanced in both directions before smirking in satisfaction. He would put his plan in motion the next day as he didn't want to wait until after his coronation to deal with his brother and his newfound companion.

*

Drawing a deep breath, Erabus opened the door and made his way down the long corridor that would bring him back to his father once more. It did not take him long to notice the guards his brother left were still guarding the door even though there was no longer any reason to. What was the point in trying to keep him from his father any longer? Not that he would let his brother's guards stop him from saying good-bye.

Realizing they were moving in to stop him from reaching the door, Erabus punched the guard closest to him, silently daring Dlivion to prevent him from entering the room. Apparently thinking better of it, both he and Azemar parted ways so he could enter, and he forgot all about them as he rushed to his father's side. He dropped to his knees beside the bed and took Tribion's hand in his as he glanced down at his cold, lifeless form.

It seemed as though the whole idea of his father's passing was a figment of his imagination until he stood facing the reality. Erabus's heart broke again as he stared down at him and silently begged him to open his eyes. To look upon him once more and assure him the ringing of the bells had been just a cruel trick played by his brother. That he only dreamed up the haunting sound.

But his eyes remained forever closed, he spoke no more words of assurances. He was gone and Erabus never had the chance to say good-bye. He should have been by his side in his final moments, holding his hand as he did now and assuring him he would be okay. Instead, he had been forced to retreat to the forest, hide away until there was no longer any reason for him to need to.

Jydral would no longer fear him trying to save the king as he was far beyond saving now, but that didn't mean he was safe from the repercussions of what he had done. Erabus would find a way to prove to the others that Jydral murdered the king. They would know him for the monster he was, Erabus would make sure of it, but it wasn't hard for him to realize Jydral would come to the same conclusion.

He had to know Erabus wouldn't sit back and allow the impostor who killed his father take the throne that wasn't meant to be his. His father gave him a chance, kept his parentage a secret and raised him to be his heir and Jydral used every opportunity to betray him. He would pay for what he had done, but before that he would need to see to the king's funeral.

He wanted to deal with his brother right away, because having him at his father's funeral would be a disgrace to King Tribion. But it would be better to wait. The king deserved to take precedence and Jydral might even drop his defenses a little if Erabus didn't act on his knowledge instantly. Of course, any sign he moved against him and that plan would go right out the window and he would announce to all of Edith who he truly was.

Burying his face into his father's blankets, Erabus released the tears he held back and sobbed uncontrollably. "I am so sorry, Father, I did not realize his treachery until it was too late to stop him. I swear Jydral will pay for what he did to you." Within a few minutes, he cried himself to sleep.

*

After Erabus left, Xicuz could only stand there staring long after he could no longer see him. More than anything, he wished he could go to him and wrap his arms around him once more. Assure him everything would be okay, but he knew it would not change anything and a more pressing matter needed to be dealt with at that moment. He needed to inform his own king about what happened.

King Zhul needed to be prepared for the worst, which Xicuz knew would come soon with Jydral taking over as king. He would hold back on his desire to attack the satyrs for only so long now that he oversaw Edith and the army that went with it. Making his way back through the forest, he swore he made the trip more times now since he met Erabus than the entire time before he met him combined.

The moment he crossed the threshold into his village, Xicuz spotted his king presiding over a duel between two satyrs with the rising sun at their backs, although he had no idea what caused the fight at that moment. He made his way toward him and knelt in respect. "Forgive the interruption, my king, but there is news from Edith," he said, drawing the attention of not only the king but of the other satyrs in the area as well.

Once the king gestured for him to speak, Xicuz continued, "King Tribion passed away last night and Prince Jydral will be crowned soon."

"That is grave news indeed. I hoped the old man had a few more good years in him. He wasn't that much older than I." King Zhul shook his head sadly. "Xicuz, keep an eye on the human village for now in case the prince does decide to attack once the power is his. Report to me any changes or anything suspicious."

Xicuz bowed his head before turning to head back the way he came. A few minutes later, Qom and Xaaxex fell in step beside him.

"We should go with you," Qom insisted as he jogged to keep up with his pace.

"I appreciate the offer, but it is better if I go alone. Three satyrs are easier to spot than one and I would feel more confident if I knew you were here protecting the king."

They both looked as though they would refuse his request, but they eventually nodded in agreement before calling for him to be careful and making their way back to the village.

Xicuz weaved his way in between the thick trees that separated his village from Erabus's. Once he was as close as he dared get, Xicuz climbed one of the trees. From one tree to another he made his way far off the ground until he came close enough to have a good view of what went on without risking being spotted himself.

By the time he reached Edith, the sun was already high in the sky, nearly blinding him when he scanned the area below. Though the humans were usually bustling about the village by now, their moods seemed much more somber than normal, their feet barely lifting off the ground as they made their way along. Xicuz wondered where Erabus was and how he was doing.

He was probably still in the castle. No way he would be anywhere other than his father's side. As the noise rose in the village, Xicuz turned his attention back to the others wondering what caused the change in the villagers. It did not take long for him to realize the noise heralded the start of King Tribion's funeral.

*

The hand that woke Erabus just after dawn was rough and unfeeling, as though it woke a servant who was late in getting his work started and not a prince who lost their father the night before. He knew, without having to look, it was one of his brother's guards.

"Be gone," Erabus snapped, not bothering to open his eyes until he heard the door close behind him. Erabus rose to his feet and took one last good look at his father, trying to memorize every inch of his face as though it would disappear from his mind the moment he could no longer look at him.

"I'm not ready to say good-bye," Erabus admitted out loud to himself as he reached up to stroke his father's cheek and found him cold to the touch. It wasn't right; the king had always been warm and kind, his arms welcoming to all who lived within his village and even those who didn't, and now he was reduced to a cold and lifeless statue.

Erabus walked over to the basin that was filled with water the night before.

It was already icy cold, and he shivered as it hit his face. He dried himself off, undid his hair, and ran his fingers through the soft, silky strands before braiding it once more. Erabus straightened his clothes and turned back to his father as the bedroom door opened, revealing his brother and his four closest guards blocking the light from the doorway.

"Place the king on the carrier," Jydral instructed as he stepped aside so his men could follow his orders. Erabus watched in silence as the men came into the room carrying a longboard that would be used to carry his father from his room to the tomb he would be buried in. The men were not as gentle as he would have liked when they transferred him from his bed to the board and carried him outside.

It was a great honor to carry a fallen king to his final resting place and Erabus was disappointed, though not surprised, to see none of the men had earned that right. Having men there who were only loyal to his brother was insulting to his father. For a moment, Erabus thought about refusing to let them carry the king and finding someone else to replace them but he knew his brother wouldn't allow the switch.

At least his father would have one worthy carrier. Erabus stepped up to help lift the back of the board. Instead of making his way to the door with the others, he was pulled back. He released his hold to ensure his father did not fall.

"You can walk at the back of the procession, Erabus. You are liable to drop our dear king in your state and I will not allow such a travesty on my watch," Jydral informed him in no uncertain terms. Once again Erabus fought the urge to fight back. His brother could always retaliate by refusing to let him come to the funeral at all. Such a feat would require him to be locked away somewhere and not only did he know Jydral would be willing to do such a thing, but he also wasn't certain he would release him once everything was over.

What good would it do anyone, or the memory of his father, if he spent the rest of his life locked away in some dungeon? Erabus glared at Jydral's retreating form as he followed his men. He took one last look at the room his father lived in for longer than he had been alive himself and followed the others.

As the procession made its way down the long corridor and out into the bright sunlight, other mourners gathered around and fell in step behind him. Some cried, some held somber expressions, and some seemed confused by what transpired. He could understand where their confusion came from. A few weeks ago, the king was healthy, and now he lay dead.

Perhaps if he had fallen in battle, they would have been more prepared for the reality they were now faced with, but his illness and untimely passing came out of nowhere for anyone who were not aware Jydral poisoned him. *That list,* Erabus swore to himself as he glared daggers into his brother's back, *will shrink considerably once father is put to rest.*

The rest of the village would know about Jydral's treachery no matter what his father wished. He wanted him to remain silent to keep himself safe, but his father should have known that was not the type of man Erabus was. He would never sit idly by letting an evil man hurt those he loved without at least trying to stop him. He would do whatever it took, even if it meant putting his own life at risk to stop him.

That, however, would have to wait until after they laid his father to rest. He continued to follow along behind the others, much farther back than he should have been and coming after others who had no right to even be in the same room with the late king, let alone carry him to his tomb. He couldn't help but notice the absence of those who should have been the ones at his side.

His healer Jeqor, who tried for weeks to heal the king, barely leaving his side unless Erabus was there to relieve him. His advisor Odinel, who he never saw anywhere else other than at his father's side, who imparted on him just and fair words of wisdom for far longer than Erabus had been alive. The guards, Alyster and Garion, who he knew were loyal only to his father and who Jydral arrested when he prevented him from getting back to his father's side.

This is not right. Erabus glanced around once more and confirmed his earlier suspicions and found no sign of the men he sought. *Where could they be?* There was no way a single one of them would miss the king's funeral, but for all of them to be missing, it could only mean one thing—his brother had to be responsible for their absence.

Were the guards still locked up in the dungeon, and if so, had Jydral sentenced the healer and advisor to the same fate? Would they be released after the funeral or would Jydral insist on waiting until after his coronation? Could it already be too late? The latter suggestion sent an icy chill into his heart. Erabus nearly stumbled before regaining his balance and continuing without letting anyone around know of the concern that raced through his mind.

The moment the funeral ended, he would see to the fates of his father's men both for their own safety, and knowing it would be better to have them by his side when he confronted his brother about the atrocities he committed against King Tribion. If the people saw the men loyal to the late king standing at his side, they would be more likely to see his words for the truth they were.

Erabus followed the men carrying his father up the hill into the tomb overlooking the village. Some nights, when the moon grew full, it would cause the tomb to take on an eerily beautiful glow as though the spirits of those who slept within had come back to watch over them. Not long after losing his mother, he noticed it for the first time when he awoke from a nightmare late one night.

He called out to her, forgetting she was gone for a moment, and went in search of her when she failed to come to his room. He wandered the halls, searching for any sign of her when he found his parent's bedroom empty. His father remained in his throne room discussing things with Odinel that Erabus couldn't understand, but his mother was nowhere to be found.

He went outside then, figuring she must have gone for a moonlit stroll and he noticed the strange lights coming from the tomb. Curious, but unable to see well from where he stood, he climbed the tree beside their home and jumped across to the roof, landing not far from where his father spoke with the others. Though he could not hear him, it gave him comfort to know he was so close by.

The pale-yellow light of the moon reflected off strange shimmering stones the masons used to build the tombs far more generations ago than he could count. Mesmerized by the sight, he rose to his feet in awe and lost his footing when he stepped forward and a roof tile came loose. He screamed out in fear and slid down the roof, plunging toward the ground below.

The hard, unyielding impact he expected never came. Instead, he found himself in the warm, safe embrace of his father. In that moment, as he glanced up into his father's sad eyes, he remembered exactly where his mother was— in the tombs that enthralled him a minute before. She lay in her coffin in the room below the one Erabus currently stood in.

He wiped the tears from his eyes. The memory of his mother being put to rest in that room was as vivid as his father being placed there now. As he watched the men lay the king into his coffin, which sat in the middle of the circular room he would remain in for an entire cycle of the moon to give everyone the chance to grieve and say goodbye, his mind flashed back to when his father helped to lay his mother in hers.

They would be reunited soon. Once the grieving period ended, his father's coffin would be rolled down into the actual tombs below. They used a series of logs that were evenly spaced all the way to the bottom as the coffin itself was far too heavy to be carried in the small passages. All his ancestors were buried within the tombs beneath his feet and when the day came for him to leave this world, he took heart in knowing he too would be reunited with them.

Taking his eyes off his father's eternally still form for the first time since entering the tombs, Erabus glanced around. Other than a few stragglers and one of his brother's guards, Elovonos, the rest of the crowd dispersed. He couldn't blame them; the cold, dimly lit room wasn't exactly inviting for those who remained among the living. Or for the dead for that matter.

Though his brother's lack of preparing the room for their father disappointed him, Erabus couldn't say it surprised him that Jydral did nothing that he expected of him. Making his way around the circular room, Erabus used one of the few candles that had been lit to light the others so the shadows that dominated the room were chased away, leaving the soft, warm glow of the flames in their wake.

He retrieved all the long dead flowers and replaced them with the freshly cut ones people carried to the tombs. Satisfied as the sweet scent of the flowers filled the depressing room, Erabus turned his attention to removing the cobwebs and dust until the room was as clean as he would be able to get it.

*

The moment his men finished laying the king in the coffin, Jydral turned without a word and made his way back out of the tombs and into the village below. Knowing he had a small window to set his plan in motion, he wasted no time in signaling his men to follow him out into the forest where he knew the satyr would be found.

As much as he wanted to send someone out into the forest the night before to keep an eye out for him, he couldn't risk them being noticed and ruining the perfect opportunity to bring everything to a head. After that day, not only would he soon be crowned king, but he would have dealt with his pathetic brother and have the perfect excuse to wipe those filthy animals from their land.

King Tribion had been a fool, believing those animals were worthy of owning land and catering to their demands. *A man does not bow before a dog, and a king does not bow before an abomination,* Jydral thought venomously as he crossed the threshold from the village into the forest and began making his way toward where he saw the satyr embracing his brother.

If the idiot had only found a human companion for his trysts in the forest, he might have even let him be when all was said and done. He couldn't be much competition for his throne if he would be unable to produce an heir, but he lowered himself to such filth and depravity by laying with an abomination and that was something he could never forgive. At least, his brother's fate would not be in vain as it would help to secure his throne from any who might speak against him.

They would be silenced soon enough once there was no one left to take the throne other than himself. The king set his brother's fate in motion and Erabus himself sealed it. Now he just needed to acquire the remaining piece of the puzzle. He caught sight of something in the trees. He had to give the satyr credit as he doubted anyone would have ever spotted him if they hadn't known to look in the treetops, but he gave away his trick when he chose to shoot the arrows from above.

Stopping beneath the tree, Jydral glared up at the satyr, instantly catching his odd silvery eyes that had already noticed his presence. As he watched him for a moment, knowing it was only a matter of time before he tried to escape through the treetops as he did after shooting at him, he knew this would go one of two ways—the hard way or the easy.

The result would be the same no matter which the satyr picked; he would end up restrained and whipped in front of the entire village as they learned about his involvement with the assassination of King Tribion. Jydral hoped he went for the more difficult option. It wasn't every day that he got to shoot an arrow into a satyr and watch them drop from a tree like a bird guarding its nest.

"Come down without a struggle, or I will kill Erabus!" he called out as he held his gaze, watching as his eyes widened in horror at his words. "I left one of my guards with instructions to slit his throat if I do not return with you soon," he warned.

The satyr hesitated for only a breath longer before jumping down with such speed it caused a slight breeze to ruffle Jydral's hair and clothing. He landed only a few feet before him, crouched down with his hand on the ground to steady himself, and turned burning, hate-filled silver eyes to him. Jydral gestured over his shoulder for his men to tie him up. They hesitated for a moment, but it did not take long before they were following his silent instructions. Once he knew he would not be able to escape, Jydral grabbed on to the loose end of the rope and roughly commanded, "Walk."

Without a word, the satyr began leading the way back toward the village and Jydral smirked at the realization that things were going easier than he anticipated. Apparently, the animal's feelings for his brother were as strong as Erabus's were for him. *Good*, Jydral decided as the group made their way back to the village without any issues, *that affection will be their downfall.*

Crossing the threshold out of the forest, it wasn't hard to realize the moment they were spotted by the others as gasps and other cries of alarm rose up, first, by those closest to where they emerged but soon coming from all over the village. As many gathered near to figure out what was going on, Jydral made his way toward the center of the village.

Jydral grabbed a hold of the strains of rope that were wrapped around the satyr's wrists and shoved him to the ground, wrenching a grunt of pain from his lips when he was unable to protect himself from the fall.

"Before you now is the animal responsible for the poisoning of our great king!" he called out. "When the meeting of the two kings did not go in the favor of these beasts, their wretched king sent him to assassinate my beloved father and their act of war will not go unanswered!" Jydral continued.

The crowd roared. Some were cheers of agreement while others were cries of disbelief. He paid them little mind and went to call out his proof. That the satyr shot arrows into their village so his accomplice, who Jydral would name once his brother stepped right into his trap, could sneak in to poison the king again. His words, however, died on his lips when the satyr startled him by climbing to his hooves.

How he managed to do that with his arms bound behind his back, Jydral wasn't sure, but the satyr gave him no chance to figure it out as he began denying Jydral's claims. "I have done nothing to your king and my own would never wish harm on his ally. I was merely on my way here to express King Zhul's condolences for your loss when you accosted me in the forest. While I might have been on your land, it was with no ill intent and there is no charge you can lay against me other than trespassing."

"You were here to give condolences for our loss?" Jydral laughed at the thought as the satyr tried in vain to wipe the dirt off his face with his shoulder. "Exactly how did you plan on giving condolences to anyone from the treetops? Admit it, you were planning another attack after your last one failed to hit your target. You were probably the one who shot at my father during the meeting of the two kings."

"I did not want to interrupt during your funeral procession and planned to wait until you were finished to make my presence known. And I attended the meeting of the two kings with King Zhul's guard. I went with Prince Erabus into the forest to search for the archer," the satyr insisted and though it angered Jydral to hear his brother be referred to by his title, he silently pointed out to himself that he gave Erabus to him on a silver platter. Whether the satyr knew it or not, he sealed both of their fates with his words.

Chapter Eleven

Erabus had just stepped back into the bright sunlight from the soft candlelight of the tombs when he heard a commotion coming from the village below. At first, all Erabus could think was, *how dare they?* How could the others be making such a commotion after laying their king to rest? Had they no respect for the dead or those who were mourning their loss?

As Erabus stomped into the center of the village where the noise seemed to be coming from, a voice rose up above the others, causing an icy hand to grip his heart. "I went with Prince Erabus into the forest to search for the archer." Although he knew more had been said, Erabus only caught the tail end of it as Xicuz raised his voice.

Why is Xicuz here? Had Jydral caught him in the forest? Why come so close when he knew I would not be able to see him for a while? The questions echoed in his mind as Erabus rushed toward where the crowd gathered, able to make out his brother and Xicuz standing in the middle of the others. Pushing his way through the crowd, Erabus soon stood in between Xicuz and his brother.

"Enough, Jydral. The king has only just been laid to rest and already you are treating our allies like this." Erabus gestured to Xicuz, only to realize his hands were bound behind his back. *How dare he?*

"Watch yourself, brother—anyone who defends our great king's murderer is obviously in on it with him," Jydral spat at him.

Erabus was about to respond, but the cold, calculated glint in his brother's eye gave him pause. *Jydral knows*, Erabus realized, barely preventing himself from sucking in his breath and giving away his realization. Somehow, someway, Jydral knew about him and Xicuz. Jydral dared him to come to his defense further, planning to use his knowledge of their romance against him if he did.

"After all, what other reason could any human possibly have for defending one of these animals?" Jydral continued, confirming Erabus's suspicions and worst fear.

It seems father wasn't the only one who should have known that isn't the type of man I am.

"Hold back our dear prince while we deal with this animal!" Jydral called out, giving Erabus no time to react before Aothorn and Elovonos grabbed him from behind and pulled him back away from Xicuz. As Erabus fought against their hold, Jydral threw Xicuz to the ground and readied his whip. *No!*

Erabus stomped as hard as he could on the guard's foot to his right. He used his groan of pain and sudden movement to disorient the guard on his left and pulled his arms free, rushing over to Xicuz and throwing himself on top of his prone form just in time to take the lashing for him. The crack of the whip against his back wrenched an inhuman wail from his lips, causing the others around to gasp in shock and horror.

Clenching his teeth against the pain, Erabus fisted his hands as he tried to breathe through the worst of it. "Don't, Erabus. Run and save yourself. Let me take the punishment. It will be worth it if I can keep you safe," Xicuz whispered urgently into his ear. Erabus couldn't help but smile before the pain reared its ugly head again and turned his smile into a grimace.

"Never," Erabus promised, squeezing his shoulder as best as he could in their current position, before turning his angry, hate-filled eyes to Jydral once more. "You know damn well Jydral," he spat at him, intentionally dropping his title, "that Xicuz had nothing to do with poisoning the king. After all, you were the one who poisoned my father!"

"You dare accuse your king of patricide!" Jydral bellowed. The whip cracked against his back once more, wrenching an ear-piercing scream from his lips. The moment the sound tapered off, only to be replaced by his roar of anger at his brother having the audacity to whip him in full view of their entire village. *Jydral would pay for this. They will soon know him for the monster he truly is.*

"I do not accuse you of patricide, Jydral—I charge you with regicide! My brother you may be, you are no son of my father! You are a bastard born of an unfaithful queen! You are no prince of Edith; you are nothing more than a baseborn cur my father took pity on!"

The roar that came from him sounded inhuman and terrifying. Jydral cracked the whip against his back over and over in retaliation for the truth. Mercifully, Erabus lost consciousness before he suffered through the brunt of it.

*

Realizing his brother no longer screamed out in pain with each crack of the whip on his back, Jydral paused for a moment, cocking his head to the side as he studied Erabus's unresponsive form. Jydral reined back in his whip as he called out, "Lock the traitor in the dungeon! I will deal with him and his atrocious lies after this despicable animal is dealt with."

As Jydral glanced around at the crowd that gathered, he couldn't help but realize far too many of them were looking uncertain and apprehensive of him. *They were not sure who to believe, him or me,* Jydral realized in annoyance as he clenched his fist tightly around the hilt of the whip. If even a few of them had any reservations about who their true king should be, it would make his rise to power all but impossible.

He needed to get them to his side, and quick. "Have the healer see to my poor brother!" Jydral called after the men who were already beginning to carry Erabus away. "The death of our father has affected him far worse than I could have imagined if it has addled his mind to this extreme." He sighed heavily for effect. His facade would not be enough to thoroughly convince them that Erabus spoke lies, but Jydral was confident it would be enough to cause them uncertainty.

"Display the satyr properly," Jydral instructed. "This animal will pay for what he has done to our king!"

Barely wasting time to nod, Dlivion and Azemar set to work hammering two large poles into the ground. Once they were finished, they untied the satyr's arms, while a third kept his sword on him to ensure he didn't try anything stupid and cut the rope in half so they could use it to tie his hands high on the poles. When they finished tightening the ropes to his satisfaction, its hooves were barely touching the ground. *Perfect*, Jydral decided as he glanced out at the crowd once more to gauge their reactions.

Some, like himself, were obviously looking forward to the animal getting what it deserved. Others watched in shock and disbelief. Jydral whipped his own brother—why they thought he would be kinder to this animal; he had no idea. And a few others, scattered throughout the crowd, watching behind half-closed eyes, were unable to bear what was about to happen.

Jydral held his head up and threw back his shoulder, trying to look as imposing as he could. He cracked the whip against the satyr's back without any warning. The howl of pain he expected to be wrenched from his lips never came. The satyr gave barely a grunt of acknowledgment to the pain that must have been searing his back.

Not about to let it deter him, Jydral demanded, "Admit your guilt in the death of our beloved King Tribion!" When he was met with silence, Jydral cracked his whip again. "Admit to poisoning the king!" Again, his reticence held. Again, Jydral responded with his whip belting across his exposed back. Over and over Jydral demanded him to confess his guilt. Over and over he was met by an eerie silence. Soon enough red, angry welts covered his back.

"I will profess no guilt, for I have none! The same cannot be said about you!" the satyr finally called out. Jydral gritted his teeth and clenched the whip hilt so tightly in his hand it threatened to break under the assault. *No wonder Erabus has started a disgusting relationship with this animal*, Jydral thought to himself even as he cracked the whip against his back once again, this time with more force. *It is just as stubborn as Erabus is.*

*

Erabus awoke to a roar of pain echoing around the village of Edith. He leapt to his feet. "Xicuz!" Erabus cried out as he tried to get his bearings and figure out where he was and where the scream came from.

It didn't take long for his eyes to adjust to the dimly lit room. Old, filthy straw covered the floor and the stale scent of urine assaulted his senses. He was in the dungeon. Anger burned within him.

Erabus tried to look out the barred window on the far side of the cell only to find it stood too far over his head for a clear view. Another scream echoed from outside. He carefully placed his foot into a groove in the wall and climbed up enough to see through the bars.

From his new vantage point, Erabus saw all the way to the middle of the village where they had Xicuz tied up between two poles. Even from that distance, he saw the angry, red welts that covered his back. Another sound of the whip cracking and another cry was wrenched from Xicuz's lips before Jydral mocked him, "You will die this day for what you have done to the king!"

"You monster! Stop it! Leave him alone!" Erabus cried out, yet his words were drowned out before they ever reached his brother. Again, the resounding crack of the whip echoed around him, vibrating through his body as though he felt it now and not Xicuz.

If only that were the case. Pounding on the bars, not caring that his knuckles were soon bleeding from the abuse, Erabus screamed over and over for him to stop. "Please let me out so I may save him!" Erabus pleaded to the empty cell around him. "Can anyone hear me?!" Again, and again, he begged anyone who might hear him for their help, but each time only silence answered him.

Erabus felt as though all was lost. He shook his head in determination, refusing to give up without a real fight. Erabus kept his eyes turned on Xicuz's form, refusing to close his eyes or look away. "Please, I beg you, I would do anything, give anything to save the man I love," Erabus prayed in a much softer voice than he had been using—his voice hoarse from overuse.

"Anything?" a voice called out. Erabus spun around so quickly he lost his balance and fell to the floor. Grunting at the pain, he glared over at the cell door, about to chastise them for mocking him at a time like this, only to realize he remained alone. Not even a guard stood on the other side of his cell door.

"Anything," Erabus swore. He stood proudly, admitting the words that were truer than anything he ever said before. "I would die if it but meant Xicuz could live and be free."

"Be careful what you wish for," the voice said. A moment later a strange figure materialized before him. At first, it seemed to be made of nothing more than mist and smoke, but with each passing moment, the form became clearer. The figure was male and had long, midnight black hair that flowed behind him, even though there no wind passed through the cell.

He stood well over six feet tall and his body was more muscular than even Xicuz's. Much like with the satyr, the being before him wore a loincloth, though where Xicuz's chest remained bare, he wore a vest made from bearskin. Instead of being open, like his own, his was held together with strange looking bone fasteners. He wore black, fur-trimmed boots upon his feet.

"Who are you?" Erabus barely managed to squeak out.

For a moment, his strange cellmate stared back at him with an odd, almost hungry, toothy grin, which unnerved and excited Erabus at the same time.

"I am Ith'tar, a bargaining devil. I have it in my power to grant you the wish you so desire, but beware, there is always a heavy price to pay," the devil said, as he stepped closer to Erabus, towering over him.

"I will pay any price you demand of me. I will do whatever I have to in order to save him," Erabus said. "I would die, I would kill, I would destroy this entire village if it meant Xicuz could be saved, and they could be saved from having Jydral as their king. Their fate will only be worse if he is allowed to rule over them. Vile, evil men do not make for good kings."

The being gave him a strange look. *Was that regret in his eyes? Did a devil even know the concept of regret?* "He will be king, unfortunately. That cannot be changed; this outcome, someone has already bargained for. I am not the only bargaining devil to have come through your little village of Edith. Another has come before me and he made a deal with Jydral. A deal for the crown he was never fated to have in exchange for two lives."

As Erabus stood there with his mouth agape, he wasn't a bit surprised. Of course, that was how his brother managed to secure the throne even after poisoning his father. Even less surprising than that was the fact Jydral bargained with innocent peoples' lives. Because what else would he have done? Jydral would never bargain with his own life when he could give up someone else in his stead.

No doubt the two Jydral named were father and Xicuz, Erabus decided to himself before saying out loud, "How is that fair? How can Jydral sacrifice someone else to get what he wants?"

The devil cocked his head to the side as though Erabus asked a ridiculous question. "I never said it was fair, Erabus. I am not in the business of fair, nor is any other devil. But fret not—all is not lost. I cannot stop your brother from being king or from a second life being lost, but I did not come here for naught. There is one way for you to save this man you claim to love. You merely must sacrifice your own life in place of his."

"Take it, take my life and give it to him. Save Xicuz," Erabus pleaded with him as he stepped toward him with his arms open wide as though the devil would stab him there right then. As the devil stepped closer to him, Erabus closed his eyes waiting for the pain to come, only to feel his hot breath on his ear a moment later. As Erabus opened his eyes, he found the devil standing just in front of him, leaning down so he could whisper into his ear.

"Alas, Erabus it does not work like that. You must make a bargain with me in order for me to interfere," the devil said. "That would give you what you want, but what about me? What would I get out of that deal?"

"The deal I make with you is this: you will not die, and neither will Xicuz. You will live half the life you are meant to as you give the other to him. You will not be able to live your short lives out together, though, as one of you would only live with the sun and the other with the moon. There is something in your future that cannot be changed, that you must be alive for, and it is why your brother couldn't sacrifice your life as he originally planned."

This was taking too much time—any moment now, there would be another crack of the whip. "Very well. I accept," Erabus said. "Now, what do you want in return?"

*

One moment Xicuz was tied between the two poles and the next, he was wrenched away in a puff of mist and smoke. Before he could realize what happened, he stood in the middle of the forest, the thick canopy of leaves overhead blocking out nearly all the sunlight. Even with as dark as it suddenly became, Xicuz could still see Erabus standing in front of him, next to a strange looking man wearing a loincloth and bearskin vest.

Before Xicuz could even begin to wonder who the stranger was, a sudden thought occupied his mind; his back no longer felt as though it was on fire. The raw, burning pain from the whip that covered his entire back was gone. As though the entire encounter with Jydral never happened. In fact, had it not been for the fact he could still hear the whip crack echoing in his mind, Xicuz might have been inclined to believe he hallucinated the whole thing.

"Say your good-byes. You have until sunset," the strange man warned them before disappearing in a cloud of the same mist and smoke that delivered them from Edith into the forest. For a moment, Xicuz could only stand there staring at where he stood only a moment before, trying to wrap his mind around everything that happened in the last few seconds, but he found himself with nothing more than other questions.

"What does he mean?" Xicuz wondered out loud as he turned his attention to Erabus for the first time since noticing he was there with him. Without giving him the chance to respond, Xicuz voiced every other question he had at that moment, desperate to receive the answer for each. "Where are we? How did we get here? Who was that? And how is my back healed?"

With his final question, Erabus spun him around to ensure his words were true. "There isn't a mark on you," Erabus confirmed, standing so close to him Xicuz could feel his hot breath fanning over his bare back. Xicuz turned around, causing Erabus's fingers to slip off his back leaving a trail of heated flesh in their wake.

Erabus shook his head and smiled. "Long story short, Ith'tar is a bargaining devil. Apparently, Jydral made a deal with another one to become the king of Edith and he used yours and my father's lives as his payment. From what Ith'tar said, Jydral tried to use mine, but there is something I needed to be alive for in the future. Not sure what he referred to, but whatever it was, it kept my brother from being able to kill me.

"This devil heard me calling out for help and offered to make another bargain for you to live. Ith'tar said he could not prevent Jydral from becoming king and a life needed to be paid. Since I couldn't sacrifice myself, for the same reason my brother couldn't sacrifice me, the devil came up with another plan, but it means we will never be able to see each other again. In order to save you, I have to lose you." Erabus caressed his cheek and Xicuz leaned into his touch.

"Starting at sunset, the two of us will be cursed; one of us only living with the sun, and the other with the moon. I am not sure what that means. If I could have given my life to allow you to have the full life you were meant to, I would have done so in a heartbeat."

Xicuz cupped his cheeks and tilted his head up so he could place a chaste kiss on his lips. "I would rather never see you again as long as I know you are still alive, even if it means I have to give up half of the days I was meant to live. And know that if you had been able to make the deal with him to sacrifice your life, it would have been in vain as I would have just followed after you." Xicuz pulled Erabus close once more, this kiss anything but chaste.

When Xicuz finally pulled back, the two of them were panting for breath. He rested his head against Erabus's. Glancing up at the unseen sky, when he got his breathing under control once more, Xicuz realized there was no way to know how close they were to the sun setting. No way of knowing how much time the two of them had left together.

Not wanting to waste a single moment they had left, Xicuz ran his hands down Erabus's shoulders, hooking his fingers under his vest and removing it from his chest. Even as a light sparked in Erabus's eyes, apparently realizing what he intended to do, Xicuz leaned forward to kiss a trail over Erabus's collarbone, moving lower toward his chest with each kiss.

Xicuz ran his tongue across the pert nipple in the middle of Erabus's toned muscle, smirking to himself when he shuddered beneath his touch. He continued trailing his kisses to the other side of his chest and paid the second nipple the same service. Xicuz trailed lower still and nibbled at his hip, enticing a low guttural moan from Erabus. Xicuz loosened his pants and let them fall to the ground before helping him to step out of them.

As Xicuz sank to his knees, trailing kisses down to Erabus's inner thigh, Xicuz gently took hold of his member and was about to pay the same attention as the rest of him, when Erabus stuttered, "I want..." unable to finish his thought as Xicuz ran his fingers down the length of his shaft.

"I know and I will," Xicuz promised Erabus a moment before licking him from base to tip, breathing his hot breath on him and causing Erabus to moan as he grabbed on to Xicuz's head to steady himself. Xicuz pressed his lips against the sensitive flesh and took Erabus into his mouth even as he stroked the base. Moving in his gentle rhythm for a moment, Xicuz waited until Erabus was nice and hard before releasing him with a plop.

Rising to his feet, Xicuz smirked at the way Erabus trembled, his eyes rolled back in his head at the sensations. As he waited for Erabus to open his eyes, Xicuz undid the strings that held his loincloth up and allowed it to fall to his feet to join Erabus's clothes. Realizing Erabus wasn't going to get himself under control without a little push, Xicuz grabbed on to his member, holding just tight enough he would have his full attention but not enough he would hurt Erabus.

"On your knees, my love," Xicuz instructed, giving Erabus's shaft a good stroke before releasing it so he could do as commanded. The sight of Erabus on his knees before him, utterly bare and exposed to him, caused Xicuz's member to harden and jerk in anticipation. The moment Erabus's hot breath fanned over the tip, Xicuz groaned as he tangled his fingers in Erabus's hair and pulled him closer.

As much as Xicuz loved the thought of Erabus teasing him, he couldn't wait to be buried deep within him and knew if they took too long, they may never have the chance. Erabus seemed to understand his unspoken urgency as he took him into his mouth and began much the same rhythm as Xicuz used on him only a minute before. Once he grew hard, Xicuz pulled back, causing Erabus to release him from his warm, wet mouth and smirked at him.

"On your hands and knees, love," Xicuz instructed, watching in satisfaction as Erabus complied, even raising his backside higher in the air without having to be told. Stepping up behind him, Xicuz ran his hands across his firm, tight ass, before leaning down to place a quick kiss and nibble upon it. Xicuz stuck his thumb in his mouth and got it wet. He pressed it into the ass that seemed to be calling to him.

A long, low moan escaped Erabus's lips and Xicuz's eyes rolled back in his head even as he pressed his thumb in farther. Feeling Erabus's body pulse around his finger, Xicuz moved it at a slow, steady pace. The more Erabus responded, the faster he moved until Xicuz added a second finger and then a third, switching out his thumb for his longer fingers.

Soon Xicuz had Erabus panting beneath him as he moved even faster. Xicuz dug the nails of his free hand into Erabus's waist to hold himself back. "Xicuz," Erabus panted, barely able to get his name out in between his moans and Xicuz knew he was ready. Xicuz pulled his fingers out and wiped them off on some damp leaves nearby and positioned himself once more behind Erabus.

"This may hurt a bit as you are stretched, but once you have adjusted the pain will cease," Xicuz assured him as he teased him with his tip, brushing it back and forth without pressing inward. Unable to speak at that moment, Erabus rocked his hips back against him and Xicuz took that to mean he was free to continue. Pushing himself forward, moving slowly, as he did not want to risk hurting him, Xicuz groaned out loud to himself at the way Erabus's body bore down on him.

Inch by inch, Xicuz pushed forward, clenching his teeth once more to prevent himself from going too quickly, but he soon realized it was unnecessary as Erabus slammed back against him, burying the last few inches in a second. Even as Xicuz moaned in ecstasy, Erabus cried out in pain, his muscles clenching around him. Before

Xicuz could even think to back up, Erabus dug his nails into the flesh of his thigh and growled out, "Don't move. Don't stop," thoroughly confusing Xicuz for a moment.

As Erabus wiggled against him, Xicuz soon realized *don't stop* referred to him not wanting him to pull out and stop their encounter altogether. Gently kneading his backside to assure him he understood, Xicuz moaned out, "When you are ready, my love," as his sword pulsed within its sheath in anticipation. As Xicuz wondered if he would be able to stand the wait, Erabus started moving against him, pulling a moan from both of their lips.

Ever so gently at first, Erabus rocked back into him so Xicuz held himself still, allowing Erabus to lead the pace and depth. As each moment passed, each thrust going deeper than the one before, each moan from Erabus's lips growing more breathless, each thrust stretching his body further to accommodate his girth, Xicuz could feel him moving faster, his body telling him what Erabus couldn't form the words to.

Grabbing hold of his hips, Xicuz pulled out to the tip, slamming his full length into him once more, enticing another cry from his lips. This time, there was nothing but pleasure behind the sound and it spurred him on further. Beginning to thrust into him, Xicuz moved faster and deeper with each moment until Erabus's body was forced onto the ground as his arms could no longer support his weight or the wholly enjoyed assault against his body.

"Xicuz," Erabus groaned out his name, the lustful sound seeming more animalistic than human enticed him to move even faster with each thrust. The tingle in his balls alerting him he was close to his release, Xicuz reached under Erabus and grabbed hold of his member, stroking the length of the shaft every time he thrust into him. Soon they were both panting, Erabus unsuccessfully trying to say his name as he couldn't catch his breath well enough to speak and Xicuz continued to increase his speed and depth, moving them both to completion.

At the same moment Erabus cried out in ecstasy, his member pulsed in Xicuz's hand and his muscles clenched around Xicuz sending him to his own release. "Erabus," Xicuz groaned as he collapsed on top of Erabus and pulled them both to the ground, allowing his softening member to slip from Erabus. Xicuz rolled onto his back and pulled Erabus on top of his chest, holding him close.

Glancing up toward the sky, as he ran his fingers through Erabus's hair that was slicked back with sweat, Xicuz noticed regretfully that it had grown far darker than it had been when they first appeared in the forest. It wouldn't be long now before the sun set and their curse activated. Xicuz placed a gentle kiss upon his brow.

"Our time is almost up, my love. If by chance, our curse is ever broken, and you are standing before me once more, I want you to know you will be mine forever. My life, my love is yours, now and forever." Xicuz held him as close as he could, unable to bear even blinking as he feared the moment he did, Erabus would be gone from his sight forever. He wasn't ready to lose him, but then again, he never would be.

"I was yours the moment I met you, Xicuz. My life, my love is yours, now and forever," Erabus swore as he rolled over on to his stomach, so he could look into Xicuz's eyes—love and unshed tears shining within them. Even without having to look at the sky once again, Xicuz knew the sun set at that moment as the light seemed to go out of his eyes and Erabus collapsed upon his chest.

Terrified he lost his life, even so, Xicuz shook Erabus forcefully, trying to revive him. When that did not work, and his heart stop in fear, he leaned down toward Erabus's face. After a terror-inducing moment, Xicuz felt the hot breath fanning against his cheek and sighed in relief.

Pulling Erabus onto his lap as he sat up, Xicuz held him close as the reality of what happened finally registered in his mind. It was Erabus who would be "dead", though unconscious seemed like a more accurate description, during the night, which meant it would be himself who would fall unconscious when the sun rose in the morning. Xicuz brushed the hair off Erabus's face before leaning down once more to place a gentle kiss on his forehead.

He still felt warm to the touch. Xicuz wondered if Erabus would remain that way for the entire night or grow cold as if he were dead. It did not matter as they would need to have shelter from the cold nights one way or the other, especially since the weather would soon begin to change. Xicuz placed Erabus gently upon the hard ground and dressed him in his discarded clothes before replacing his own loincloth.

Glancing back in the direction of Edith, Xicuz swore, "One day we will break this curse and have our revenge on Jydral," out loud as though there was someone there who could hear him. *Can Erabus hear me?* Somehow, Xicuz doubted it. Carefully lifting Erabus into his arms, he glanced around the dense forest for a moment, trying to get his bearings, before heading northeast away from the human village and from his own.

With each step Xicuz took, the face of Jydral appeared in his mind and he gritted his teeth against his image. Jydral would see his retribution one day, of that Xicuz was certain, but for the moment he refused to allow him any more control over his thoughts. Turning his eyes to Erabus, Xicuz smiled as he gazed upon him, able to pretend for a moment Erabus merely lay asleep before the reality came crashing back with full force.

"Someday," Xicuz promised Erabus softly once more before pulling him tighter to his chest and continued to weave his way in between the thick trees, not sure where he was headed but knowing they needed to get far away. Further away than Jydral could ever hope to find them as it was only a matter of time before he began looking for them. *If he wasn't already.*

*

Jydral refused to accept what he saw with his own eyes. Or, more accurately, what he no longer saw with his eyes. The satyr hung there not a moment before and now was nowhere to be found. The ropes and poles remained. Even the blood spilled upon the ground, flung in every direction each time the whip flew through the air remained, and yet the animal who bled it did not.

Where was the satyr and how had it managed to disappear in front of his eyes? Did the strange animals have a magic Jydral wasn't aware of? *No, that couldn't be it.* If the satyr had a way to release himself, it would have done it long before Jydral inflicted such pain upon him. But then where did the power come from suddenly? Even as Jydral asked himself this, thinking the same question he could read on the faces of those around him, the answer dawned on him.

He followed my example once again, Jydral silently growled in annoyance and a minuscule amount of admiration. The latter he quashed down in disgust before turning his attention to his men who were still standing around trying to figure out what happened. "Search the forest for the animal; it couldn't have gotten far!" Jydral called about, deciding there was no reason to tell them what truly happened right before their own eyes.

No reason for them to know that just as the animal had when it climbed the tree to shoot the arrows at them and hide his tracks, it inexplicably did the same thing as Jydral once more by making a deal with the devil. How it managed to do so without being seen, Jydral didn't know, but then again, he wasn't convinced anyone else would have seen the devil he spoke with had they been there.

But even if the devil were only visible to the one who made a deal would they not have seen him speaking to thin air? Or did the devil somehow stop time when he made his deals? Finding he had too many questions and no answers, Jydral decided to get to the bottom of things the moment he was alone. Until then, Jydral needed to make sure there wasn't a second escaped prisoner on the loose.

As his guards made their way out into the forest to search for the animal, Jydral made his own way toward the dungeon where he already knew his brother would not be waiting. Sure enough, the moment Jydral stepped down into the dimly lit, rancid smelling dungeon and stopped before the cells, he found each to be empty. Had saving his brother been a part of the satyr's deal or...?

No, it was Erabus, Jydral realized as it dawned on him the otherwise empty dungeon would have been the perfect place to summon the devil and make a deal with him without being interrupted by others. Jydral had Erabus to blame for ruining his plan, but he would rectify that soon enough. The devil he called claimed some nonsense about Erabus needing to be alive for some unchangeable future event, whatever that meant, but Jydral looked forward to seeing how well that held up when he went after him with his own hands.

Especially since the devil already broke his side of the agreement; the satyr should have been dead already. "Droz'gamal!" Jydral called out. When the devil didn't immediately appear before him, Jydral called his name again and again, his voice growing louder with each call.

After the fourth or fifth time, a disembodied voice finally demanded, "What is it you want, human?" The figure appeared with a cloud of mist and smoke as Droz'gamal had the first time Jydral saw him. The king had informed Jydral that he would not be inheriting the throne as destined, claiming some ridiculous lie about how he failed to live up to his expectations and would not make a wise and just ruler.

Jydral stormed out of his father's room and went in search of Erabus, knowing if his brother were gone his father would have no choice but to make him king, and the devil stopped him not long after entering the forest. "I can give you what you desire, but there will be a heavy price to pay," a voice called out but as Jydral spun around in a circle, no one else was there.

"Who is there? Show yourself!" Jydral demanded as he continued to spin around, refusing to allow anyone to come up behind him. They could try to scare him all they wanted; Jydral wasn't fool enough to fall for it. Instead of being answered, Jydral soon found the area covered in a strange cloud of mist and smoke, as though he stood too close to a fire that was lit behind a waterfall.

"I am Droz'gamal, a bargaining devil and I can give you what you desire, but there will be a heavy price to pay," the voice said again as the devil materialized in front of him. Droz'gamal had long fiery red hair, not unlike his brother's, but where Erabus pulled his back into a braid, the devil's fell down his shoulders in waves. He had strange orange eyes that seemed to look straight through Jydral the moment they turned to him.

He wore dark brown pants made of an animal skin, wolf or bear it seemed, with a strange web of bones strung across his chest, protecting him from nothing and leaving most of his flesh exposed. As Jydral took a closer look at the bones, he quickly wished hadn't, as they seemed to be small finger bones that had a hole drilled through the middle so they could be strung.

Each bone had a large, intricate knot tied on either side, holding them in place no matter how much the webbed shirt moved. The devil wore a pair of thick, hide boots and bore no weapon Jydral saw. "You can make me the king like I was meant to be?" Jydral questioned in disbelief when he could finally take his eyes off the strange man, or devil apparently, before him. The devil laughed at him and Jydral's blood boiled.

How dare he mock a future king? Before Jydral could voice his outrage out loud, Droz'gamal explained, "You were never meant to be king, silly child. One must be of legitimate birth to inherit the throne."

Stunned beyond belief Jydral could only stand there and stare at him in silence. *Had my father sired me with a woman other than the queen?*

"No, no, silly child," the devil said again, apparently reading his mind and annoying him with the less than flattering nickname. "The queen was your mother. It is the king who is not your blood."

Jydral's whole world crashed down on him, destroying everything he ever knew to be true. He was not the son of King Tribion? Erabus was only his half-brother and the true heir to the throne? His mother had an affair that resulted in his birth? Had the man Jydral believed to be his father known from the beginning? Had Tribion only just found out and that was the real reason why he decided to steal the crown from his head?

Once again, Jydral found far too many questions and no answers. Did any of it truly matter if this devil could give him the crown anyway as he claimed? "And what would be the heavy price you claim I would need to pay to have my throne?" Jydral demanded.

"The life of two," Droz'gamal said and before Jydral could say that it wasn't such a heavy price at all, the devil continued, "One life in payment for the change in your destiny and one for the change in Erabus's, but you may not pay with the life of your brother as there is a fate for him in the future that cannot be changed even by me. You must pick another besides King Tribion.

"But you needn't name him now. Simply whisper my name when you are before him and it will be done. Know this, future King Jydral, the crown will not adorn your head until after the price is paid in full."

Jydral nodded in understanding, already knowing the perfect way to deal with his nonfather. As the devil disappeared in the same fashion as he appeared, Jydral was drawn back to the present as he did it again.

"What I want to know is why that animal escaped me when his life was supposed to be forfeit. I named him as my second sacrifice, and you assured me you accepted him. Why is it my brother's apparent deal with a devil was able to save his life? Was it you who allowed him to undo my deal? Isn't that a conflict of interest?" Jydral demanded, each question spoken in a louder and angrier tone than the one before.

For a moment, the devil only stared at him in silence, as if he debated if his questions were even worth answering, before finally shaking his head. "Your deal was not undone by another's; it cannot be. His life is still forfeit; your brother has simply given him half of his life to allow him to continue living. And no, it wasn't one of my deals, but that of another named Ith'tar. He is the reason you are not able to sacrifice Erabus's life out right.

"For now, my king," Droz'gamal said with a mock bow, "the crown shall be upon your head as promised soon enough. Do not summon me again unless you have another deal to make." The threat heavy in the air, Droz'gamal disappeared once more, but Jydral called out for him to wait. Though he reappeared, the expression on his face spoke to his unhappiness.

"Forgive me, Droz'gamal, I have but one final question. What does it mean that my brother gave him half his life?"

For a moment, Droz'gamal stared at him in silence once again and Jydral worried he had no intention of answering even one last question.

Eventually, Droz'gamal smiled at him, showing off his rather sharp and pointed teeth. "Erabus gave up all his nights to Xicuz so that he may live them," the devil explained cryptically before disappearing. *Erabus gave him his nights? What does that even mean?* Jydral wondered. This time he chose not to call the devil back and risk his ire.

He'd already annoyed him enough by summoning him. No need to push it further even if he still had unanswered questions, and even a few new ones with his parting words. Taking a deep breath, Jydral calmly pointed out to himself that his questions didn't matter at the moment. He would still be crowned king; everything else could be dealt with and the answers learned in due time. Either way, for the moment at least, the two of them were out of his way and his coronation could go on as planned.

Chapter Twelve

As Erabus returned to consciousness for the first time since the curse activated, for a moment, he could not remember what happened, or where he was. His head still felt groggy and out of sync, as if his mind ran a minute or two behind reality. Along with the lag, Erabus felt as though he overslept, his eyes barely able to open and show him the dark world around him.

Question after question filled his mind. Erabus rubbed the sleep from his eyes, first with his fingers and then with his palms when his eyes still felt resistant to opening. A warm pressure across his back held him down, but Erabus lifted himself up as best he could. Erabus blinked rapidly as he tried to clear his vision but still could not see anything. Was he in a cave, or maybe a room?

Erabus still had no idea where he was and would not be figuring out the answer until he managed to get himself up. Reaching behind his back, he grabbed hold of Xicuz's arm and gently pulled it off him to get up. Pushing himself up with his hands, Erabus felt something rough and somewhat prickly in some places and caressed the bedding with his fingers.

Leaves and pine needles. Erabus stood up. Glancing around as best he could with no light to see by, Erabus found himself even more confused. There was cold dirt beneath his bare feet instead of the hard rock of the cave.

It was far too dark for them to be outside. Erabus knew it couldn't be nighttime as he had "died" when the sun set.

As the memory flashed through his mind, Erabus was thankful for the darkness as it would hide the blush that covered his cheeks, though it wouldn't matter as no one would see it anyway. No, Xicuz remained awake during the night and apparently moved them to some place safe, but that still left the question of where they were and why it was so dark.

The satyrs' village? Even as Erabus wondered this, he already knew the answer; Ebrein was well known to not have any buildings. They did not believe in being surrounded by walls or sleeping beneath roofs.

And, even if, Xicuz built a house for him within the village, Erabus would have heard the others moving about by now. Since he was awake, it meant dawn had arrived and the satyrs would, no doubt, be as busy as his own village during the rising of the sun. That only left one real option; they were inside a building somewhere far away from both villages. But who would have built something that far out?

They had to be deep into the satyrs' land to ensure Jydral would not find them and they would have no use for a building so far out into the forest. *Unless Xicuz built it last night? Is that even possible?* Realizing he had no way of getting the answers for now, Erabus pushed his questions from his mind. The first thing he needed to do was get some light into the room.

Erabus walked forward with his hands in front of him until he ran into something solid. He scraped his fingers across the hard grain of the wood and guessed the wall stood only a foot or two away from the bed. Continuing to feel along the wall, Erabus soon found a door and pushed it open.

Instead of it swinging outward as Erabus anticipated, it fell forward to the ground with an echoing *thud*. Crying out in surprise, he glanced back to Xicuz, who could now be seen with the warm rays of the sun illuminating the room behind him. Erabus worried the sudden noise might wake him. Even as Erabus assured himself that he hadn't, he remembered nothing other than the sunset would be able to wake him now.

Taking his first real look around the room, Erabus realized he guessed the size of their home accurately. Only about two feet stood between the door and their bed and maybe another foot on the other side from the far wall. The logs that made up the walls around him were caked in still drying mud. Erabus was grateful he had not pushed too hard on the wall when he found it in the dark.

He turned back to the bed to watch Xicuz sleep. He lay in the middle with his arm once again draped over Erabus's side of the bed. Erabus made his way over to him but stopped short when he noticed markings in the dirt.

It was a note Xicuz wrote on the ground just beside where Erabus got up. "My love, I moved us far into the forest. We shall be safe here. I will build a permanent home for us over the next few nights. This one is to keep us warm until I finish. Careful, the door is not attached yet." As he read the words out loud, Erabus laughed at the last line.

Of course, Xicuz left him a note in warning; it just hadn't done him any good. "Xicuz must not have realized he made the hut impenetrable by light," Erabus laughed once more before reminding himself to leave a torch burning so Xicuz would not have the same problem when he awoke that night. "Still cannot believe Xicuz got all this done in the dark," Erabus admitted as he glanced around again before his eyes landed on Xicuz's sleeping form.

Erabus made his way back to Xicuz, knelt on the bed and kissed his brow. He rose to his feet once more and began making his way out of their new home for the first time. Though it was much brighter in the one-room hut once the door fell, there was still a stark difference with how bright it was outside and Erabus found he had to shield his eyes the moment he stepped past the threshold.

Glancing up, Erabus discovered the reason as Xicuz managed to find and build their hut within a small clearing devoid of trees. Smiling as he looked at their new home, Erabus could already see the small garden he would plant off to the side. Erabus could see the bigger hut that Xicuz would build, basing its appearance on a larger scale of the one they had now.

He could practically see the smoke rising out of the chimney, feel the warmth of the fire burning in the hearth. A hearth they would never be able to sit in front of or share the warmth of together. Shaking his head to clear the dark thoughts, Erabus headed over to his future garden when he noticed black smudges on the side of the hut. Curious, Erabus made his way over and realized Xicuz left another note, this time using a burnt stick from the nearby campfire that had since reduced to embers, instead of his fingers in the dirt.

"My love make sure to return to hut before dusk. It will be difficult to find your body in the dark." Smirking at the note, he made his way over to the spot designated for his garden and removed the rocks, sticks and weeds that littered the area.

He found a piece of bark large and strong enough and tilled the soil within the garden. Though it wasn't anywhere near as good as having one of the well-made wooden gardening tools they used back at Edith, it would have to do for now until Erabus had the chance to whittle a better one. Satisfied for now, Erabus made his way into the darkened forest, barely able to see a foot or two in front of him due to the thick canopy overhead.

"How did Xicuz manage to find wood to chop down in here at night?" Erabus wondered as he made his way through the forest in the immediate area around the clearing, tripping over more than one exposed root he couldn't see.

He stopped and laughed as an obvious explanation crossed his mind. "A torch!" Xicuz had used a torch. Chalking his lack of grasping the obvious up to his mind still being groggy from the effects of the curse, Erabus decided to grab a few sticks and dry leaves to rebuild the fire so he could make one for himself.

Once his arms were full, Erabus made his way back to the clearing and dropped them near the smoldering embers. Building the fire back up ended up being easier than anticipated with the still hot coals catching the kindling quickly and soon a nice, roaring fire was going. Grabbing a large stick he noticed protruding from the ground, Erabus realized it was the torch Xicuz used.

Xicuz wrapped it with the same thick, dry vines Erabus remembered seeing on the torches in the cave. Taking a closer look at the vines, Erabus knew they didn't grow on the human side of the forest and he never saw them before meeting Xicuz. "I wonder if they can be used for anything else?" Erabus found himself asking the empty clearing as he lit the torch and began making his way into the forest once more.

This time, instead of being engulfed by darkness Erabus found himself surrounded by the eerie dancing shadows caused by the flickering flame. Concentrating on the warm, orange glow it cast around him, Erabus soon spotted a wild onion and went to pick it before something else obvious dawned on him; he would not be able to carry too much back with only one free hand.

Securing the torch into the ground so it would not fall over, Erabus set to work gathering up broad leaves and weaved them together, soon making himself a small, but sturdy basket. Braiding leftover strips of leaves, Erabus weaved them into the basket to create a handle and sat it down in the middle of the area lit by the torch light.

Making his way back over to the onion he spotted before, Erabus pulled it up, roots and all to plant whatever they didn't use in the garden. Dropping it into the basket, Erabus walked around the area, grabbing any edible berries, nuts, and greens he could find. They soon joined the wild onion, and Erabus grabbed the torch and basket before making his way a little further into the forest before repeating the process again.

It wasn't much of a haul, but better than nothing. Erabus grabbed a thick, arched stick that could bend without snapping in two and dropped it over the basket before making his way back to the clearing. Erabus put out the torch and sat his stuff down beside the fire, then got to work removing the parts of the plants they would eat, which went back into the basket, and made his way over to the garden with the leftovers.

It did not take him long to plant them in the freshly tilled soil and Erabus surrounded it in the stones removed earlier to mark its location. Scribbling a crude "garden" in the dirt beside it, Erabus made his way back to the fire and ate about one-third of the food gathered, leaving the rest for Xicuz. Placing the food on a large leaf, Erabus grabbed the basket and the burnt stick Xicuz used to write the note on the hut and relit the torch before making his way out into the forest again, this time heading in a different direction.

Marking every few trees with an X so he could find his way back, Erabus headed off in search of water, though he had no idea of how to carry any back to the clearing as the basket wasn't waterproof.

*

Xicuz woke up to the greatest feeling he had ever known. Without having to open his eyes, he knew it was Erabus in his embrace. Nothing had ever and could ever feel that warm and comforting to him. Pulling him against his chest, Xicuz breathed in his enticing scent and quickly grew hard from it.

Sighing to himself, Xicuz leaned down to kiss Erabus's forehead before whispering, "Goodnight, my love." Noticing that a warm, orange light bathed their temporary hut, Xicuz glanced toward the open door and found a torch planted in the dirt. Smiling to himself for Erabus having the forethought to make sure Xicuz could see, he crawled over him out of the bed to check to see if Erabus found his first message.

Xicuz realized the moment he lay down and closed his eyes that Erabus wouldn't see it until it was too late, but the curse activated before he could do anything about it. Xicuz chuckled at the new words scrawled into the dirt—replacing his own note. "Need a window. Too dark. Started garden. Water to the south. How did you fell the trees?"

Once again, Xicuz chuckled before shaking his head, having no intention of telling him that he ended up wracking them with his horns. First thing Xicuz needed to do was make an axe especially since his way would do Erabus no good. As the image flashed through his mind, Xicuz laughed at the thought of Erabus dragging his unconscious form around the clearing to use his horns as an axe.

Shaking his head to clear the ridiculous image, Xicuz went outside to rebuild the fire. Unsurprisingly, not only had Erabus done so right before turning in for the night, but he also gathered up a nice pile of firewood to keep the fire going long into the night. Beside the roaring fire, Xicuz found a large leaf with some berries and greens with the single word "eat" scrawled into the dirt beside it.

Realizing how hungry he became at the sight of the food; Xicuz emptied the leaf and made his way around the clearing to see what changes Erabus made. He found the small garden and a pile of sturdy sticks and flat stones.

"Spears and a bow. Spear, arrow and axe heads," Xicuz decided, noticing the different sizes of stones. "Apparently Erabus has been busy." Xicuz grabbed the torch, picked up one of the baskets, and began making his way south of the clearing. It did not take Xicuz long to find the tree he tied a trap to, made with the same vine he used on his torch, and his stomach rumbled at the sight of the rabbit hanging in midair.

He unwound it before placing it in the basket and setting the trap once more. Searching the area, Xicuz found much of the same as Erabus and added them to the basket. Back in the clearing, he set to work on preparing the rabbit and set it to roast over the fire before making his way back south again.

In only a few minutes, Xicuz made his way to the nearest water source that Erabus mentioned and had visited the night before. Xicuz leaned down to take a drink and rubbed water on his face and neck. He set the basket aside and stripped off his loincloth before slowly stepping into the cool water until it reached his muscular thighs. Cupping his hands, Xicuz used them to pour water on his chest before gliding his hands across to remove any sweat and dirt from the night before.

As his fingers brushed over his nipple, Xicuz shuddered at the sensation and could already imagine it was Erabus's hand covering him and not his own. The thought of him standing before him, close enough to touch his bare flesh had Xicuz reacting before he realized where his thoughts were turning. Even though he would much rather it be Erabus's, and not his own, hands exploring his body, Xicuz had to take what he could get.

Closing his eyes, Xicuz rubbed his fingers across every inch of his chest, flicking and pinching his nipples in turn and imagined Erabus's tongue and teeth. Moaning, more from the image his mind supplied him with rather than what he felt, Xicuz moved his hand lower as he caressed his way down to his inner thigh. Licking his lips, Xicuz watched Erabus take hold of his member and stroke it in his mind.

Erabus smirked up at him as he lowered himself into the water. He ran his tongue across the tip and Xicuz sucked in air through his teeth as he ran the pad of his thumb across it to match Erabus's actions. His hand became Erabus's mouth as Xicuz closed his fingers around his hardened member and stroked the entire length.

Xicuz heard Erabus moan around him, the vibrations coursing through his manhood as he picked up the pace and pressure. With each stroke Xicuz thrust into his hand and the lovely friction the movement caused allowed his fantasy to be even more believable in his mind. "Erabus," Xicuz moaned out as he felt himself drawing nearer to completion.

Xicuz went faster, applying more pressure, even as Erabus grabbed a hold of the base with his hand and moved along the length in time with his mouth. Panting, the image of Erabus smirking around his shaft as he looked up at him, spurring him on, Xicuz soon found his release and screamed out Erabus's name as his seed shot into the water. Opening his eyes, Xicuz groaned when he caught his own reflection in the calming water, breaking the spell of his fantasy.

For a moment, Erabus stood there with him, alive and well. In that moment when Xicuz felt Erabus's hot mouth embracing his manhood, the curse ceased to exist, and everything went back to the way it should be. Roaring in rage, Xicuz closed his eyes once more and allowed himself to fall back into the cool water, letting it wash over him and numb his thoughts. When Xicuz finally had to return to the surface for air, he grudgingly made his way back to the shore and shook himself to remove the excess water.

After wrapping his loincloth around his still damp waist, Xicuz retrieved the basket and made his way around the stream to travel further south than he had the night before. Xicuz couldn't be gone for too much longer; the rabbit would need to be checked on soon, but there was time for a quick scan of the area to see if there were any more plants to pick for Erabus. It did not take long before Xicuz filled the basket with more wild onions, roots, berries and even a few small, thick branches that could be whittled down into bowls, and he made his way back to their new home.

Xicuz set the basket down beside the fire and turned the rabbit. He gathered up the stones with the second basket Erabus made, grabbed a large rock, and sat down next to the fire to work. It was slow going, the rabbit finishing long before he did, but Xicuz managed to sharpen the stones into two axe heads, a half dozen arrowheads, three spear tips, and a couple of small knives. He stopped midway through eat his share of the rabbit and wrapped the extra in the leaf Erabus left his food on and placed it into the basket with the other food.

Once the stones were all sharpened, Xicuz used the vines to secure them to the axes but decided to leave the arrows and spears for later as their wooden bases would need more preparation before they were ready. After checking on Erabus, Xicuz made his way into the forest and began the long, tiring process of chopping down the trees he would need to make their permanent home. *At least,* Xicuz had to admit, *this time it won't give me such a headache.*

*

Erabus found it strange to wake up next to Xicuz when they would never have an actual conversation again, knowing they would remain close enough to touch but unable to hold on to each other. Erabus couldn't help but wonder if he would ever grow used to it or if he would one day find it unbearable to remain. For now, at least, there was far too much for him to do each day for him to worry about anything else.

He sat beside the fire and searched for the food he knew Xicuz left him even without having to see the note. Erabus could smell it upon awakening. Unwrapping the leaf, he found a slab of cooked but cold meat, and a quick sniff informed him it had once been a rabbit. Erabus hung it above the fire and glanced around at the changes the clearing had undergone during the night.

Xicuz started laying the foundation for the much bigger hut, apparently deciding to lay a wooden floor instead of leaving it dirt as he had with their current home. No doubt it will help keep them a bit warmer. On the far side of where Xicuz started laying the floor, there stood a large pile of stones in mostly the same size and shape. Erabus made his way over to take a closer look even though he already figured out what they were for.

On the northernmost side of the floorboards, where a few of them were cut smaller to leave a few feet in the middle open, he laid a foundation of the stones in lieu of the wood. Those already laid were covered in a dark grey clay that turned to a much lighter color as it dried. Erabus ran his fingers along one of the stones in the pile before making his way back to the fire as the scent of the rabbit made his mouth water.

After carefully removing it from the fire, Erabus gobbled down the hot, savory meat. All too soon it was gone and Erabus pouted at his empty hands. For a moment, he couldn't understand why he was so disappointed for it to be over, but realized it was the first. The first time Xicuz cooked something for him. The first time Erabus ate something prepared by the man he loved.

Pushing the realization from his mind, Erabus stood once more as he glanced around the clearing to decide what needed to be done next. To the side of his garden were a few more plants that needed to be planted. The stones Erabus gathered were sharpened, but still needed to be fixed to the arrows and spears, no doubt by the pile of thin vines Xicuz stacked up next to them. The pile of firewood was low.

Another rabbit lay inside one of the baskets near the fire needing to be tanned and Erabus wondered if Xicuz had left it for him to do or if he ran out of time before the sun rose. He decided to start with the rabbit since it would need time to cook. Erabus set to work skinning it before putting it on the spit Xicuz set up. Preparing the hide, he removed the one Xicuz left hanging and put the new one in its place on the tanning post.

Next, Erabus grabbed the axe and the empty basket and made his way into the forest. Sticking to the logs and branches already on the ground as much as possible, Erabus chopped up firewood and piled it up before going deeper into the forest and doing it twice more, adding anything edible he could find into the basket. There wasn't much left in the immediate area surrounding the clearing, but it would keep them for now.

He carried the wood back to the clearing before pausing to turn the rabbit and add another log to keep the fire going. Once done, Erabus turned his attention to the arrows and spears, wrapping the heads to the shafts with the vines Xicuz left there, testing the spears by throwing them as hard as he could into the nearest tree. The first one missed, bouncing harmlessly to the side, but as it hit the trunk hard and the vines did not come undone, Erabus considered it a success.

Turning to the bow next, Erabus ran his fingers over the intricate carvings Xicuz added into the wood after sanding it. Erabus gasped at how beautiful the horns and the crown, the trees and the rain, and the sun and the moon looked dancing across the wood. It was as if Xicuz told their story in each and every detail he added. Erabus wiped a stray tear from his eye and ran his fingers across each pattern before placing a gentle kiss on the horns.

Erabus set the bow aside for the moment and grabbed another vine. He tested it to make sure it could be used as a bow string before stringing his bow and testing the first arrow on the same tree. Much like with the first spear, it pinged off the trunk harmlessly and Erabus adjusted the string before trying again and hitting directly in the center where he aimed. It was perfect. Erabus tested the rest of the arrows to ensure they were tied properly.

"All that's left now is a quiver," Erabus realized as he made his way over to the tree to retrieve his arrows. He set them off to the side with the other weapons and made his way into the forest once more to gather up as many of the larger leaves as he could find.

Once they were ready, Erabus weaved them in a spiral, pulling the cylinder tighter the higher it went. When it was big enough for his needs, he wove in the extra pieces and braided the strips together to make another handle.

Sighing in relief once finished, Erabus wove the ends into the quiver and tested it over his shoulder before adding the extra weight of the arrows into it. Satisfied it would hold, Erabus checked on the rabbit and turned it once more, deciding it would be ready by the time he returned. Though Erabus doubted he would have enough time to hunt anything down now, he wanted to test out his new weapons today in case Xicuz needed to check them when he awoke.

Shouldering his bow, Erabus made his way into the forest, taking extra care to keep his footsteps silent. He followed the path marked out with charcoal X's before stopping to listen to the sounds of the forest around him. The animals seemed intent on keeping quiet.

Erabus kept himself still, barely even breathing, as he listened for his cue that the forest forgot about his presence and came back to life. As Erabus was about to give up, he heard the flapping of wings and notched his first arrow, aiming into the trees where he knew his quarry would be.

Sure enough, a few moments later, the bird took to flight out of the trees overhead and Erabus aimed his arrow and released it as he exhaled. Though it caught the bird and caused it to plummet to the ground, Erabus realized his aim hadn't been as true as he hoped, and the bird lived still. Erabus rectified the situation the moment the bird was in his hands, not wanting the poor creature to suffer, and retrieved the arrow and cleaned it off before adding it back to the quiver.

He ran his fingers across the feathers; they would be perfect for giving his arrows the stability and accuracy they were lacking, as naked as they were. Listening for a moment for any other signs of life in the area, and finding none, Erabus began making his way back to the clearing. Before Erabus could even cross the threshold out of the forest, the scent of the rabbit hit him, and he quickened his pace back home.

He removed the rabbit so it could cool down and plucked the bird, adding the feathers to the basket. Glancing up at the sky and realizing there were still many hours before sunset, he held off adding the bird and instead added another log to the fire. Eating half of the rabbit, Erabus wrapped the extra meat and set it aside before grabbing the basket of feathers and cutting some down to the size he needed with the axe.

Then he carefully added a split in the end of the arrows and secured the feathers to them. Once he finished his six arrows, Erabus took them back to the tree and practice again. Already he saw the improvement and returned them to his quiver before grabbing his bow, and the basket, and decided to make his way down to the stream. Erabus stripped down and slowly made his way into the cool water, shivering at the sudden change in temperature even as he rubbed his hands across his body to clean quickly.

Erabus only remained in the cold water a minute or two before he rushed toward the shore. After drying off as best he could, Erabus redressed and took a scenic route back to the clearing. By the time he stood before the fire once more, Erabus managed to shoot a squirrel and a rabbit, and gathered a few more wild onions and edible roots, and a few handfuls of nuts from the ground.

He would need to go back later for more, knowing they would come in handy later during the winter when his garden died. "If it worked for the squirrels," Erabus joked to himself as he set the basket down and picked up the empty one without tending to the meat. He would do that later as it was not time to put the meat on the fire yet. Checking on Xicuz, finding him as unconscious as expected, Erabus wondered how long he would continue to check.

At what point would Erabus give up and accept the truth for what it was? When would he stop looking at Xicuz and expect him to open his eyes and smirk at him? Erabus already knew the answer—never. He would never give up hope of seeing him again or accept this was truly the fate they were dealt. To find each other, against all the odds.

To fall in love, to mean more to each other than the air they breathed. Only to be ripped from each other's arms forever by the curse. Surely there must have been something, some way to break the curse and allow him to have the life he was supposed to have with Xicuz. Erabus had no idea what that might be yet.

Making his way into the forest again, Erabus smiled when he stumbled upon one of Xicuz's traps with a rabbit caught in it. He added it to the basket, reset the trap, and continued on. Though Erabus came upon a few more traps in his search, none of the others were sprung. Looking down at the rabbit, Erabus smiled as a thought came to mind. They would have extra meat today.

"We could salt it," Erabus realized and began hunting once more with a newfound zeal at the thought of being able to really help Xicuz. Erabus left the hut building to Xicuz, not wanting to mess things up as he had no idea how he wanted things set up, but if he could gather more meat for them, Xicuz wouldn't have to and could concentrate on finishing their home so they would have a place to store the dried meat.

Erabus set the basket down and made his way a bit deeper into the forest, climbing up into a tree when he knew there were animals in the area. Their tracks and the small stream, barely a few inches wide, but perfect for a watering hole, were more than enough to assure him of his chances. But as the hours passed without any sign of life other than a small bird chirping in one of the trees nearby, Erabus wondered if the tracks were older than he first thought.

Glancing up at the sky, able to make out the position of the sun as he was high enough in the tree that its leaves were unable to block all the sky from his view, Erabus estimated he only had an hour or so before he needed to be back in the clearing. Just as he gave up and went to make his way back empty handed, other than the rabbit of course, Erabus heard the soft footfalls below him.

Glancing down, Erabus spotted the small buck as it broke through the tree line into the area beneath him. Holding his breath as he stared down at the magnificent creature before him, he couldn't help but remember how annoyed Xicuz had gotten when they first met, and Erabus mistook his goat-like horns for a deer's antlers. Though it was easy to tell they were different, once he got a look at them, Erabus honestly couldn't figure out why Xicuz had been so annoyed by the comparison.

The antlers on the deer before him were things of beauty, not that Xicuz's smaller, curved horns weren't also amazing to see and touch. Lining up his sight, Erabus exhaled and let his arrow fly. At the same moment he released his breath, the wind shifted slightly and caused his arrow to ping harmlessly off the tree beside the deer, scaring it away.

Before Erabus could curse under his breath at his misfortune, the noise from the frightened deer, making its way back into the forest, startled a rabbit out of the underbrush. Not wanting to lose his second chance in as many minutes, Erabus took aim once more and took the animal down with one arrow. Smirking at the fact he would have plenty to show for his day, even if his preferred target did get away, Erabus climbed down from the tree and collected his catch before making his way back toward the basket.

He didn't have much time left now, so Erabus quickened his pace back to the clearing, dropping the basket near the other for Xicuz to deal with later. Erabus climbed onto the bed beside Xicuz, and he traced the outline of his face with his finger, whispering, "I love you, Xicuz," as he lost consciousness.

*

Once he reset his trap, finding an animal tripped it during the day without getting caught, Xicuz turned his gaze toward the south and watched the silent forest for a few minutes, as though he could see through the trees all the way to the man he wondered about. There were miles in between them, but what was there to stop him from coming in search of them anyway?

A week passed since the curse first activated and Xicuz nearly had their larger hut complete and yet there was no sign of anyone else in the forest in that entire time. He thought for sure Jydral would have been hunting them down by now.

Surely, Jydral knew they were still alive and found it odd they disappeared out of thin air. No matter the reason for the delay, Xicuz would be unable to relax until he knew for himself.

Xicuz calculated how long it would take him to get there and back before the sun would rise; he would only have maybe a few minutes to watch the human village and it would be late into the night. Would there even be anyone awake for him to spy on? Certainly, a guard or two, but from what he saw the last time he was there, they tended to speak little while on duty.

Would the whole thing be a waste of time? Time Xicuz could spend working on their home instead. Even as Xicuz wondered this, he felt his feet already beginning to move him in the direction of Edith. Deciding to commit to his plan since his instincts apparently were already, Xicuz picked up the pace as he weaved in between the trees, making his way quickly.

Once Xicuz reached the border, he would have to be far more cautious. As hour after hour ticked by, Xicuz never slowed down his pace or stopped for a break, even as his muscles protested against the strain, he put them under. Ignoring them, Xicuz waited until he crossed the human's border before finally coming to a stop.

It lasted only long enough to ensure there was no one around before Xicuz took off again but at a much slower pace this time. He made good time coming through the forest and if there was no one out hunting or guarding the forest between his location and Edith, Xicuz figured he could give himself an entire hour to watch instead of only a few minutes. The former Xicuz doubted, as it was far too dark for the humans to see their prey, but he had to admit the latter was possible.

Especially after their disappearance. Did Jydral station sentries in the forest in case either of them came back? Much as Xicuz was doing at that moment. As the hours continued to pass without any other sign of life, other than an occasional squirrel moving around in the trees overhead, Xicuz soon realized he worried about nothing. Apparently Jydral was so arrogant he did not believe they were a threat.

As he picked up speed once more, Xicuz realized how strange that was; Jydral tried to convince everyone the satyrs were a threat when he was just a prince. Wouldn't Jydral be even more set on attacking them now that he was king? Surely, Jydral would have been crowned by now. He grew even more confused the closer he got to the human village without coming across any guards, Xicuz wondered if he was running right into a trap.

For a moment, Xicuz debated turning around right then and going back to the clearing empty handed but decided it was worth the risk to find out for sure. He couldn't go back to Erabus without making sure there wasn't any danger. Xicuz planned to make his way back through the trees at the first sign of trouble, certain the humans would not be able to keep up with his speed that far off the ground. He found his way to the same tree he spied from before and climbed up into its thick branches.

Minutes ticked by without any sign of the humans, other than the guards on the far side, and certainly no one came close enough for him to hear any conversations, let alone one of substance. As much as he dreaded the idea, Xicuz would have to make his way into the village if to hear anything at all.

But how? How was Xicuz supposed to make his way into the village without being seen? Even if he managed to find a cloak big enough to cover his horns and hooves, and that was a big if, it would render him far too tall to ever pass as an actual human. He would have to go in as is without being seen by any of the guards who were suspiciously moving around more than they had been a few minutes before.

As he watched them from the cover of his tree, noticing some of them were even beginning to pass within feet of his hiding spot, Xicuz soon understood what they were doing. *Their patrols are random.* Though he figured it made sense to them, as none of the guards seemed to be the least bit confused by their assignments, Xicuz figured no one on the outside would be able to figure it out.

At least not in the short amount of time Xicuz had before he needed to be making his way back home. Once again, Xicuz wondered if he shouldn't go back to the clearing without learning any information and once again his conscience refused to allow him to leave without assuring himself Erabus wasn't in any danger. That left him with only one option. Xicuz would have to sneak in without having the foggiest idea what the pattern was for the patrols and with nothing more than the shadows to cover him.

This wouldn't be easy, but Xicuz was running out of time to even try. He scanned the area beneath him for an opening in the patrols and dropped to the ground once he found one. Running as quickly as his hooves could carry him, without risking noise, Xicuz pressed his back up against a nearby wall. Xicuz bathed himself in shadows a moment before a patrol he miscalculated, passed right in front of him.

Surely, they must have heard his heavy breathing, the adrenaline pumping through his veins at the thought of being so close to getting caught, yet they walked right past him unaware. "Can you believe the king went after them?" one of the guards whispered to the other, and Xicuz smiled at the thought of his luck turning around and being in the exact spot he needed to be to overhear their conversation, but as the second guard answered, he found his luck hadn't changed at all.

"Of course, even if they were the late king's men, King Jydral couldn't allow them to go unpunished after they were spouting such nonsense about him and questioning his right to be king. He gave them the option to be banished, to live out the rest of their day in the forest, but they refused and questioned his legitimacy again. The only option left to King Jydral at that point was to execute them."

As the men moved farther away from him, preventing him from hearing anymore of their conversation, Xicuz turned his attention back to what he heard. The men they referred to, no doubt, were those loyal to Erabus's father, those who tried to help him protect the king from Jydral's treachery. *So, they had lost their lives in the end?* Xicuz wasn't surprised, though he did find it a bit strange their executions were so recent that the guards were still talking about it.

Then again, the first guard mentioned needing to go find them. Perhaps they hid well enough in the forest to avoid capture until recently. Had they been looking for Erabus? How far out were they when they were finally captured? Anywhere near the clearing? Had they found Erabus one day and led Jydral's men away from him for his safety? No, Erabus would have left him a note of warning if anyone, friend, or foe, showed up near their home.

After coming to the village, Xicuz found he had even more questions than when before, but one thing was for certain as he waited for an opening and began making his way back into the forest; he would not be telling Erabus. The last thing Erabus needed was to know that more men died due to his brother. That he had been unable to save them too.

With his newfound knowledge weighing on his mind, Xicuz quickened his pace as he admitted to himself that, at least, the news meant Jydral and his men weren't currently searching for Erabus and him. If they were, the guards would have had a lot more to talk about rather than something that already happened.

Xicuz saw the moon in a break in the canopy and realized he miscalculated things again. If he were not careful, Xicuz would not make it back in time before sunrise. Running faster than he could ever remember running before, Xicuz made it back into the hut panting, gasping for air even as the sky brightened to the predawn blues and greys.

Crawling into bed beside Erabus, Xicuz smiled before placing a gentle kiss on his brow. "Our day will come, my love. This I vow."

*

Time seemed unable or unwilling to make up its mind as some weeks passed faster than Xicuz could blink and others seemed to last an eternity. Each night passed the same; he spent his time building their home and checking his traps. Once it was complete, and with Erabus soon keeping up with the traps, he had nothing to do except chop more firewood and dry the extra meat they had.

Even with the much bigger hut giving them plenty of room to store both, there was only so much he could stand of repeating the same two mundane tasks. After a few days with little else to do, Xicuz started hunting the elusive deer Erabus mentioned in one of his daily notes, but so far, he had yet to even catch a glimpse of him. But even the thrill of the hunt couldn't keep him busy for too long and he tried anything to keep himself occupied through the long nights, the ones that never seemed to end.

One night, Xicuz barely found the will to even get out of bed, doing so only so he could read Erabus's notes, eat, and rebuild the fire as needed. The rest of the time, countless hours spent in silence and passing impossibly slowly, Xicuz spent lying on the bed beside Erabus. Just holding on to him and even falling asleep with him in his arms. He woke up every few hours, happy until he remembered Erabus would not be awake soon as well.

When Xicuz could no longer stand the painful reminder that night, he got up and cooked the rabbit Erabus caught earlier. He never complained in his notes, but Xicuz knew his days were as long, as boring, and as lonely as his nights. But much like Erabus undoubtedly did, he left only content notes, reminding him of his love and telling him about the roasting meat.

If Erabus realized how unfruitful his night had been, he never said a word in any of his notes since. After that night, Xicuz decided he needed something to break up the endless cycle of nothingness. When he began to get too stir crazy, usually about once a week, Xicuz would go check on Edith to make sure Jydral wasn't making any plans to move against them.

Spending his entire time awake running back and forth made for a great way to keep himself occupied and forget about how much he missed Erabus. As long as the breeze fluttered through Xicuz's hair, his lungs burned with the desperate need for air, and his calves screamed for him to stop, he could lose himself in that moment. The nights Xicuz took the trip were over faster than he could blink.

It was too bad Xicuz couldn't make the trip every night, but each time increased his risk of getting caught. Tonight proved to be such a night, and he hid in the shadows outside the throne room. He came here on a few occasions before, but each trip ended up being a complete waste of time. Jydral seemingly slept during most of his visits, and even in the ones he was awake for, the human king never said anything of substance.

Usually Jydral complained about whatever was not going the way he wanted it to on that particular night: his new room—the late king's old one—wasn't finished being redecorated as he demanded, repairs not being completed after a fire, hunting parties not bringing back enough meat for the winter stores. It had never been anything of importance, but that night everything changed.

Instead of Jydral yelling at whichever guard met with him, after apparently waking up in the middle of the night, he seemed to have called the meeting, but Xicuz couldn't for the life of him figure out why he held it in the middle of the night. Perhaps Jydral worried about spies in his village spying on them and overhearing something he didn't want them to.

Xicuz smiled at the thought as it proved to be exactly what he was doing. "The preparations will be completed soon, my king. Your army will be ready to move on schedule," one of the guards told Jydral, though the one who spoke after him was either too quiet or too far away for him to hear. Not wanting to miss any more of the conversation, Xicuz moved closer to the source of their voices, exposing himself more than he would have preferred.

Xicuz glanced around to ensure no one had discovered him yet and pressed as close to the wall as he could in time to catch Jydral's reply. "Good. It's time we deal with those animals once and for all. The sooner the full moon rises, the better." The moment Jydral finished speaking, Xicuz didn't bother waiting to see if they would say anything else of importance. Xicuz glanced up at the sky, judged if he would have enough time to make it and began running back into the forest, barely pausing to make certain there were no patrols in the area.

He didn't need to see the current shape of the moon to know it would be full in two days. Traveling through the forest, Xicuz weaved his way in between the trees barely noticing the miles as they passed him by. As he raced through the forest, only one thought penetrated his mind; he was running out of time.

The crunch of the dirt beneath his hooves, the nocturnal birds screeching in protest overhead, the rustling of the leaves as Xicuz pushed his way through the low-hanging branches were barely registered in his mind. Weak, panting for breath as his lungs burned from overuse, Xicuz finally crashed through the threshold into the village he spent his entire life in. Qom was at his side in an instant and Xicuz waved him off.

"Get the king!" Xicuz commanded, gasping for air between each word. Qom took off running as Xicuz doubled over and tried in vain to calm his racing heart. Seeing a shadow fall over him, Xicuz glanced up to find it wasn't Zhul towering above him as expected. It did not take him long to notice the crown upon his head confirming what he already knew would come to pass; King Zhul had died.

Before the thought had fully formed in his mind, Xicuz already dismissed the idea Jydral might have something to do with it. The last time Xicuz saw him he knew it wouldn't be long, and the satyrs weren't acting like their king had been murdered. "You have finally returned to us, Xicuz. We have been worried," the new king said as he placed his hand on his shoulder.

Glancing up to get a better look at him, Xicuz soon realized who it was. *Heoltos*. He wasn't at all surprised the satyr before him became the next to be crowned king. Heoltos was one of the best hunters and fighters the village of Ebrein had ever seen, and though Xicuz had never been as close to him as he was with Qom and Xaaxex, he remained his closest companion after them.

Heoltos stood well over six feet with a body covered in lean, well-toned muscles. His long dark hair flowed over his shoulders in waves that were occasionally interrupted by a lock of hair tightly twirled upon itself and fastened with carved wooden beads or wrapped in thin strains of orange twine. His dark skin glistened in the torch light.

He wore a small animal hide draped across his shoulders and held in place by straps tied under his arms. Upon his head sat a circlet of bones and teeth. "My king," Xicuz greeted as he knelt on one knee and bowed his head in respect. "I come bearing warning from Edith. King Jydral plans to move against you at the full moon," Xicuz warned, barely catching the widening of his eyes before the king sighed and returned his expression to a more relaxed state.

"I do not know the numbers Jydral brings with him, but you should prepare for the worst." The king nodded in understanding. Xicuz wished he had more information for him, but he could not risk staying in Edith any longer. Turning toward the north, Xicuz started making his way back home, even knowing he would not arrive in time, but realized that even the short journey he planned would not be possible. "It's too late," Xicuz whispered out loud to himself, his eyes staring up at the soft grey light that could be made out on the horizon.

"What do you mean, Xicuz?" King Heoltos asked, but before Xicuz could respond, a weakening sensation overcame him as the curse took effect once more and he collapsed to the ground. Xicuz whispered Erabus's name as he lost consciousness.

Chapter Thirteen

Erabus knew something was wrong as he awoke. Their home had become far colder than it should have been and Xicuz was not on the bed beside him. As icy fingers seemed to latch on to his heart, Erabus shot up in bed.

"Xicuz!" Erabus called out as he leapt from their bed and made his way out into the greying sky. Finding the outside fire as dead as the hearth inside, Erabus spun around screaming out, "Xicuz!" even though there was no way for him to hear him, let alone reply. Grabbing his bow and quiver, he hurried into the forest, praying Xicuz lost track of time while out hunting.

"Xicuz!" Erabus continued to scream out every few minutes as he searched the area around his traps and the stream, finding them equally empty. Gripping his bow so tightly the wood groaned under the pressure, Erabus willed his mind and heart to stop racing so he could figure out where Xicuz was. It did not take him long to figure out there were only two options—he went to visit the satyrs, or Jydral captured him.

Erabus decided to try the satyrs' village first. Not only was it closer to his current location, but if Xicuz had been captured by Jydral, he would need their help to get him back.

Erabus ran as fast as he could go. He barely noticed as the miles passed under his feet as Erabus weaved his way through the trees, finding their thickness tapering the farther south he got. The forest came to life around him as the sun rose, but even as he heard the wildlife, they heard his approach and scurried off further into the forest.

Long before Erabus reached the threshold of the forest, the sounds of the bustling village permeated through the trees. Keeping his bow shouldered, Erabus raised his hands in the air, hoping to look as nonthreatening as possible. He had no way of knowing how the satyrs would react to seeing him enter their village uninvited. Even if Xicuz was there, he had no way of knowing if he informed them that Erabus was a friend.

And, perhaps more importantly, Erabus had no idea what his brother might have done in his absence to destroy the treaty between them. Had Jydral already attacked them? Did they suffer heavy losses if he had? Though, judging by the sounds coming from Ebrein, that did not seem to be the case for them. As Erabus burst through the trees into the late afternoon sunlight, all eyes turned to him, but paid the satyrs little mind as he scanned the area for any sign of Xicuz.

"I am not a threat!" Erabus assured them, raising his hands higher when a few of them started to move closer. "Please just tell me, where is Xicuz?"

A large group of the satyrs parted and a dark-skinned, giant of a satyr stepped forward. The circlet of bones and teeth upon his head identified him as the king, though he wasn't the one his father had known. Erabus sank to his knees and bowed his head in respect. "He is here. Why are you?" the new king questioned in a stern, but soft voice and Erabus fell forward in relief, barely catching himself with his hands before he would have face planted in the dirt.

Xicuz is here. He is safe. Getting control of himself once more, Erabus glanced back up at the king with another respectful bow. "I am—" Erabus fell forward once again, only this time he couldn't move his hands out in front of him in time to catch himself. For a moment, Erabus wondered if one of the satyrs hit him without him feeling it, but as his eyes were closing against his will, he noticed how dark it had grown.

He was out of time.

*

Xicuz knew something wasn't right when he felt Erabus's body beside him upon waking up. At first, his mind couldn't figure out why it was so strange—after all, before tonight not waking up beside Erabus would have been what caused him concern. As the remaining traces of sleep cleared from his mind, Xicuz soon discovered what unsettled that night; Erabus shouldn't have been sleeping beside him this time.

The cold, hard ground beneath him and the cool night breeze blowing goosebumps on to his skin informed him he remained outside and not in their hut lying on their bed. As everything came rushing back to him from the night before, Xicuz sat up, causing a gasp from someone nearby. He had gone to check on the human village and overheard Jydral's plans for an attack.

He made it to Ebrein in time to warn the king—*the new king*, Xicuz reminded himself—but he didn't make it back to the clearing before sunrise and yet Erabus lay beside him. Smiling once he realized what that meant, Xicuz had to admit he should have known this was the only way for things to work out. Of course, Erabus would go in search of him the moment he awoke and realized Xicuz was missing.

Xicuz glanced down at Erabus and smiled at his peaceful expression. It was as if Erabus knew he laid beside him even in his unconscious state.

"Care to explain who he is and what is going on?" a voice demanded from behind him. Xicuz turned to find King Heoltos standing a few feet away, arms crossed in front of his bare chest.

Xicuz bowed his head. "Forgive me, my king. I did not have enough time to fill you in on everything last night. This is Erabus, son of Tribion, the late human king. It has come to be that Jydral made a deal with a bargaining devil to become king, sacrificing mine and Tribion's lives in exchange.

"Once he realized what happened, Erabus made a deal with another devil to save me and gave me half of his life in exchange. Our curse, as such, is that I only live during the night and Erabus during the day."

"Why would this human sacrifice all of his nights to let you live?" the king questioned, though something in his deep, golden eyes made Xicuz think he already knew the answer. Had Heoltos already figured out the truth about him? If so, when? Did he already know before Xicuz disappeared or had Erabus told him the day before when he arrived? And if Heoltos already knew, why did he insist Xicuz tell him himself?

"He is my chosen, my king," Xicuz finally admitted out loud as he turned his eyes from the king and smiled down at Erabus, brushing a lock of hair from his eyes. "He, and our curse, are the reasons why I never returned to Ebrein before now. I had to make certain Erabus would be safe." The king stared in silence for a long moment and

Xicuz finally had to turn his eyes back to him, expecting to see anger or disgust in his.

Instead, Xicuz saw the same calm, yet stern expression that Heoltos wore on his face since he met up with him the night before. "Your chosen is safe here, Xicuz," Heoltos informed him before turning his golden eyes on Erabus for a moment and speaking to him once again. "Are you aware of how to break the curse?"

Xicuz stood stunned. He always figured the only way to break the curse was for the devil who cast it to remove it. A little spark of hope ignited in his heart.

"To break the curse, you must destroy the magic it stems from," the king continued. "In this case, the magic lies within the deal Jydral made. Something you do not know about we kings is that there is much knowledge passed between us during our ascending. For a moment, we are connected to the kings of the past and their wisdom is shared with us. One of our past kings made a deal with one of these devils himself asking to live far longer than he was ever meant to by sacrificing the lives of his fellow satyrs every time he grew old or injured in battle.

"In his case, they gave him a talisman that would transfer their life force to him and the only way to break the deal, as the satyr who would become the next king after him did, was by destroying the talisman. In the case of the human king, I believe it would be Jydral himself you would need to destroy to break the magic."

There was no way Xicuz could kill Jydral. As much as the monster might deserve to die for the evil he had done, and would continue to do if left unchecked, Jydral was still Erabus's brother. And if Xicuz knew anything for certain, it was that Erabus wouldn't wish his brother dead just to save himself from the curse. "It is not possible to kill the human king," Xicuz insisted. "He is Erabus's brother and even if that wasn't a factor, it would be impossible to get close enough to do so."

For a while, the king watched him in silence, before finally nodding. "That is not up to me to decide but know your people will stand with you no matter what you choose. Getting close might be easier than you think with the human king marching on us soon. And you should have known, Xicuz, your chosen would have been safe and welcome here with us." Apparently noticing the startled expression on Xicuz's face, the king admitted, "I have always known you were not interested in the embrace of a woman; we all have."

Undoubtedly seeing how confused Xicuz became at his words, King Heoltos laughed before explaining, "It was rather obvious to anyone with eyes, Xicuz."

*

Waking up in Xicuz's arms once again, Erabus wondered if he imagined the whole thing the day before. Then Erabus realized how cold and hard the ground beneath him was. They were not back at home, in the comfort of their own bed, and everything he hoped was imagined, actually happened. Coming to terms with reality left him with far more questions than answers. Why had Xicuz gone to the village in the first place?

Had Xicuz done it before and never left him a message to let him know? What kept him from returning home on time? Was he being selfish expecting Xicuz to stay out in the forest with him instead of letting him return to his village, to his friends and family? And what kind of welcoming should Erabus expect that morning? Knowing there was no reason to put off the inevitable,

Erabus opened his eyes to find himself in the satyrs' village as expected and wondered why Xicuz hadn't just carried him back home during the night as he did when the curse first activated.

Glancing around in the dirt, hoping to find a note Xicuz left for him, Erabus found one of the satyrs sitting nearby, his bright silver eyes, not unlike Xicuz's own, staring at him in question. Qom—or was it Xaaxex? Erabus still had no idea which was which—watched him for a moment before rising to his hooves and bowing his head ever so slightly at him.

"The king wants to speak with you," he explained, starting away without waiting to see if Erabus would follow. Erabus glanced at Xicuz and refrained from kissing his cheek as he wanted to. He wasn't sure how the others might react. Instead, Erabus rose to his feet and hurried after his "guide".

As he ran to catch up, Erabus realized his bow and quiver were missing but knew they wouldn't have done him much good even if he still had them.

He was outnumbered, and Erabus had no intention of starting a fight with the satyrs. As he was led further into the village, all eyes turned toward him as they passed. Not that Erabus could blame them for their apprehension or curiosity. It wasn't every day they had a human walking around their village; at least not a male one.

As he glanced around once more, Erabus realized none of the human women who lived there were anywhere to be found. Apparently, they were hiding from him, perhaps worried he might be there to try to take them back, but Erabus decided against saying anything that might assure them this was not the case. It wasn't as though they would believe him anyway.

He was curious as to where they might be hiding as there was nothing to provide cover in the entire area that he could see. *Maybe they are in the forest*, Erabus thought.

His guide stopped to kneel before the king. Erabus stepped up beside him to follow suit and bowed his head before getting another look at the dark-skinned king, wondering what happened to the one he met before.

"I am King Heoltos," he said. "My predecessor, King Zhul, has ascended to the endless night. You are Erabus, son of Tribion, the late human king." It was not a question, but Erabus nodded anyway.

"I will tell you the same thing I told Xicuz the night before. If you wish to break your curse, you need but kill the cause of the magic."

For a moment, Erabus knelt there in silence, trying to figure out if Heoltos expected him to kill Ith'tar, but soon realized that was not what he said. "You mean Jydral. If he is dead, there would be no need to sacrifice Xicuz's life for his deal anymore and my own deal would no longer be needed to save Xicuz. But how does that work? His deal has already been completed. Jydral is king and Xicuz's life, along with my father's, were sacrificed. How would killing him now undo what has already been done?"

"There is an old game that we satyrs play, though I do not know if you humans have it as well. It is called Towering Stones. You take flat stones and pile them one on top of the other until you have built your tower. Once complete, you pull out the second stone from the top and place it on your tower again. Then you take the third, then the fourth, and so on until your tower collapses. Eventually it will, as any foundation would.

"The same could be said for bargains made with these devils. If you remove a piece from far enough down, the whole thing will collapse, taking down the intertwined deals with it. If your deals weren't connected, then there would be nothing you could do, but because your deal saved Xicuz from Jydral's they are linked. If there is no more Jydral, there is no reason for his deal and with his deal gone, yours will no longer be necessary.

"Alas, it cannot bring back your father as any truly dead cannot be resurrected." Though Erabus already assumed as much, it still broke Erabus's heart to hear that nothing could be done to save his father from his cruel and undeserved fate, no matter how long it had been since King Tribion was placed in the royal tombs.

"Thank you, King Heoltos. I understand," Erabus said as he bowed once more and tried to figure out what to do with his newfound knowledge. He wasn't given much time to process it before the king interrupted his silent dilemma to throw him off balance.

"Are you aware your king is planning to march on us this very night?" Startled beyond words by his sudden question, Erabus could barely process what he heard, let alone respond to it.

"What will you do now that you know your king is starting a war with us?" the king inquired. Oddly, even though Erabus never allowed himself to think about it before, knowing no good would come from dreading the future, Erabus knew the answer without having to think about it.

"He is not my king; Jydral never was, and I will do everything in my power to stop him from hurting your people. I do hope to get my own people to see the truth of him before it is too late, but I will not allow any innocent lives to be lost because my fellow humans were too foolish to see him for the monster Jydral truly is." If he were being honest, Erabus didn't know if he could take the life of another human, men he had known all his life, but he would be able to do anything short of taking their lives to stop them.

The silence settled over them once again as King Heoltos stared deep into his eyes. Finally, after what seemed like an eternity to Erabus, a faint smile crossed his lips and his golden eyes blinked, breaking his hold over him. "You are welcome to stay in Ebrein, Erabus chosen one of Xicuz, but be warned, you shall not find a roof over your head."

Blinking at him in disbelief, Erabus tried to decide if heard him right. The slight twinkle in his eyes assured him he had. The satyr king just told a joke. Erabus chuckled. "I do not need one. I need only Xicuz to keep me warm."

*

With Xicuz's warning, the preparations were done well before the scout returned to inform them that Jydral and his army were nearing the designated battleground. Though the humans had no idea, the satyrs' army would descend upon them long before they could get close enough to Ebrein to put anyone left behind in danger. That, of course, included the women who could not be expected to fight against their own friends and family who they cast aside to be with the satyrs, the elderly who were far past the age of fighting and the children who had not reached it yet.

And most importantly, Erabus remained in the village, his unconscious form being watched by the others who were left behind. As much as Xicuz would have preferred to be the one protecting Erabus himself, he was needed on the front lines. He grabbed his engraved spear, which had a leafy vine carved down the handle, and tested its weight in his hand before hurrying to catch up to the king and his guards. Noticing his approach, King Heoltos nodded to him and Xicuz fell in step beside Qom and Xaaxex.

The farther they traveled out into the forest, the more they heard the approaching army. In contrast to the loud stomping created by their heavy boots, the satyrs' hoof falls were nearly imperceptible, allowing them to keep their element of surprise until they were certain they were just on the other side of a rather thick grouping of trees from the human army. Even before he saw them, Xicuz knew this battle wouldn't be easy.

They would be fighting in the middle of the thick forest, with barely a foot or two between each tree, giving neither them nor the humans much room to maneuver. It would be difficult enough for a one-on-one fight to take place between the trees, but this would be a full-on battle between the two clans. It would be nearly impossible for both sides to fight, but it was the only option that didn't risk the humans getting too close to the village.

Drawing a deep breath, Xicuz pressed his back up against one of the thicker trees and moved out of view as he waited for his king to give the command to attack. A moment later, the first wave of humans broke through the tree line and King Heoltos stepped out into their view, stopping them in their tracks with his sudden appearance. From his current location, Xicuz saw a few of the humans move into a defensive position and Jydral raise his sword, sneering at Heoltos.

"You are trespassing on our land, human king," Heoltos warned. "You shall receive but one warning to return from whence you came before I view your behavior as an act of war.".

"Animals can't own land, you foolish beast," Jydral spat. "The late king may not have understood this simple fact, but I assure you I most certainly do. You, however, will receive no warning to retreat as my people will never be safe as long as you monsters are allowed to live," Jydral raised his sword above his head even further. "Attack!" Jydral cried out, bringing his sword down on the king's head.

Heoltos swung up his battle hammer just in time to block the attack, and both sides moved against each other. Xicuz stepped out from behind the tree and raised his spear in time to block an attack from one of the humans behind Heoltos. Two strikes of his spear were all it took to take down the coward, and Xicuz turned from him to his next target before his body even hit the ground.

Parrying the sword strikes of the human he faced now, his footwork resembled a dance more than a battle as Xicuz kept himself out of his reach. It did not take long before his human opponent lost his patience and plowed toward him. Xicuz spun, dropped to the ground, and thrust his spear into his chest, using his own momentum against him. His strangled battle cry became his death rattle that spit blood in Xicuz's face, but he wiped it away without a thought and turned his attention to his next target.

One after another, the humans fell at his feet and Xicuz wondered if they were someone Erabus knew well. Each man who lost their lives at his hand was born and raised in the same village as Erabus. As much as he tried to push it from his mind, Xicuz couldn't help but dread the worst with each human cut down.

Had the man, who Xicuz pinned to the tree with his own sword when his spear was knocked out of his hand, been his cousin? The one who screamed in agony when Xicuz was forced to finish him off—had he been a childhood friend? Had the one who took advantage of his opening and got the tip of his dagger into the flesh on his back before he could move away, been a teacher or mentor to Erabus?

With each man who fell before him, their faces ingrained in his mind, Xicuz made a silent promise to learn their names from Erabus if they were ever reunited in the future. As much as he hated the position Jydral forced upon them, despised the way his spear cut through their unprotected flesh, sending blood spraying everywhere, Xicuz knew without a doubt he preferred it to be them and not his own friends and family who were falling before them.

Each human Xicuz slaughtered was one less who could harm one of the other satyrs. One less human to put his king, or his love, in danger. Holding on tight to that thought, he continued to make his way through one opponent after another as the hours passed them by as if they were seconds ticking away on a clock. Xicuz was worn out, tired, bleeding from more wounds than he could see or count but refused to allow it to show on his face.

No sense in letting his enemies know how close to his limit he grew. Another human fell to his spear, and Xicuz found a small lull in his attackers, the rest too busy already fighting with other satyrs. Taking the first breath he could remember since the battle started, Xicuz glanced around the area and figured out why he was being left alone. Jydral seemed to be losing his fight with Heoltos and the other humans were moving in to assist.

Glaring at their cowardice, Xicuz drew in a deep breath before rushing toward the fray, leaping into the air with his spear raised just before he reached them. Coming down on top of the nearest human, Xicuz slashed at him with his weapon faster than he could react and turned from him even as his body dropped to the ground. The next opponent did not go down as easily, as he parried his spear with his sword for a few moments before Xicuz spun his weapon above his head before dropping to sweep his legs out from under him.

A spear to the chest took him out quickly enough, and Xicuz moved on to his next opponent. A quick glance at Heoltos informed him he would not be able to hold off the three humans, Jydral included, for much longer. As it was, Heoltos bled from a wound in his back and his movements were far slower than they should have been. Charging into the fray once more, Xicuz blocked one of the swords and pushed him back before turning on the second, leaving Jydral for Heoltos to deal with for the moment.

Back and forth Xicuz moved between the two, parrying one's attacks and then the others, keeping them both off their feet so they wouldn't be able to use their numbers against him. It would not last long, but as neither were giving him any real opening, there was little else he could do. The clashing of their weapons reverberated throughout the forest, the sound echoing around them, and he realized it was far quieter than it should have been midbattle.

Either there were far fewer men still fighting than expected, or some of the battle moved away from the area. Neither sounded like a good scenario. Hearing a grunt coming from behind him and knowing the king made the sound without having to look, Xicuz decided he was running out of time to deal with his two opponents. King Heoltos was one of, if not the best warrior Ebrein had, and in any normal situation, Xicuz would never have insulted him by assuming he needed help.

Especially when Heoltos was down to a one-on-one fight with Jydral, but as he saw the wound on his back still bled heavily, Xicuz decided he could deal with his injured pride later. Ducking under one of the swords coming at his head, Xicuz stabbed his spear into his opponent's foot, grabbed his sword with his free hand and thrust it into the other's chest as he pitched forward. Xicuz grabbed the small dagger from the man's boot and stabbed it into his thigh and chest as he rose back up once more and wrenched his spear free as his opponent collapsed.

Rushing to Heoltos' side, Xicuz blocked an attack that would have cut him down, his injuries slowing his reaction time too much for him to keep up with the mostly unharmed human king. Catching Jydral off guard, he pushed his spear back knocking him and his sword off balance. Using the brief opening he created for himself, Xicuz positioned himself between the two kings and raised his spear in defense.

Without looking over his shoulder to make sure they were there or would follow his directions, Xicuz called out, "Qom, Xaaxex, tend to our king." Xicuz heard others moving behind him and he knew without having to look that it was the two he trusted most in the world. He felt their presence behind him. Xicuz focused his full attention on Jydral as he regained his balance and came charging at him with more skill and precision than expected.

"Seems your pitiful king is too much of a coward to fight me to the death!" Jydral taunted, the smirk on his face mocking.

"Coming from you, that's absurd, Jydral. Your men out numbered him and still stabbed him in the back. Obviously, it is you who are the coward, but everyone already knew that. After all, you poisoned your own king," Xicuz spat at him a moment before jumping back to avoid his blade as it came down in an arch from above him.

Realizing goading him was working, Xicuz continued to tease and mock him even as he dodged one strike after another that all seemed to be aimed at his head. If he could egg him on a little more, get him to lose his temper, Xicuz knew he could ensure himself the upper hand and take him out once and for all. But even as he dodged another strike, sweeping his spear under his feet as he came around, Xicuz realized that was not going to be an option. So wrapped up in the battle, so focused on taking Jydral down for all the pain and suffering he caused, he forgot to pay attention to the time.

Even without looking, Xicuz knew the sun would soon rise. Xicuz felt himself weakening as his eyes grew heavy and his steps slowed as though his hooves were stuck in thick mud. Each time Xicuz parried a sword strike, each time he side stepped his lunge, he felt Jydral's blade growing closer and closer to drawing blood.

So close now Xicuz felt the tip of the blade cutting through the air an inch from his skin. It would not be long now before he lost all consciousness, and Xicuz would need to be far away from him before that happened. As much as he hated running from a fight, there was not much he could do that wouldn't result in the loss of more satyrs' lives, his own included. Even if Xicuz stayed there and allowed Jydral to kill him when he could no longer defend himself—not that he had any desire to do so— the others would attempt to protect him; even at the cost of their own lives.

No, Xicuz needed to get away to where hopefully no humans would stumble upon his body or assume he was already dead if they did. But try as he might, no matter how much Xicuz backed away from Jydral or tried to weave the fighting between the trees so he would assume he ran away and go after someone else, Jydral just continued to follow after him. As Xicuz grew even weaker, the glint in Jydral's eyes soon confirmed his worst fear; *Jydral knows.*

Somehow, someway, Jydral knew not only about the curse, but how it worked. Jydral intentionally prevented him from getting away so Xicuz would be at his complete mercy the moment the curse activated.

*

The instant Erabus regained consciousness, he knew something had gone terribly wrong. Not only was Xicuz not lying beside him, though his still foggy mind soon remembered the night before had been the full moon and Jydral was due to attack, it did not take him long to realize the warriors had not yet returned from the battle. Though there were still plenty of satyrs left in the village, including an elderly male who watched him with curious silver eyes the moment Erabus woke up, he doubted any of them saw a battle recently.

Each satyr Erabus spotted, most sitting around fires and talking quietly amongst themselves or staring off into the forest with worried expressions on their faces, were either too young or too old to have gone to war the night before. *They weren't back yet.* The battle hadn't ended yet, but the curse had activated. Xicuz was out in the forest somewhere, unconscious, and vulnerable. *No,* Erabus reminded himself, *Xicuz had Qom and Xaaxex with him.*

They would keep him safe. Even though he was quite certain about that, it did little to ease the worry in his mind and Erabus jumped to his feet, instantly regretting it as the sudden blood rushing from his head made him lightheaded and dizzy. Steadying himself on the hand offered, Erabus smiled his thanks before glancing around the village once more. Erabus needed to join the fight, needed to protect Xicuz, and most importantly, he needed to stop his brother from hurting anymore people, satyr and human alike.

The elder satyr, who seemed to be left in charge of watching over him while Erabus slept, held out his bow to him along with his quiver. "Thanks," Erabus said with a smile as he shouldered the quiver and gently ran his finger over the carvings Xicuz etched into his bow.

"They are fighting about two kilometers to the northwest, or at least that had been the plan. They sound closer now," the elder informed him.

The fighting grew too close to the village. They would be in trouble if the humans got past the satyrs and attacked those left behind. "If there are any weapons left, I suggest you arm anyone who is able. I doubt we have long."

Even as he said that, Erabus heard the battle, now within his own hearing range. Swearing under his breath, Erabus made his way to the forest's edge. This was the moment Erabus dreaded since he learned of his brother's plans. He would be forced to face off against those Erabus had known his entire life because they were incapable of seeing their king for what Jydral truly was.

Or because they lacked the courage to stand up against him if they, in fact, knew exactly what kind of man he was. Still not sure if he would be able to take a life, Erabus knew he was about to find out one way or another. "Tell the women and children to hide!" Erabus called over his shoulder, not bothering to wait to see if anyone would listen before pulling his first arrow from the quiver and notching it on the bow. *Inhale.* The sounds were getting closer. Erabus could now make out the clashing of swords and screams of pain in the distance.

Exhale. He saw movement in the trees, could catch the glint of the sunlight off their blades in the few places the sun could penetrate the canopy overhead. *Inhale.* They were in range now, but the dense trees kept his bow useless for now. Anyone who was watching could easily step behind one of the innumerable trees for cover. *Exhale.* Erabus spotted one of the satyrs losing the battle between two humans; one of which was about to bring his sword down on the now defenseless satyr.

Inhale. He aimed at his first target and drew the bow string taunt. *Exhale.* Erabus let the arrow fly and a moment later it struck the man in the midthigh; he roared in pain and dropped his sword, grabbing his leg with both hands. *Inhale.* He turned angry eyes toward him, realizing exactly who shot him and yelled something Erabus couldn't hear.

As the second attacker turned from the satyr and began charging toward him, it became rather obvious what his instructions were. Notching another arrow, Erabus locked eyes with the man charging toward him. He increased his speed as he got closer. Waiting until there were no more trees for him to hide behind, Erabus took his aim and pulled the string taunt once more.

Exhale. Erabus released and his arrow *whooshed* through the air, catching the man in the calf as he jumped out of the way at the last second. "Help protect the women and children," Erabus called out to the satyr who was already making his way over to him, a startled expression on his face. Turning his attention from him before he even reached him, Erabus notched another arrow and searched for the next human approaching the village.

"Any man that does not turn back is a coward! This isn't the battleground!" Erabus called out in warning. One or two of the men seemed to hesitate, especially once they realized who he was, but the majority changed their direction toward him. Erabus couldn't begin to imagine all the lies his brother had been telling them about him in the weeks since they disappeared. Did they believe Erabus was responsible for the death of their king?

Did they know of his relationship with Xicuz and hate him for that? Whatever the reason behind their individual hatred, there was only one outcome for all of them. They would battle and Erabus would win. There was no doubt about that in his mind. Not because Erabus was better than them or because good conquered evil, but for the simple fact he had to.

There was no telling what orders Jydral might have given them for when they reached the village. They were not there by accident, at least not all of them. Were they there to kill the women for "abandoning" them or to force them to return to Edith? Erabus wasn't sure which would be worse. Were they there to slaughter the children to prevent the next generation from rising up in retaliation?

Or, what seemed most likely in his mind as an icy chill ran down his spine, were they there to slaughter the entire race of satyrs and wipe them from existence as his brother always wanted to do? How loyal to Jydral were they and how far were they willing to go to make his despicable dream a reality? *Inhale.* Notch an arrow and take aim. *Exhale.* Release and let it fly. One after another the humans dropped with arrows protruding from their arms and legs; none were fatal, but usually sidelining them for the rest of the battle.

Grasping for another arrow, Erabus found his hand came away empty. Staring at the man only a few yards away from him, his arrow still protruding from his calf, Erabus rushed toward him and wrenched it free without warning. His blood-curdling scream was drowned out by the blood that seemed to be echoing in his ears. Notching the arrow, blood dripping from it to stain his fingers and the string, Erabus searched for his next target. Elovonos came straight at him; not far away from him, another man charged toward an elderly satyr who had his back turned as he fought off another attacker.

Erabus shot the coward through the back of his leg, causing him to tumble over himself as he could not stop his momentum. A split second later, Elovonos was upon him and Erabus barely had the time to spin around and raise his bow in defense before Elovonos swung his sword down at him. They both grunted from the impact. The wood cracked. His bow would not be able to stop his pressure for long before it gave away completely.

"You should have stayed dead, you disgusting abomination!" Elovonos spat in his face as he pushed the sword down with more strength and Erabus felt his bow giving way. With all the force he could muster, Erabus pushed back against Elovonos and knocked him off balance enough to get out of the way of his sword as he released his bow. Elovonos went tumbling forward once the resistance had gone slack.

Elovonos roared in anger, as he tossed the bow aside and regained his balance before spinning back around at Erabus. With no weapon left to defend himself with, Erabus could do little more than attempt to dance around his strikes, moving out of reach each time Elovonos lunged forward. It took everything Erabus had to keep himself from getting more than a few shallow cuts whenever he didn't get out of the way quickly enough.

But his luck would run out soon. If Erabus did not find himself a weapon, he would no longer be needing one. As if the elder satyr read his mind, Erabus heard his voice call out to him and turned long enough to catch the sword that was thrown. He had no time to call out his thanks before Elovonos attacked again. Blocking his attack at the last second caused the vibrations of the sword strike to reverberate through Erabus's arms. Clenching his teeth, Erabus refocused himself on offense and began meeting him strike for strike.

"You are as disgusting as those animals and you deserve to die with them," Elovonos taunted, spitting each word at Erabus. Erabus refused to fall for his goading. Erabus knew their fight was evenly matched enough that if either of them lost their temper, it would be all they needed to tip the scale in the other's favor. "It is a good thing your brother is king and not you. Could you imagine you ruling with that beast at your side?"

Though Elovonos obviously meant it as an insult, Erabus smiled at the thought of doing just that. "I can, and wouldn't that be grand? With or without him, I would make a far better king than that regicide committing bastard. Jydral had no more right to the throne than a piece of rubbish like you. Once this war is over and your pitiful uprising has been squashed like the bugs you are, I will make sure everyone knows who you and your useless leader truly were.

"I say 'were' because neither of you will be leaving this battlefield alive." Erabus taunted as he continued to parry strike after strike, eventually getting in a couple of good cuts himself. Seeing more men approaching from the forest, Erabus realized they were out of time. The men would be upon them soon and he would be left vastly outnumbered. Elovonos would need to go down, now, if Erabus stood any chance of dealing with the others.

Drawing a deep breath as their swords continued to clash, Erabus looked over his opponent trying to find a weak spot. He sought an opening in his defense; his body language telling Erabus what his next move would be. Though neither of these made themselves known, Erabus caught the sunlight glinting off metal at Elovonos' waist. It was small, a dagger no doubt, but as he had yet to reach for it, he either forgot it was even there or, more likely, thought it wouldn't be needed.

Either way, his oversight would work in Erabus's favor. Putting more strength behind each strike of his sword, Erabus pushed him farther back on his feet to keep him off balance, waiting until his sword had Elovonos' pinned up in the air to reach for the dagger. In one smooth motion, Erabus pulled it free from the belt at his waist and thrust it into Elovonos' neck. As he used his nondominant hand, the angle was off and the blade did not go in as deeply as Erabus would have liked, causing Elovonos to choke on his own blood instead of dropping instantly.

Pushing Elovonos' sword from his hand with no resistance, Erabus brought his own sword down and thrust it into Elovonos' chest without ever releasing his hold on the dagger. A moment later, his full weight came crashing down on Erabus, causing him to release Elovonos. Erabus rolled him over on to his back and wrenched his weapons free, wiping the blood off on Elovonos' pant leg before turning his attention to the other incoming humans.

"I am Prince Erabus, rightful ruler of Edith! A fight against the satyrs is a fight against me! Throw down your weapons or soak my blades in your blood!" Erabus called out. All the approaching men turned their attention to him as he raised both blades in the air.

Chapter Fourteen

Jydral was livid. He knew that animal cowered around there somewhere, but they were keeping him hidden. It should have been dead by now, its blood dripping from the end of his blade, but as the sun rose and he moved in for the kill, two other satyrs had gotten between them and held him off while a third carried the body away somewhere. At the least the animals' king faced off against him once more, but even that did not last long.

Once again, before Jydral could get the death blow in, two other satyrs replaced the king. "Who knew animals could be such cowards!" Jydral spat at his current opponents, making quick work of them before going in search of those who ran away.

But as Jydral searched, he realized finding them would not be an option. At least not for now. No doubt they were planning to keep it hidden until the sunset once more and it regained consciousness, but Jydral soon decided that would work for him too.

When it awoke again, it would be to find itself to be the last of its kind. *What a fitting way to leave this life.* Jydral smirked. *To wake up just long enough to know that you would be the last to die.* Smiling darkly to himself at the thought, he went in search of their king. Even as he began investigating every movement he saw through the trees, Jydral smiled once more to himself as a twisted thought sprang to mind.

A fitting end to the animal absurd enough to think himself a king. To watch, strapped to a tree, as Jydral slaughtered every one of the animals it was supposed to protect. Now, he just needed to find the animal.

*

Time passed far quicker than Erabus realized with the humans spacing out their waves just enough for Erabus and the elders to breathe for a moment before the next wave hit. There were never many men, usually less than two dozen with each assault and Erabus wondered if they weren't heading to the village on purpose, as previously thought, but instead simply followed the sound of the fighting.

With each new wave, Erabus called out the same warning, the same plea for them to lower their weapons, and more and more of the humans complied. Whether it was because he demanded it or because of their ever-increasing collection, for lack of a better word, of injured and disarmed humans, which were now being guarded over by two of the elders armed with bows.

Thankfully more than a few of the humans had gone in to battle with his weapon of choice and Erabus replaced the one Elovonos broke and refilled his quiver. Now, with his advantage of range and not having the trees to block his view, Erabus held the encroaching army off. As long as they didn't start appearing in larger numbers; at least. But as he took out the most recent wave, adding four to the list of men who surrendered at his voice alone and more than a dozen to the injured pile, Erabus realized his luck finally ran out; the sun was setting.

In the darkness, especially with the large number of injured but alive and mostly mobile humans in the village, vastly outnumbering the satyrs now, the chances were high that some of them would realize this fact and try to get revenge while Erabus was incapacitated. Moving as far away from their prisoners as he dared, Erabus caught the attention of the elder left in charge of him, realizing even after all these hours of fighting side by side, he still had no idea what his name was, and gestured for him to come closer.

Once he was within range, the humans nearby unlikely to overhear them, Erabus instructed, "You need to lead the others away from the village and find a place to guard the women and children. My curse will activate soon, and I will no longer be able to help protect this village. I am afraid the moment I lose unconsciousness, those already dealt with will be emboldened and rise up once more."

"And what of you, chosen of Xicuz? As skilled a warrior as you are, even you cannot defend yourself while unconscious," the elder pointed out.

Erabus smiled. It seemed he wasn't the only one who never learned the other's name.

"Erabus is fine," Erabus said with a smile before turning serious once more. "Worry not about me, elder. Save yourselves and those who need defending. Perhaps my sudden collapse will distract them long enough for you to put some distance between you." As Erabus watched, the elder signaled something to the others he didn't understand, and the satyrs filed out of the village.

"I am Veom, Prince Erabus, and even if Xicuz had not tasked me with keeping you alive, I still would not leave you here to die. You have saved my life, at great risk to your own, and for that I owe you my life. As I live, so will you," Veom said with a tilt of his head before gesturing for him to follow. Taking one last look at the injured humans, Erabus prayed they were out of the fight for good before following him.

As they ran to catch up to the others, his bow slapping against the back of his thigh with each step, Erabus soon realized they were meeting up with not only the elders who were fighting within in the village, but the women and children too. From behind, he heard the confused shouts coming from the humans as they tried to figure out what was going on, perhaps wondering if they should be running away as well, but as none of the voices seemed to be growing closer, Erabus felt confident that, at least for now, they were not being followed.

About to question where they were headed, Erabus was silenced by a form that came crashing through the forest behind them. Instinctively spinning round as he notched an arrow and raised his bow in the direction the noise came from, Erabus froze in shock when he realized who came barreling toward them. *Elovonos.*

*

Xicuz's muscles protested the sudden movement as he sat up straight the moment he awoke, his body remembering the danger he was in long before his mind could recall the events of the night before. "Your spear is at your side," Qom's voice called out to him. Xicuz glanced over to find him standing on guard near him even as his fingers wrapped around the shaft of his weapon.

"What have I missed and why are you not fighting with the others?" Xicuz demanded as he rose to his hooves and worked out the kinks before glancing around the area, barely able to make out the trees that surrounded them as darkness consumed them. Once the waning moon rose more in the night sky, they would be able to see anywhere the light penetrated the canopy, but for now they were in the dark.

"The king has commanded I look after you and Heoltos outranks you," Qom quipped. "Many of the king's guards have fallen, but he is well. Xaaxex is with him now. The battle has moved to the southeast."

Qom didn't need to tell him what that meant, and even without the dread he heard in his voice, Xicuz would have figured out exactly what happened. Jydral moved his army toward Ebrein. Did Jydral know they left no warrior, and planned on attacking them to show what a coward he truly was? Or was Jydral after Erabus? Did he know his brother had been left behind with them?

No, he couldn't. Xicuz closed his eyes and listened to the few sounds coming from the surrounding forest. Realizing he heard little more than Qom's and his own breathing, Xicuz opened his eyes once more and gestured for him to lead the way. With a quick nod, Qom started running through the dark forest, gracefully leaping over exposed tree roots, and fallen branches.

His step wasn't as poised or silent as Qom's, and Xicuz realized his mind was still rather foggy. He stopped trying to copy his movements consciously. Allowing his body to do the guesswork seemed to work much better, and he turned his attention instead to the surrounding forest. Occasionally, Xicuz heard a single clashing of swords, as though that one strike was louder than the others and managed to echo further, but he could never pinpoint its origin.

No two strikes seemed to come from the same fight as they were spaced out too far and coming from different directions. After a while, Xicuz wondered if he wasn't, in fact imagining the noises, but soon decided it didn't matter. He couldn't waste time chasing down real or imaginary sounds that could have been coming from anywhere. They needed to get to Ebrein before Jydral attacked and Xicuz had no way of knowing how much of a head start he had on them.

As they grew closer to the village, actual sounds of battle cropped up around him and Xicuz made his way toward each one; dispersing the problem as he searched for both the human king and his own. But each similar battle Xicuz stumbled upon seemed to end the same with no sign of either king. The closer they came to the village, Xicuz realized there was a larger number of humans to fight, as if they were all intentionally migrating that way during the battle.

As Xicuz took out another who decided to attack him, it dawned on him that was exactly what they were doing. No doubt at Jydral's instructions. Had that been their plan all along? To go after those who could not defend themselves. And if so, to what end? They must have known the warriors would eventually make their way there and destroy them after they figured out what they had done. And only a monster would attack unarmed children.

Though, it did not surprise him in the least that Jydral would order a cowardly attack like that, Xicuz had to admit he was more than a little startled that the majority of the humans would go along with it. Surely there must be more men like Erabus within the human army instead of just those like Jydral, but Xicuz knew he couldn't rely on hope alone to keep the younger satyrs safe.

"Ignore the stragglers! Head straight to Ebrein! They are after the children!" Xicuz called out in warning even as he quickened his pace and leapt over a man who turned to attack him. His sudden change in pace threw him off balance and Xicuz soon heard him face planting in the dirt but paid him no further attention as he weaved his way in between the trees at a desperate pace.

Pushing any attacker out of his way without wasting time to stop and fight them, Xicuz soon realized they were intentionally trying to prevent him from reaching the village. *Why?* Surely, they could not tell which satyr he was in the dark, even if Jydral gave them instructions about him, so why were they so focused on him? *Unless...* Xicuz soon realized as he pushed a man's head into a tree as he ran past and he tried to block his way, *they think I'm the king.*

He gave out instructions, and the others all followed them without hesitation. It appeared to be enough to convince the humans Xicuz was their leader and telling them to concentrate on the king made sense. Sighing, Xicuz decided this both worked in his favor and against him. As long as they were focused on him, they would not be searching for the actual king.

But it also meant Xicuz would be unable to get to the village in time to do any good. Praying the others would be enough, he leaped back away from an incoming sword, drawing his spear up in defense, before calling out to the others, "Follow my orders! Defend Ebrein!" Qom turned and gave him a confused expression, but Xicuz shook his head and turned his full attention to the men who were converging on him already.

Knowing he couldn't afford to waste any more time on each opponent than unavoidable, Xicuz gave himself three strikes per each one to take them down; knowing any more than that would give them too much time to overpower him. For the moment, his luck held out as the trees were too dense for more than one of them to attack at once, but it was only a matter of time before they figured out how idiotic that was.

Sure enough, by the time Xicuz took down the fourth or fifth attacker since he sent Qom and the others ahead of him, a few men who were charging after him split off and fanned out into the trees. They would come up from behind him in a moment or two, but there was little Xicuz could do to prevent their actions. Taking the moment of reprieve between the dropping of one opponent and the attacking of another to glance up, Xicuz realized the trees would not be a viable escape plan for the moment as the first branches were well out of his reach.

They were close enough to the village now that the lower branches of all the trees in the area had been stripped away to prevent spies from being able to sneak up into the trees to watch their village. *It is rather ironic,* Xicuz realized, *that I was the one to suggest to King Zhul to strip them.* A second too late turning toward his next opponent and Xicuz couldn't block his entire attack, suffering a rather large gash to his upper arm.

He grunted at the pain but pushed it from his mind even as he drove his sword arm back with the shaft of his spear and swung it back in a large arch, catching him just below the chin. Before he even hit the ground, Xicuz spun around to block the attack from behind, kicking him square in the chest with his hoof and sending him flying back into an unyielding tree. The resounding *crack* his body made on contact echoed around them but was drowned out as Xicuz spun around once more in time to block the next attack.

Realizing his luck had already run out, knowing he would not be able to keep the battle up long with opponents bombarding him from both sides, especially once they began attacking simultaneously, Xicuz decided he needed to come up with a plan of escape, and quick. Back and forth Xicuz moved, taking out one human after another, suffering a new cut to his arm or gash to his leg for practically every fight.

Each new injury slowed him down even further, each one deeper than the one before as a result. It took him far longer than Xicuz would have liked to realize that his only choice was to outrun the humans to the village. As long as he got a big enough opening, being faster than them wouldn't be a problem, but their attacks were coming so close together now that they were pretty much attacking in groups.

Finding an opening between them would be nearly impossible, but at least the others had enough of a head start to push the humans out of Ebrein. Which means Xicuz would have plenty of back up once he could get to them. Even if he didn't, fighting them would be much easier when there was enough room to use his spear at its full potential. Quickly understanding an opening would not be an option as he feared, Xicuz decided it was time to make his own.

Tightening his grip on the shaft of his spear, Xicuz rushed forward even as his next attacker started his way, taking him out before he realized what happened. Instead of turning back to the one behind him, Xicuz spun out of his way, barely registering his strike came down on one of his own men as they screamed out in pain, and buried his spear into another who was too caught off guard by the sudden change in direction to defend himself successfully.

Finding a small space between him and the next man in his way, Xicuz ran as fast as he could, launching his spear and catching him in the chest. The force of the blow sent him flying backward and Xicuz had to run to retrieve his weapon. Though it put him at a disadvantage for a moment if anyone caught up with him, it was worth the risk as Xicuz used the spear embedded in his chest and his own momentum to launch himself forward, pulling his weapon free as he sailed over the body.

It didn't propel him far, only a few yards away from his most recent foe, but it was enough to cause the rest of his attackers to have to chase after him. Within moments Xicuz heard their breathing right behind him, running faster than expected, but he did not need to have the advantage for long. Just long enough to cross the threshold into the village and as the trees began thinning before him, Xicuz didn't have far to go.

The tip of a blade managed to slash the back of his arm, but thankfully he was too far away from its owner for him to suffer more than a flesh wound. It did manage to knock him off balance enough that Xicuz tumbled forward, rolling out of the trees before hitting the bottom of the hill with a dull *thud*. Rolling over as he heard one of his attackers catching up, Xicuz managed to barely avoid the sword strike that was meant for him and stabbed him with his spear before he could try again.

Xicuz grunted as the man's weight collapsed on top of him and he tried in vain to remove his spear from his opponent's chest to block the next attack that came but was pinned under the man's dead weight. The moment before his blade would have struck him down, another sword blocked the attack and Xicuz glanced up to find Qom staring down at him with a smile. A split second later, his second sword swept over Xicuz's head and caught the human in the chest.

Qom pulled his sword free as he kicked him back before plunging one blade into the dirt near his head, so he could push the human off Xicuz. No longer trapped, Xicuz was back on his feet in a moment and rolling his shoulder to relieve the pain the rather large body caused when he dropped. "Elders were already gone," Qom informed him even as he turned back to the incoming army and yanked his blade out of the dirt.

"No sign of your chosen or either of the kings." Each word was spoken between the thundering sound of one of his blades meeting an opponent's, but the effort needed to speak didn't even seem to faze him. As he turned his attention to his own opponent, Xicuz decided that it was both good news and bad. It went without saying that if either King Heoltos or Erabus had been found and captured by Jydral's men their bodies would be out on display, meant to frighten the satyrs and inspire the humans.

But it also meant Jydral was out in the forest with them, no doubt searching for one of them at that moment. And one of his targets was currently unconscious and unable to defend himself. Turning his full attention to the fight before him, Xicuz made quick work of every opponent who came rushing at him, his desire to end the battle as soon as possible leaving them little chance against him.

As hour after hour passed without much respite, Xicuz couldn't help but wonder how many humans were heading their way through the forest and if the assault on the village would ever end. Beside him, Qom was beginning to slow. It finally dawned on Xicuz that while he was able to "rest" during the day, the others had been going at it for over twenty-four-hours now.

Though, judging by how much stamina the humans seemed to have left, they had not been. Confused, Xicuz glanced at those around him. He realized how rested and full of energy they all seemed to be. *That's impossible. How could they still be...?* Dispatching of another human, Xicuz yanked the tip of his spear free and was about to turn away to find his next target, when something caught his eye.

Xicuz grabbed on to the loose shirt that blossomed with blood, tore it free and stared down at the wound his weapon left in his chest. Just beside it was another wound of the same shape and size, the flesh red and raw but no longer bleeding. Turning back to the shirt in his hand, he searched for the piece that lined up with the wounds, and though hard to spot at first as the color of the shirt was almost the same color as his blood, Xicuz soon spotted a second, already-dried pool of blood.

It overlapped with the stain he just created, but upon closer inspection you could tell the blood had already crusted on the fabric. *He was already dead. Possibly by my own spear even*, Xicuz realized in shock before releasing him and letting him collapse to the ground. "Qom," Xicuz warned, turning to him as he dispatched another opponent and glanced at him in question. "Before you attack the next, look at his clothing. Do you see the blood?" Xicuz questioned even as he turned his attention to his own opponent and scanned his chest for wounds.

Finding a dried spot of blood among the rich, red fabric, Xicuz defended his attacks for a moment and then sliced the top of his spear down the front of his shirt, slicing through the strings holding it closed. As his next swing caused the fabric to fly open completely, Xicuz got a good look at his chest where the blood from the material corresponded and found a large, puncture wound. It was longer and deeper than the one caused by his spear, and if Xicuz had to guess, he would say it was most likely caused by a sword.

"That was a fatal wound," Xicuz accused before punching him in the nose and knocking his sword from his hand when he was off balance. Xicuz grabbed hold of his shirt and pulled him close, not bothering to threaten him with the tip of his spear as he usually would have done since killing them seemed to be pointless. "How is it you continue to live with a mortal wound?" Xicuz demanded; his face so close to the human's he felt his breath on his face.

Instead of answering, the man continued to attack him as if he hadn't heard his question at all. "They are not dying, Qom, or at least not staying dead. This is why this battle seems to never end." Even as his words sounded strange and impossible to his own ears, Xicuz caught a glimpse of the man Qom was about to fight next. "I killed that one myself. Slit his throat." Sure enough, as Qom dispatched his attacker, the crusted wound on his neck could easily be seen.

"How is the human king doing this? I was not aware any of the humans possessed enchanted blood," Qom pointed out as he stared down at the twice, at least, dead human at his feet.

"They don't. Jydral must have made another deal to ensure they would win this battle. I fear what he might have sacrificed this time." Sighing to himself in disbelief, Xicuz dealt with his current opponent and then paused for a moment to glance down at the bodies that littered the ground beneath his feet. None of them had risen, yet, but there was no way for them to know how long it would take them to rejoin the fight.

"It is pointless to continue this sham of a battle. We must find Jydral. He must be the key to ending this. There is no one here to guard, let these abominations have the village. Follow me into the forest! Search for the human king and execute him on sight!" Xicuz called out before turning and making his way into the near pitch-black forest without waiting to see if they would obey. He already knew they would.

As Xicuz blindly made his way through the dense trees, he couldn't help but wonder how Jydral managed to see anything out there himself. *Maybe he wasn't*, Xicuz wondered as the minutes passed without him coming across anyone. *Perhaps Jydral is hiding somewhere waiting for dawn.* The more Xicuz thought about it, the more he realized how much sense this made.

It would explain why he was unable to find him and why the humans, if you could even call the walking corpses that anymore, were converging on Ebrein. It was the only place in the battle where there was enough moonlight to see everything. Though the moon was still nearly full, barely any of its light penetrated the canopy overhead. *That's not right*, Xicuz realized after a moment, coming to a stop, causing Qom to run into him before he could stop.

"Xicuz?" Qom questioned, but Xicuz ignored him for a moment as he glanced up through the trees to the dark sky above. The trees in the area were not that dense. More of the moonlight should be getting through and illuminating the forest around him. The fact it wasn't meant that the moon already sank further than Xicuz thought and once again his time was nearly up.

"Qom, the sun will be rising soon. This time you must leave me behind and deal with Jydral. Our people will not survive if Jydral is allowed to continue raising his dead. I entrust it to you to hunt him and strike him down. Hopefully with his death, the enchantment that affects his people will end, but if not, find Erabus and have him speak with the devil he made his deal with to find out how to fix this."

Though Xicuz could tell by the pained look on Qom's face, he did not want to abandon him when he was vulnerable, but he nodded reluctantly after a moment and assured him that he would do just that. Since Xicuz didn't feel the curse activating yet, he had a bit more time and continued making his way through the forest. He felt himself weakening before they found more than a few stragglers and dispatched them.

"My time is up, Qom. Continue on and do as I have instructed. Hopefully by the time the sun sets once more this will be over and done with. Be safe, my friend," Xicuz bid him his tone pleading. They clasped arms and Qom nodded before releasing him and calling out for the others to follow him as he continued their search again. Xicuz watched them go before glancing around at the trees in his immediate area.

Thankfully, they were far enough away from the village that the lower branches hadn't been trimmed off, but it still took him a few minutes to find one to suit his needs. Discovering a rather large branch that forked off a little ways out before coming most of the way back to itself a few feet later, Xicuz decided it was the best he would be able to find in the short time left and glanced around the area once more to make sure there were no humans waiting to attack him the moment his back was turned.

The fact that it was too dark for him to find anyone reassured him that he was as invisible to anyone who might be around. Xicuz put the shaft of his spear in his mouth and climbed the tree up to the sturdy branch he spotted, realizing how strange a feat it was. Glancing up toward what little of the sky he could see through the leaves above, Xicuz noticed the sky began to lighten.

The predawn grey light allowed him to see the branches above, but it had not been able to penetrate to the ground below yet. Turning his attention away from the encroaching dawn, knowing his time would soon run out and the last thing Xicuz needed was to lose consciousness while still climbing, Xicuz scrambled the rest of the way up to his chosen bough as quickly as he could. By the time he positioned himself in the fork, Xicuz already felt himself starting to lose consciousness.

Retrieving the staff from his impromptu hold, Xicuz weaved the staff between the branches and his legs to give him a bit more stability; though he already knew he would not be rolling over. Erabus never did. Resting his head back onto his temporary bed, Xicuz's eyes grew heavy as he barely managed to whisper, "Be safe, my love," before the sun rose and Xicuz lost consciousness once more.

*

It took Jydral nearly all night, but he finally found Erabus. The animals were keeping him well hidden within the darkened forest where his eyes stood no chance of seeing two feet in front of him, let alone spotting something well shrouded in shadows. They hadn't realized it, but they gave away their location in their attempts to protect their unconscious charge.

Throughout most of the forest Jydral trampled through since he gave up the search for the two animals at the top of his kill list, he barely passed one or two of the satyrs, assuming they were hiding in the treetops like the cowards they showed themselves to be. They were, no doubt, lying in wait, to pick them off one by one as they spread out to search for them, but Jydral wasn't worried about his chances with them.

Pretty soon they would be figuring out no matter what they did, no matter how cowardly they acted, they stood no chance of being the last one standing at the end of this battle. You could not defeat an army who could not die, at least not permanently. With each wave of attacks, they would lose more and more of their numbers, but Jydral knew his own were still holding steady at the three hundred he came to war with.

Even if some of them were out of commission for a while, it wouldn't be long before they joined the rest once again and took out more of the animals on their next pass. Each death brought him one step closer to his ultimate goal, and it was getting so close now Jydral could practically taste it. They all but confirmed his suspicions by hiding in the trees. If there were hundreds of them still, as there were when the battle started the night of the full moon, Jydral would still be practically falling over them as he searched the forest.

Instead it seemed empty other than himself and his own men. Come dawn, when he could once again see the state of things around him, Jydral planned to call his men to the animals' village, rounding up whatever was left of them and dealing with them once and for all. Before they killed all of them, though, Jydral would be certain to find out exactly how they knew the attack was coming.

Though, it was most likely they had a spy watching Edith, he needed to make sure there wasn't another traitor hidden in their midst as Erabus had been. *He too will be dealt with soon enough,* Jydral realized with a gleefully evil smile when old, decrepit satyrs jumped out of where they were concealed and defended their hiding spot. Even though Jydral had trouble seeing them in the darkness, there was enough light that he saw it glint off their metal blades, giving him just enough time to raise his own sword in defense.

If they stayed eclipsed by the underbrush and shadows, Jydral would have never known they were there and would have continued past them none the wiser. The fact they were willing to come out and risk their own safety was enough to inform him that something still hid worth protecting—something worth dying for. If they were younger, real warriors like the ones they had been fighting since the battle began, he might have believed they protected their king.

But it wasn't young, vigorous satyrs that sprung out of the shadows to attack him, but old, weak, slow elders. Surely no king would ever hide behind those so far past their prime, even an animal king. It could have been their women, those that were vile enough to leave their own kind behind to be with those animals, and their young they were protecting, as Jydral did by leaving them back at Edith instead of bringing them into the battle.

If he believed that to be the case... Well, Jydral wouldn't have let them go. No point in trying to eradicate an entire race if you leave their young alive to repopulate their village down the road. Perhaps Jydral would have made sure to give those guarding them a quicker, less painful death than what he had in store for them. It truly did not matter how he would have reacted as it was obviously not who they were concealing.

Their hiding place was far too small to hold much more than themselves and perhaps one or two others. No, there was only one that would have need to be protected and wouldn't warrant stronger, younger guards to protect them. *Erabus.* Jydral found his brother's obscured hiding spot all because his guards feared for his safety. A fitting end for Erabus, poetic even, to be unintentionally betrayed by those he betrayed his own people for.

Slashing his sword through the elderly guards as if they weren't even there, it did not take Jydral long to make his way through what little opposition he faced and soon towered over the underbrush that hid his brother from his view. Without hesitation, Jydral stabbed his sword into the dense bushes but felt no resistance. He struck again and again, but each time his blade came back with no fresh blood coating it.

Starting to doubt his brother was even where he thought, Jydral reached into the bushes and searched around blindly until he felt the silky strands of Erabus's fiery hair in his fingers, yanking him out of the thicket in what certainly would have been a painful manner if he was conscious to feel it.

Though there wasn't much light to see by, just a bit from the pre-dawn greying sky, Erabus's skin glowed a pale, eerie blue, looking even more unnatural than the animals that protected him. Raising his sword above his head, his fingers twitching as though the blood running through them itched to strike, Jydral couldn't help but think what a pity it was to be forced to do this.

Long ago, before he betrayed his people to be with one of the animals, Erabus was a good man. He might not have been the type that Jydral would have wanted at his side, but Erabus had always done what he thought best for their people. Perhaps if things went differently, and their father hadn't turned them against each other, Erabus's fate wouldn't have been sealed.

If Jydral didn't know that Erabus would betray him again, he might even have allowed him to live, banished from Edith forever, but breathing. But there was only one outcome that would come to pass if he let him go and Jydral worked far too hard, sacrificed way too much, to risk it all now. Especially not for some weak, inconsequential feeling of a familiar bond.

No, Erabus would die as Jydral planned from the beginning because nothing was too great a sacrifice if it meant the crown would rest upon his head. It was he, and he alone, who could save Edith from the weak and feeble shell of a village it became since they crowned Tribion king. Stories of the wise and conquering kings who came before had been told to him since he was a child.

Stories of how kings should have been: strong, ruthless, powerful, and, above all else, loyal only to their own clan. Not weak and spineless, bending to the will of animals like King Tribion. For the first time since Jydral found out the truth, a truth he refused to believe for a long time, he could honestly say he was grateful, honored even, that Tribion was not, and had never been, his father.

It meant Jydral had none of his weak blood or traitorous beliefs, beliefs Erabus seemed to share. It meant he could do what needed to be done for his people; that he could put their needs first, above all else, as a true king should. The man Jydral always called his father, never seemed to understand that simple fact. All that mattered to him was his ill-conceived treaty between his people and the animals.

A treaty that would be broken the moment said animals showed their true cowardly and greedy ways, wanting more than the already unbalanced amount they had received. King Tribion, who could never see them for the animals they truly were, chose instead to see them as equal to humans. Equal to even himself, a king. That foolish belief would have brought about his ending even if Jydral hadn't been there to hurry his demise along when Tribion finally told him the truth and tried to keep him from his birthright.

It didn't matter if his mother had an affair and Jydral sprouted from the seed of another man; King Tribion claimed him and raised him as his heir. To steal that away from him after he already proved himself to be a capable ruler would have darkened the people's view of him beyond repair. They would have wondered, naturally so, why Jydral was no longer heir and if Tribion chose not to admit the infidelity of his wife, which he very much doubted the king would ever do as it did not look favorably on him, the people would have no choice but to see him as lacking.

No matter what Jydral did after that moment, no matter how many times he proved himself worthy of their respect and loyalty it would not make a difference. He would be seen as less than a man for the remainder of his life.

He was not about to let his mother's mistakes upheave his entire life twenty-eight years after the fact. As a sudden heat spread across the back of his neck, Jydral glanced behind him to discover his thoughts had dragged on for longer than he intended. The sun was rising. Knowing what it meant, that the man before him would also be rising soon, Jydral turned back and began swinging his sword down upon Erabus; he would not let him live to awaken again.

*

Even before his mind had the chance to clear and Erabus realized he lay on the hard ground, an occasional twig or rock poking him in the back, a strong sense of foreboding fell over him. Something was wrong. Terribly wrong. So wrong in fact, his barely conscious mind knew something needed to be done now or it would be too late. Erabus's eyes shot open, and he reached up and stopped the sword that came down on his chest, mere moments before it would have struck him down.

The sudden, painful pressure on his arms caused him to cry out in pain, nearly giving his attacker the advantage they needed to get the upper hand once more. Feeling his arms being pushed down toward his chest, Erabus ignored the pain shooting up his arms and pushed back with all he had. Though he could not launch much of a defense from his current position, it was enough to throw his attacker off balance long enough for him to scramble to his feet.

The moment he steadied himself, Erabus reached across his shoulder for his bow only to find himself unarmed. Though his borrowed bow was probably in the area somewhere, Erabus knew better than to waste precious time to look for it. He spotted a discarded sword and dove for it just in time to miss the strike aimed at his head.

Turning back to face his attacker, Erabus wasn't the least bit surprised to see Jydral standing there with his sword raised in anticipation for another attack. Jydral sneered at him. Erabus raised his borrowed sword in defense. It felt strange in his hand, as Erabus had long grown accustomed to holding a bow, but even if he held one at that moment, Jydral would never allow him the space that would be needed to make use of such a weapon.

"I know what you have done to our people, Jydral," Erabus said. "I know what you have turned the dead in to. The only question I have is what did you sacrifice to make this deal? Which of my people's lives did you give in exchange for this unnatural army of yours?" Instead of answering, Jydral roared out as he slammed his sword down on Erabus's, the impact causing a sudden jolt of pain to course through the length of his arms.

Gritting his teeth against it, letting little more than a grunt escape his lips, Erabus pushed his own sword back against him and managed to put a few inches between them, but it did not last long. Barely enough time passed for him to raise his sword in defense once more before Jydral closed the distance between them with his next attack. Erabus needed to turn the table on him, and soon, if he stood any chance of being able to hold out against him.

Hold out against what, Erabus wasn't sure, but he was already at a disadvantage when fighting against his brother. Erabus was stuck using a borrowed weapon that he not only had less practice with, but seemed to weigh a good deal more than the swords they used back at Edith. Jydral, on the other hand, fought with the same sword Erabus saw him training with for his entire life.

Even the countless hours Jydral had been awake fighting, the numerous battles he fought against the satyrs, the fact that they were surrounded by endless trees, none of it seemed to be slowing his brother down any. If anything, everything he went through seemed to spur him on even more, giving him an unnatural amount of energy. But maybe that was it. Had Jydral asked for more than an unkillable army when he made his second deal with the devil?

Did whatever affected them, affect him too? Had Jydral already been killed by countless others only to return to the battle as if death were not permanent? Judging by his lack of response and the way he stared at him with hatred in his eyes, Erabus might have believed it to be true. That was how Elovonos behaved when he attacked again after Erabus killed him. Only, Jydral wasn't the kind of person who would allow such a fate to befall himself.

When the battle was over, no matter who came out victorious, the men who died on the battlefield would not be going home. Whatever enchantment kept them coming back to life would not continue to do so once the fighting concluded. Jydral would not want the animated dead back in his village, even if they all died for his cause in the first place, and their behavior after rising did not indicate any of who they used to be was still there.

They were mindless, futureless, expendable warriors who Jydral would not lose a moment of sleep over and his brother would never allow himself to become the same. Knowing this did little to explain his continued silence, but Erabus soon decided it didn't matter. Erabus knew exactly what Jydral would do if he did speak to him—distract him with taunts about Xicuz.

It was only a matter of time before Jydral brought him up, undoubtedly waiting until Erabus finally had the upper hand to throw him off balance. Pushing the obvious tactic out of his mind for the moment, Erabus blocked another few strikes from his brother, hissing in pain when the tip of his blade managed to slice a shallow cut across his knuckles. Sparing the new injury no more than a passing glance, long enough to make sure it wasn't bleeding badly enough to turn his sword's hilt into a slippery mess, Erabus was about to return his brother's attacks when he noticed a subtle movement out of the corner of his eye.

For a moment, Erabus was afraid one of Jydral's men came to join the fight, putting him at even more of a disadvantage, but soon realized one of the elders on the ground had caught his attention. As much as Erabus had wanted to check on them when he first regained consciousness, and even more so now that he knew at least one of them were still breathing, he could not risk drawing Jydral's attention to them.

Jydral would undoubtedly try to use them against him. Either as a living shield or by threatening to kill them if Erabus didn't surrender. Neither one was an option he would chance. Instead, Erabus backed away from Jydral as they continued to fight, knowing Jydral would think him a coward trying to run away. *Let him think that*, Erabus thought as he continued to move away from the injured elders without taking his eyes off Jydral.

As long as Jydral thought Erabus was running away from a losing fight, he wouldn't pay the assumed dead satyrs any attention. Apparently his "retreat" was all the motivation Jydral needed to begin taunting him, as Erabus knew he eventually would. "Fear not, dear brother," Jydral spat out the term of "endearment" as a strange, cruel smile spread across his lips. "You will be joining that animal of yours soon enough.

"No need to run from the inevitable. The quicker you are reunited in death, the better it will be for all of us." His laughter was dark and foreboding as he sped up his pace, backing Erabus into a tree in his attempt to get away. The meaning behind his words was evident, and even though he knew better than to believe a single thing Jydral said, Erabus sucked in a breath.

Xicuz was dead, or at least Jydral wanted him to believe it so. Erabus knew it wasn't true, he would have felt something or, perhaps, would have even awoken before dawn as the curse would undoubtedly be broken with Xicuz's death. Still, his heart clenched painfully at the thought of him being gone. Somewhere at the back of his mind, Erabus could hear his earlier self-pointing out that he already knew Jydral would try something like this.

The reminder was enough to push back the fear, and Erabus launched himself off the tree to throw Jydral off. He barely managed to give himself enough time to block the next attack, and Erabus retreated once more, hoping to give himself some more room to maneuver in. With each step back he took, Jydral swung his sword down over his head, and Erabus soon blocked less and less of the strength behind the strikes.

Each impact sent jarring vibrations down his arm and Erabus had to fight against the rising desire to flinch away. Ducking behind a nearby tree as his brother raised his sword once more, he grabbed hold of one of the lower branches and pulled it back with him. It did not take Jydral more than a moment or two to catch up to him and Erabus released his hold once he was too close to dive out of the way in time.

The branch whipped back in to Jydral's chest and it propelled him back, allowing Erabus to put a little distance between them. Not much, a few yards at most, but those few seconds were all he needed to glance back at the elders and make sure they were far enough away from the battle.

Catching Veom's silver eyes staring at him in concern as he slowly rose to his hooves, Erabus shook his head. He saw the determination in his eyes to rejoin the fight, and even though Erabus could use the help, it could only end one way; Jydral would use him against him. Veom seemed about to refuse to stay out of it, but he must have seen the pleading look in Erabus's eyes for he nodded after a moment and lay back down as Jydral turned back.

Apparently catching where Erabus's attention was, Jydral glanced back at the area the elders were before turning back to Erabus with a dark laugh. "No one is coming to help you, Erabus. They are all dead, just as... What was his name again?" Jydral questioned, apparently not noticing at least one of the elders still lived even if gravely injured, before shaking his head and continuing without letting Erabus answer him.

"Don't suppose it matters much. He's already dead. And soon there will be no one left to mark his grave. Or yours," Jydral taunted before rushing forward once more with his sword raised. As Erabus attempted to block the attack, Jydral changed tactics at the last moment and kicked him square in the chest instead. Unable to react in time, Erabus felt himself being propelled backward and knew it was only a matter of time before he crashed into an unyielding tree, hard.

Tensing in anticipation of the pain, Erabus made a last-ditch effort to slow himself down before impact and grabbed a hold of a branch with his non-sword hand as he flew underneath it. He cried out in pain as the rough bark scraped off more than a few layers of skin, but Erabus refused to release his grip. His hand would be all but useless now, as he could already feel the blood seeping on to the branch, but it was a fair price to pay in light of the alternative.

Though Erabus couldn't stop the impact entirely, the resulting blow merely knocked the wind out of him for a moment and he was able to right himself before Jydral could catch up to him. Erabus flung the blood from his hand with a flick of his wrist and clenched his fist to apply what little pressure he could and swung his sword at Jydral before he had time to put him on the defensive once more.

His surprise was short lived and a moment later, Jydral attacked Erabus. Things were not going his way. Erabus would not be able to hold out against Jydral indefinitely and was already beginning to grow weaker. *That's not right,* Erabus thought perplexed by the way he felt. *The sun has only just risen.* That he knew for certain.

There was no way Erabus had been fighting against Jydral all day and yet he felt as he did everyday just before sunset, weak and tired. As though he might pass out standing up at any moment, though Erabus would not remain on his feet long if he did. It wasn't quite as strong a feeling as usual, but the realization only caused Erabus to be even more confused. Erabus saw a dark shadow fall over Jydral's face and glanced up as his brother did, both noticing the darkening sun at the same time.

"An eclipse." His voice came out as a breathy whisper, so quiet, in fact, Erabus wasn't sure he spoke out loud until his brother turned back to him with the same dark, foreboding smile he showed earlier.

"It would seem, my pitiful brother, that your time, and luck, has all but run out. There is no way for it to get here in time to save you once the animal awakens. Such a pity, for you," Jydral mocked as he stopped his assault and stood back to watch him as the full weight of what would happen flashed through his mind. With the sun gone, soon to be covered by the moon, Erabus would lose consciousness and there would be nothing standing in Jydral's way.

Jydral wouldn't even bother trying to fight him anymore, content to wait until Erabus could no longer defend himself to strike him dead. If Xicuz did awake, it would take him much longer to find them than Erabus had left. There were always the elders nearby, though they were far enough away now he could no longer see them, but Erabus prayed they already left the area.

The last thing Erabus needed, or wanted, was for someone else to lose their life for him. *But at least*, Erabus realized with a smile of his own, as he turned unconcerned eyes to his brother, *I know Xicuz is safe*. Apparently Jydral did not realize what he had done, but by trying to taunt him with the fact that Xicuz would be unable to get there in time to save him, he confirmed Xicuz still lived.

Erabus already knew this deep down, but having it confirmed was a huge weight lifted off his heart and he could breathe freely for the first time in a long time. At least, if he were to die, if this were to be his last few moments of life, Erabus would go out knowing that his love remained safe. And he would go out with a bang. It was too bad if Jydral wanted to wait for the moon to overtake the sun completely so Erabus would be defenseless.

Erabus never said he would wait. Smirking to himself as his brother continued to taunt him about the hopelessness of his future, Erabus drew a deep breath and took off toward Jydral before he could notice the change in his expression. Erabus leaped into the air and drew his sword down on to Jydral's, knowing that even though his brother would manage to get his up in time to block the strike, the force at which his came down on him would jar his arms painfully.

Giving neither of them the chance to adjust to the vibrations, Erabus swung again and again; each attempt being met by his brother's sword, but each managing to push him back a little more. *I will take you down with me,* he swore as Erabus kept up his assault, refusing to allow Jydral even a moment to take a breath. *Even if it's the last thing I do.* If so, Erabus had to admit to himself it was a worthy cause to go out on.

The grunting seemed to echo through the surrounding forest, though Erabus wasn't sure who it came from. Certainly at least some came from both. Again, and again Erabus beat his sword against his brother's, not bothering to hold back on his strength or his energy as he did not have much longer now. Erabus grew weaker with every passing moment.

Each rumble of thunder that came from the impacting of their swords signaled another moment that passed; another moment Erabus no longer had left. Darkness seemed to be settling around him now and he knew, without having to look up, the corner of the sun now only peeked from behind the moon. How long had it been since Erabus was awake in the darkness? *The first morning after the curse activated.*

He awoke to find himself in the pitch black of the temporary home Xicuz built, but it wasn't real darkness. This was the first time since the last night Erabus shared with Xicuz he saw the moon. Not that Erabus would get the chance to do so today as it would only be a black dot covering the sun and he would lose consciousness before he had the opportunity to see even that.

Jydral continued to taunt him, at one point even counting the passing seconds as though Erabus didn't already know his time grew short, but Erabus refused to allow it to distract him. His brother parried one strike and then another, each met by a mocking quip, but Erabus only responded with another strike. *We're too even*, Erabus realized with rising dread. There was no way he would be able to overpower him with the way things were going; especially not in the small amount of time left to work with.

At least not as long as Erabus fought honorably. Even though the thought of using less than honorable methods against his brother had his stomach turning, the only thing that would make him feel worse was not doing everything he could do to stop him. But as Erabus subtly glanced around without missing a beat with Jydral, he realized there was little he could do anyway.

There were no other weapons in the area, even if his injured hand could even manage to hold one. The dirt beneath his feet was far too packed down for him to be able to grab a handful to throw in his eyes if Erabus managed to get to the ground in the first place. There were no branches in the immediate area he could pull back to release on his brother and Jydral would see them coming even if there was.

Apparently, fate decided to prevent him from dishonoring himself before death. If it didn't mean Jydral would still be allowed to harm others after he was gone, Erabus might have seen the beauty in that. Erabus would be able to die as he lived, but when staring down your worst fears in the form of your own brother, beauty wasn't exactly a word one would use to describe things.

One moment Erabus glared at his brother's taunting face and the next they were covered in complete darkness. It did not last long, just long enough for the moon to settle over the sun completely before a bright ring of fire encircled the void in the sky. As if he blinked and all had gone back to normal, except for his brother. In that brief moment Jydral took advantage of Erabus's momentary distraction, and before he could even realize his brother had moved, he felt a sharp pain in his side.

Instinctively knowing it was his brother's blade, Erabus twisted to the side, pulling himself away from the attack. As Jydral wrenched the sharp blade from him, he screamed out in pain, but paid it no further attention as even a quick glance at it to see how bad it was would only result in his brother getting another opening. Instead, Erabus assured himself that it wouldn't kill him, yet, and raised his sword in defense once more.

Throwing himself into the fight once more, Erabus couldn't help but wonder why he hadn't lost consciousness yet but was given no time to dwell on it. It would happen soon, either due to the curse activating or to loss of blood, but as the minutes passed without either, Erabus soon realized something that caused his heart to sink. Xicuz wasn't coming. The eclipse weakened him, but there was no real reason for him to think Xicuz would have been awakened as well.

Just because the moon was out, it did not technically mean it was nighttime. Though Erabus had not seen it since they were cursed, he could remember more than one morning from his life before that the moon was visible in the sky even though it was daytime. So not only would Xicuz not be there in time to save him, but he would not be waking for hours. Perhaps it was better this way though.

Xicuz could finish the battle without ever knowing Erabus had died until it was too late to affect his chances of winning. If Xicuz had to find his dead body at all, Erabus wanted it to be long after Jydral was dealt with. Though Jydral would undoubtedly taunt Xicuz with his death the moment they fought, hopefully he would do a better job of not believing him than Erabus had done.

Dismissing Xicuz from his thoughts for now, Erabus fought back against Jydral with everything he had, ignoring the shooting pain in his side that seemed to flare up with each and every movement, until he caught a blade to his hand and Jydral kicked the sword out of his hand before he could even react. Before his mind could register where the sword went, Jydral kicked him square in the chest, sending him flying once more.

This time, both of his hands were far too injured for him to slow his descent. As Erabus flew for those few moments, the only thought that had time to cross his mind was the fact he would not land anywhere near where the sword had. As he impacted the ground, Erabus let out a grunt of pain, simultaneously grateful he had not struck a tree and disappointed he remained conscious.

The pain seemed unbearable, but at least on the bright side, Erabus would not have to feel it for too much longer. Jydral made his way over to him with his sword raised in anticipation of the killing blow. *I have failed*, Erabus admitted to himself even as he tried to move only to realize he had no control over his own body. It would heal, in time if Erabus had the luxury, but as he knew since the eclipse began, time was the one thing he did not have.

Forgive me, my love. I pray you can do what I could not. The sword raised above his head but Erabus refused to shrink away or cower. Erabus would meet his death with dignity and courage, the way he lived his life. He would not give Jydral the satisfaction of seeing him scared or begging for his life. It wouldn't change the outcome anyway. "When Xicuz kills you, know I will be smiling down on your demise.

"Know that I will be blocking your path to Eternity and will see to it you are banished to the Void. Know this, my dear brother, the monster you are now, the monster you have always been, will prevent you from joining us in the afterlife, but many decades down the road when it is finally time for Xicuz to pass peacefully in his sleep, he will have a place beside me for all eternity.

"For it is you that are the animal and not him, Jydral," Erabus said in a voice so cold and steady that it didn't even seem like it belonged to him. Unphased by his words, or tone, Jydral continued to advance on him until his brother towered above him with a cruel and hateful scowl on his face. "Do you know what is sad, Jydral? I have never once treated you like anything other than my brother. My father never treated you as less than his own son although he knew the truth from the beginning.

"If you were but a decent man, the throne, the crown, they would have been yours. I never wanted them, never wanted the responsibility and obligations that went with them. Even after I discovered the truth about your parentage, I never once thought to stop you from taking the throne even though you had no real right to. Not until I saw you for the type of man you truly are. Though I can honestly say that until you killed my father, the man who raised you as his own son, I never truly knew the depth of your depravity."

"As interesting as that is not, Erabus, the truth is I never once thought of you as my brother. If I were told then that our mother had an affair and borne an illegitimate child, I would have assumed it was you as you have always been too wretched to truly be of royal blood, but in truth, I am grateful that it is me who was not his son. For I am not cursed with his weak and feeble blood coursing through my veins.

"But it does not matter if I am king by right or if I am not but a usurper, for I am still king. And you," Jydral paused to raise the sword up and flip it over in his hand to plunge the tip into Erabus's chest, "are dead." Erabus refused to close his eyes as he watched the sword coming down on him, seemingly in slow motion, but before it could reach his heart and strike him down, another blade swung over his head and the resounding clang of the swords had him crying out in alarm.

Even before he glanced up and saw who it was above him, Erabus already knew. The angry, disbelieving roar his brother let out told him all he needed to know. Tilting his head back, even as Jydral's sword was pushed away from him, Erabus wasn't the least bit surprised to see Xicuz towering over him. Turning his silver eyes to him for a moment, they seemed to twinkle with the same unspoken happiness Erabus himself felt at that moment. "Miss me, my love?"

Chapter Fifteen

Xicuz stepped around Erabus and reached down to clasp his wrist, as there seemed to be no wounds there, and hauled him to his feet. Though they did not have the time to be wasting on such things, it had been far too long since Xicuz felt Erabus's soft lips on his and his only desire at that moment was to rectify that. He pulled Erabus to him by their clasped arms and pressed his lips against his feeling him respond as though that was the only thing he wanted in that moment too.

Sensing the attack moments before Jydral could reach them, Xicuz pushed Erabus away none too gently even as he raised his sword to block his assault. As he fought against him, catching Erabus moving away out of the corner of his eye and wondering if he was going for his weapon or running away as both his hands seemed to be already injured, Xicuz couldn't help but realize how close he came to losing him.

If I had been but a moment later... Xicuz could not finish that sentence, even in his head. He could not bear the thought of even allowing himself to think Erabus could have died. It was an unbearable future that caused his heart to squeeze painfully in his chest. And that was only at the mere possibility something could have happened that he already knew didn't.

Xicuz did not want to imagine the pain he would be in if it was a reality. All he knew was he demanded to die first. He wouldn't survive if Erabus passed before him, and as soon as the battle ended, Xicuz would make certain Erabus knew this new rule. Turning his thoughts away from Erabus and back to the task at hand, he focused all his attention on Jydral.

Giving him no time to react, let alone plan his next move against him, Xicuz swung his sword in rapid succession. The more he kept him on his toes, the fewer openings he gave for him to go on the offensive, Xicuz knew the better his chances would be to defeat him. Much to his dismay, Jydral seemed to be able to meet him thrust for thrust, parry for parry. Xicuz couldn't say he was surprised though.

When he awoke a little while before, Xicuz knew instantly he ran on far less strength and energy than usual. At first, when he jumped down from the tree and began heading out in search of anyone who could give him an update on the battle, Xicuz chalked it up to his body being unaccustomed to so much fighting and the fact he could not remember the last time he ate something.

It wasn't until a few minutes later, when he finally got a decent look at the sky above, that Xicuz realized they were in the middle of an eclipse. Two thoughts crossed his mind at that moment, each seeming to echo in his mind even as he started running knowing his time was short. *Wasn't it always these days?* Xicuz would think to himself as he ran, but before that, it was the fact that it wasn't nighttime and Erabus probably lay somewhere vulnerable, that were vying for dominance in his mind.

Erabus would have been in a battle when the eclipse started as Xicuz doubted he wasted any of his time awake hiding. Which meant his opponents would have little issue with disposing of him now that Erabus could no longer fight back. As much as Xicuz would have preferred to see the other humans as noble and honorable as Erabus, considering what Jydral turned them in to, it was more likely they took after the less than desirable brother.

Yet, even stranger than Xicuz could have imagined himself, Erabus was still conscious when the sound of their sword fight drew him to their battle. Considering the state of his hands and the fact Erabus lay on the ground when he finally reached them, he felt the same effects of the eclipse as Xicuz. Neither of them fought with 100 percent, and even though it had been quite a while since the last time he saw an eclipse as complete as this one, Xicuz knew it would only last for a few minutes.

Most of which Xicuz wasted trying to find them. *How much time do I have left? Enough to defeat Jydral once and for all*? Deciding not to squander what precious little time he had left, Xicuz came down on him hard with another swing of his sword before drawing Jydral's in a loop as he arched his own and elbowed him in the face before he regained his balance.

Growling in frustration, Jydral moved to attack him once more, but Erabus stopped his sword before it could even reach him. Seemingly unphased by his brother's reappearance, Jydral fought both of them off in a strange three-way of swords crossing that sent the sound of clanging metal echoing throughout the forest around them. Even with the two of them weakened due to the eclipse, their desire to defeat him once and for all was enough to tip the battle in their favor.

It was not long before Erabus caught his eye through the fray and gestured with his eyes, signaling what he wanted him to do. Unable to nod without giving things away to Jydral, Xicuz blinked even as he blocked another attack from the human king. In the next breath, Xicuz leapt into the air and brought his sword down on Jydral's head. Jydral reacted swiftly, raising his own blade to block the assault, and left his midsection exposed.

Taking advantage of the opening the moment it appeared, Erabus slashed his sword across his brother's chest, causing Jydral to scream out as he fell backward, his sword easily removed from his slackened grip. Before he could even think to try to get up, Xicuz stood above him with the tip of his blade pressed against his unguarded neck. Erabus stepped to the other side of him and glared down as he demanded, "Call your devil and undo your deal."

"I will do no such thing. I am the rightful king!" Jydral spat at him. Much to his surprise, Erabus laughed at his words instead of being taken back as Xicuz assumed he would. You would think, or at least Xicuz had, that Jydral would be begging for his life, or at least doing anything to keep it, and yet he tried to antagonize his brother further as though Erabus didn't hold his life in his hands.

"If you were the true king, Jydral, you would never have needed to make a deal with a devil in order to steal the throne," Erabus said, far calmer than he had a right to be at that moment, without a hint of mockery in his voice. Instead, it sounded like Erabus was sympathetic toward the man who did everything he could to, not only kill him, but to erase an entire clan from existence.

Then again, it was his brother. Blood ties run deep. Instead of answering with the same calm and steady tone Erabus used, Jydral shrieked at him something unintelligible before practically leaping at him, unphased by the blade that drew an angry red line across his throat. Jydral landed on Erabus, knocking them both to the ground and in that same moment his hands closed around his neck.

His feet moving before his mind managed to catch up, Xicuz yanked him off Erabus and tossed Jydral's body to the side. As Xicuz turned to make sure Erabus was all right, he saw him clearer than a moment before. Glancing up at the sky, it did not take long for him to realize the eclipse was ending. He'd runout of time. Hearing Jydral getting back up and running toward them, undoubtedly, to attack again, Xicuz turned toward him even as he raised his sword.

*

Taking the hand Xicuz held out for him, Erabus allowed himself to be pulled to his feet before finally turning his attention to his brother's lifeless form. The sad truth was things could have only ended this way. Even if Erabus wanted to give him another chance, to offer him banishment, his brother would have never stopped.

He would have healed up and come back in search of revenge against at least one of them. No, this was the only way for things to truly end. Now Erabus needed to deal with the aftermath of the destruction Jydral left in his wake. Turning tired, concerned eyes to Xicuz, he started to ask what would happen now only to be silenced by a sudden cloud of smoke that appeared out of nowhere.

For a moment, Erabus thought it might be Ith'tar returning to break the curse on them as the eclipse would be ending soon and judging by the way he seemed to sway on his feet, Erabus was certain Xicuz would not be able to remain standing for much longer. Instead, the being who appeared before them was a complete stranger. He had long, fiery red hair, not unlike his own, that flowed freely down his back in waves.

His eyes were a bright orange and Erabus wondered if they were made to look even more so by the color of his hair. He wore pants made from a dark hide and a strange web of bones across his chest, each bone held in place by an intricate knot tied on either side. He carried no weapon Erabus could see but judging from the power that seemed to be coming off him in waves, Erabus figured he had no use for one.

His lack of a weapon didn't make him seem any less imposing. The being turned his harsh orange eyes to them for a moment before seeming to dismiss them as he reached down and touched his hand to Jydral's bare chest. Erabus held his breath as a dark light pulsed just beneath Jydral's skin. A moment later, Erabus realized it beat in sync with his own heartbeat and dread filled his mind.

Was he being raised from the dead? Were they going to have to go through all that again? Only to lose this time as Erabus knew Xicuz would not be much help in the battle in a few short minutes. About to call out for him to stop, Erabus was stunned into silence once more when the dark light seeped out of his chest and onto the palm of the devil's hand. Or, at least, Erabus assumed that to be who he was.

The bargaining devil who Jydral made his deals with. When the devil finished, he stood up with a dark orb of pulsing energy in his hand, occasional sparks of light visible in the mass reminding him of lightning strikes on a stormy night. Before Erabus could ask any of the million questions running through his mind, the devil glanced at him for a moment before disappearing as suddenly as he arrived.

Unable to even call out "wait" before he was gone, Erabus could only turn to Xicuz in question and found him kneeling on the ground, using his hands to support his weight. Erabus dropped to his side as he pulled him onto his lap. "It is okay, my love. We have defeated him. The danger has passed. Rest peacefully now. I will try to get us back to Ebrein before dusk."

Seeming to use the last bit of strength he had left before the curse would activate once more, Xicuz rolled over so his head rested in his lap and gazed up at him with love-filled eyes. "It is not fair, my love. Our time together was far too short today and most of it wasted on that monster. Until the next eclipse?" The look on his face, the heat in his eyes, assured Erabus of exactly how Xicuz planned to spend their next eclipse together and he couldn't help but laugh despite the situation they were in.

Leaning down to kiss him, ignoring the pain that shot through his overused and tired muscles at the weird angle he was in, Erabus pulled back after a chaste moment to caress his cheek. "I love you, Xicuz," Erabus whispered before kissing his forehead, hiding the unshed tears from his sight; he could cry afterward. He wasn't going to waste what few precious seconds they had left weeping for things they could not change.

Before Xicuz could respond, though Erabus already knew what he would have said and desperately wanted to hear the words again, a voice called out from behind him. Glancing back, Erabus found Ith'tar standing there staring at them with a strange, intense look in his eyes. Ith'tar turned to Jydral for a moment before settling his gaze on Erabus once more and beginning to close the distance between them.

He felt Xicuz tense in his arms and assured him that it was okay. "Ith'tar," Erabus greeted with a nod, far too tired and sore to do anymore. "The other devil already came for him. I assume he took his soul as payment for the second deal Jydral made with him. Though I am rather surprised he would willingly give up his own soul in exchange, even if it were for a never-ending army."

Instead of speaking, Ith'tar stopped mere inches from where they were situated and leaned down to caress Erabus's cheek. Though he found the gesture strange, Erabus said nothing, even as Ith'tar turned and did the same to Xicuz. "The greater the request, the greater the sacrifice must be. For what Jydral wanted, his soul was the only price in balance. Speaking of," Ith'tar paused for a moment as he turned his eyes from Xicuz to Erabus, "the next time we meet, I will be here for your payment."

Ignoring the tensing of Xicuz in his arms, knowing he would have to explain things eventually, but unsure of how much longer Ith'tar would remain and having far too many questions to leave them unanswered, Erabus turned his full attention to the devil. "What happens to my brother's army? The men who died and came back to life? Is there any way to undo the death and destruction Jydral left in his wake?"

For a moment, the devil stared at him in silence before finally sighing and explaining, "Dead is dead, my dear Erabus. Any who died on the battlefield, even once, are dead. They always were. The life was never brought back, only the animation. Any who died, but were standing when Jydral himself died, went with him. Bury your dead and move on with your life," Ith'tar said before turning and disappearing in the same cloud of smoke and mist that the devils always seemed to.

"What payment?" Xicuz demanded after a few moments, no doubt as distracted by his disappearance as Erabus was. Glancing down at him, Erabus was rather surprised to see him still conscious; though Xicuz did look quite a bit weaker than the last time he looked at him. It took him another moment to realize what he said. Erabus tried to dismiss it, assure him that Ith'tar would not be returning for a very long time, but unsurprisingly, Xicuz refused to accept such a vague answer.

Sighing, Erabus explained, "The deal I made with Ith'tar, to save us, was in exchange for an heir. When I die, an old man in our bed, because I have no heir to leave my throne and crown to, he gets to choose one for me. Ith'tar will pick the next human king." Xicuz continued to stare at him in silence for so long Erabus thought the curse finally activated, and he forgot to close his eyes before losing consciousness.

With that thought, Erabus realized how bright Xicuz's face was, how clearly, he saw all his features and glanced up to find the sun had passed from behind the moon. A startled breath caught his attention, and Erabus glanced back down to find Xicuz staring at him with a shocked and, somehow, amused expression. "That means you are the human king now. My king," Xicuz said with a slight nod, the best he could do in his current position, that seemed to be only slightly teasing.

"Technically, I've been king since my father died as Jydral wasn't his son, but the product of our mother's affair with another man. Though I'm not even sure my father knew who he was. To save our mother's life, my father accepted Jydral as his own and decided to name him his heir as long as he proved himself worthy. I suppose you know as well as anyone how that turned out.

"I can only assume my father finally told him the truth, and that was why Jydral poisoned him. But none of this matters anymore. None of that is important. What is important is the fact that the eclipse is over, and you are still awake," Erabus said with a smile, watching as Xicuz glanced up at the sky to confirm for himself before turning shining eyes back to him. Seeming to regain the strength he lacked since the eclipse started to wane, or more likely ignoring how weak and tired he was, Xicuz pulled Erabus down and rolled them over, so he lay on top of him.

Without a word, or giving him the chance to respond, Xicuz pressed his lips against Erabus's in a rough and hungry manner. Erabus smirked against his lips for a moment before responding with the same fire and passion.

*

As much as they would have preferred to stay exactly where they were, doing exactly what they were doing and more, Erabus knew there were far too many things that needed to be dealt with at that moment. And they would have plenty of time later to make up for the time they missed. Reluctantly pulling his head back to break their rather heated kiss, that had Xicuz's hands exploring his chest, his fingers leaving trails of goosebumps in their wake, Erabus panted for breath.

"We need to deal with the aftermath, my love. After the unpleasantness is dealt with, then we can continue this," Erabus promised with a sultry smile before biting on the corner of his lip when he caught the hungry way Xicuz's eyes flashed at the prospect. About to change his mind, desperate to have his hands on him once more, Erabus was more than a little disappointed when Xicuz seemed to disappear only to pull him to his feet a moment later.

"As you say, my king," Xicuz said with a deep, exaggerated bow that Erabus rolled his eyes at before retrieving his sword and glancing down at his brother's body. "What do you want to do about him?" Xicuz wondered, his voice hard and cold as he stepped up beside him and followed his gaze. In truth, Erabus had no idea what he wanted to, or should, do about his body. Obviously, Jydral would not be joining their mother in the tomb, but Erabus couldn't leave him out here for the animals either.

"We'll leave him for now," Erabus decided. "I'll come back after the others are dealt with. That's already more than Jydral deserves." Glancing around the forest for a moment, Erabus realized he had no idea how to call off any who might still be attacking the satyrs. No way of knowing where they might be in the forest at that moment and if any of them were even still alive.

Seeming to sense where his thoughts went, Xicuz took his hand in his and gave it a reassuring squeeze before tilting his head back and giving off a strange, echoing cry. It was a horn-like sound, though Xicuz made it with his lips alone. Before Erabus could even think to question what he was doing, other calls cropped up throughout the forest, each in a different note, but the general tune stayed the same.

Soon the forest was alive with music as each note echoed around them far longer than the satyrs had been giving them. "The others will meet back in the village. I don't know about the humans, but at least there will no longer be anyone left in the forest for them to attack. Most likely the satyrs will explain to those they see that the battle is over, but you may want to bring Jydral with us now to convince any humans who happen to follow them to Ebrein."

Glancing back at his brother's lifeless body, Erabus had to admit Xicuz was probably right. If there were even any humans left alive, there was no reason for them to believe anything he said without proof. Sighing, Erabus moved to collect his brother only to have Xicuz step in before him and effortlessly lift him into his arms. "Your hands," Xicuz explained as he nodded to them and Erabus glanced down at them, the caked-on blood, and angry red wounds beneath reminding him of the injuries he sustained.

"Grab the weapons," Xicuz instructed and Erabus watched as he turned around and made his way back toward the village for a moment before grabbing Xicuz's spear and his sword, leaving Jydral's where it lay and hurrying after him. Their walk back to Ebrein went far faster than he anticipated and Erabus had no more idea of what to expect when he arrived than before they began. Were there any humans left alive?

Would they obey him now that Jydral was dead or would they call him a usurper and avenge his death? Would any of them be waiting in the village when they arrived? And what happened to those who surrendered before Erabus and the elders were forced to flee? At least they knew there were still satyrs left alive, as they answered Xicuz's call, but there was no way of knowing who or how many survived.

Not until they got there anyway. Drawing a deep breath, Erabus stepped through the tree line into Ebrein with Xicuz beside him, the three of them catching the attention of everyone in the area. Most appeared to be satyrs, but Erabus saw a few humans scattered about, and even from a distance, he could see their frightened eyes turned toward Jydral. "Do any of you carry a battle horn?"

He rose his voice to make sure everyone heard him and glanced around at each of them trying to find the instrument that would allow him to call an official end to the battle. In all honesty, Erabus found it more than a little strange Jydral himself hadn't been carrying one. Undoubtedly, he planned on having one of his guards signal the end when it got to that point. Probably thought they would still be by his side at the end.

"Aye, Prince Erabus. I have a battle horn," a voice called out after a breath and Erabus turned to find an older man walking toward him with the horn raised in his hand. He recognized him as one of the farmers back in Edith, but also as one of the men who surrendered to him when he was last in Ebrein. Reaching his hand out for the horn, Erabus nodded in thanks once he passed it over to him and brought it to his lips.

Drawing in as much air as he could hold, Erabus pressed his lips down and blew into the horn, sending the echoing blast for miles around. Anyone who lived to hear it would be able to and would make their way toward the sound. Now they just had to wait. Returning the battle horn to the farmer, Erabus sighed before turning back to Xicuz and finding him staring at him in silence, Jydral still in his arms.

"Put him with the others," Erabus instructed, gesturing toward the pile of the dead that the others gathered up. It did not take him more than a quick glance for him to confirm it was only dead humans who were placed there. Apparently, the satyrs were keeping theirs somewhere else; not that he could blame them. Turning his attention back to the others, Erabus watched in silence as the survivors trickled in.

"The battle is over! Jydral has lost!" Erabus called out, gesturing to where Xicuz placed him. Seeing the scared, confused expressions on most of their faces, Erabus wondered how many of them he should actually feel sympathy for as they were only doing what they were forced to do, and how many were as loathsome as Jydral was, who came in to the battle believing what hatred their false king spewed at them.

"You need not mourn for the death of your king, even with Jydral lying dead before you. He was never the king! Jydral murdered my father in cold blood after discovering he was the product of an affair our mother had. He made a deal with a bargaining devil in exchange for King Tribion's life in order to get the throne. Once he had that, the usurper made another deal so his army would rise once more after they were killed.

"For that, Jydral sacrificed his own soul and wherever it is, I hope he feels the torture his actions has brought upon our people and our allies. Countless lives were lost because Jydral was a greedy monster of a man who wanted to wipe out an entire clan simply because they were different from him. He was not fit to call himself human, and certainly was no king. As King Tribion's only son, I take my rightful place as the ruler of Edith!"

He let his voice reign out over them for a few moments before continuing, "My first mandate as king is to declare this war over! Any human who dares defy my order will be severely punished! All of you are to return home to Edith. Bury our dead and wait for my return there. As for Jydral," Erabus paused for a moment as he glanced back at his brother, "he is to be buried with the rest of the fallen, not in the royal tomb."

*

After placing Jydral where Erabus indicated, showing his body more care and respect than he deserved, for his brother's sake, Xicuz waited until he began speaking to what was left of his people before making his way toward King Heoltos. It had been far too long since Xicuz last laid eyes on him and concern for his continued wellbeing stayed at the back of his mind.

Now that he had confirmation his king remained safe, seemingly only sporting a few cuts and scrapes along his arms and legs, Xicuz breathed easier. "My king," Xicuz greeted as he knelt before him. Every satyrs' eyes seemed to be on him in a moment, but he paid them little mind as the more eyes that were on him meant more satyrs were still alive. Each one watching him was one less they would have to mourn and say goodbye to.

"I am glad to see both you and your chosen have come out of the battle unscathed. Though I am rather surprised to see you both are awake at the same time. Am I correct to assume that with the death of Jydral the curse broke?" Heoltos questioned as he moved toward him and placed his hand upon his shoulder, giving him the gentlest of squeezes before gesturing for him to rise.

"The curse on the humans who would not stay dead broke with his death, but ours took the devil Erabus made his deal with coming and removing it himself. I assume he did so because Jydral was no longer alive to need me dead, but I cannot be sure of why he removed it without any fuss. The only thing that matters is we are free and that Ebrein no longer has anything to worry about when it comes to Edith.

"Erabus will be a wise and just king and will honor the treaty placed by his father," Xicuz assured him as the king glanced over toward where his human counterpart addressed his people. Heoltos watched him for a few moments before nodding and turning back to Xicuz.

"Of that, I have no doubt. But what of the two of you? What happens now that Erabus is king?" Heoltos inquired.

"That I do not know, my king. We have not had the opportunity to discuss the matter yet. Right now, there are other things to deal with anyway. When the dust has settled and we have buried our dead, then I will broach the subject with him," Xicuz explained before glancing back to Erabus once more when realized the humans were beginning to move around as they gathered up their dead from the village.

Even as two were lifting Jydral into their arms, a few small groups went into the forest empty handed. No doubt they would be searching for the bodies of their missing fallen. Turning back to King Heoltos, he was already telling the satyrs to do the same. Once his instructions were given out to the others, he turned back to Xicuz. "Help gather our dead into the village. Once all are accounted for, you may spend your time with the human king.

"It will be awhile yet before our men are ready to be buried. Have your conversation sooner rather than later as Erabus may not have time after today," Heoltos warned before turning his head toward Erabus as he made his way over to them. "King Erabus," Heoltos greeted with a slight bow of his head which Erabus returned with a soft smile. "The elders have told me what you did for my people and I want you to know it will not be forgotten.

"You may ask anything of me in return for your services. If it is within my ability, it shall be yours."

Though it was obvious Erabus's response caught Heoltos off balance, Xicuz couldn't help but smile as it was exactly as he expected him to say.

"The elders? Veom? Did he make it?" Erabus inquired, his voice trembling at the name, unshed tears in his eyes. Of course, the first words out of his mouth wouldn't have been to request something of King Heoltos, even if that was exactly what he was instructed to do. No, his first thoughts were of the others Erabus probably spent a good deal of the battle with. Xicuz left Veom in charge of protecting the unconscious Erabus when it was time for the satyrs to go to war.

No doubt they continued to watch over him, and him over them, when the sun rose, and Erabus awoke once more. This he knew, but what happened to them after that, even Xicuz had no idea. "Most of the elders are fine, King Erabus. Veom lives. He suffered a wound to his chest but is already out retrieving the others who were guarding the women and children. Of those who were guarding you when Jydral attacked, two did not survive, and we lost another four here in the village before the human army overtook it, but all the others who were left behind are safe.

"In large part, I have been told, due to your courage and honor. None would have looked down on you had you taken off when the sun was setting and yet you stayed and protected those who were not your own, risking your life in doing so. For that, my people and I are eternally grateful as neither our women nor our children were harmed." The moisture in Erabus's eyes intensified but went ignored as he smiled sadly at Heoltos.

"Alas, King Heoltos, I am not worthy of the praise you have given me. My people are the ones who put yours in danger in the first place. It was my brother who tried to attack them. In truth, I did not protect them because they were unable to defend themselves. It was more so to make sure my own people did not attack the innocent. My reasons were selfish ones, certainly not one's worthy of a reward.

"But if you must insist on giving one for your own honor's sake, as I know I would in your shoes, then I ask only that you remain our allies and do not hold my brother's horrible actions against the whole of my people. I want nothing more than to retain the friendship our predecessors worked so hard to achieve; though I shall not blame you if too much has been destroyed between us that cannot be repaired."

Heoltos watched him in silence for a moment, his stoic expression unreadable even to Xicuz before he finally graced him with a smile. "Our brothers' mistakes are not our own, King Erabus. Just as we could not claim credit for their accomplishments. The treaty between our people stays as it was, for I have no greater wish than to continue our alliance as well.

"Perhaps after we have tended to our dead and a period of mourning has passed, we can come together once more as your father and King Zhul did. Thank you, King Erabus, for all you did to end this war and save as many lives as possible," Heoltos said with another slight bow of his head before making his way away to meet the elders who were bringing the women and children back in to Ebrein.

Erabus watched him go in silence for a few moments, smiling a greeting at Veom when he noticed his presence before turning toward Xicuz. "Shall we go home, my love?" Erabus inquired with a soft smile as he held his hand out for him. Xicuz was a bit thrown off by his request. As much as he wanted nothing more than to return home with him, to be able to share the life they built together now that they were both conscious at the same time, Xicuz couldn't help but realize it couldn't possibly last for long.

Erabus would need to return to Edith soon and Xicuz would have plenty of work to do himself at Ebrein in the coming days, but if this were to be the last time they were able to spend at their home, he wasn't about to darken their time together by pointing that out. Xicuz took Erabus's hand in his and led them into the forest, deciding all talk of the future and the inevitable could wait until morning. Their day finally came, and he had no intention to waste it, especially if it could be their last.

*

Walking back to their home took far longer than Erabus could have imagined, and more than once, he debated foregoing heading all the way back to their clearing and making love to Xicuz right there in the middle of the forest. It wouldn't have been the first time. Hopefully not the last either. But there was something about finally getting to have him in the home Xicuz built for them that kept his hands, and more, to himself.

Moving as quickly as Erabus could without running, it was well into the night before they finally arrived. Even with only a little light from the moon overhead lighting their way, Xicuz seemed to have no problem navigating his way through the forest so Erabus was happy to let him lead. When they finally arrived at their home, instead of being able to jump Xicuz, as Erabus had been itching to do since they stepped into the forest, he had to wait for him to build a fire.

It would be impossible for them to see anything, let alone each other, even with the moon shining brightly above their clearing. The time seemed to drag on agonizingly slow as if each minute it took for him to build the fire was intended as torture for him. Finally, after what seemed like an hour passed, though in reality had only been about five minutes, Xicuz stepped back from the now roaring fire to survey his handy work and was pulled back without warning by Erabus.

Before Xicuz could get off more than a startled gasp, he was pushed back onto their bed and Erabus climbed on top of him, staring down at him with unmistakably hungry eyes. "It's good to know I am not the only one desperate for the other's touch," Xicuz only half teased as he caressed Erabus's cheek, his silver eyes showing the same hunger and passion as Erabus's.

As if he could read his mind, Erabus saw the same complaints reflected in his eyes that were running through his own mind since they left Ebrein. It had been far too long since they felt each other's touch. An eternity seemed to have passed since the last time their lips met in a heated exchange. Weeks without any real conversation between them and no one else to keep them company other than their own voices.

Erabus didn't even want to imagine how long it would have continued to go for if Jydral hadn't decided to attack the satyrs and if Xicuz never knew about his plans in advance. If they had not been there to defeat Jydral, would the war have ended differently? Pushing that last thought from his mind, Erabus focused only on the satyr beneath him, losing himself in his silver eyes.

"Erabus, my love," Xicuz said as though it were the first time they saw each other in that moment and had not been together for hours already. In a way, Erabus supposed that was exactly what was going on. Even if they had not left each other's sides for more than a minute or two since Xicuz found him fighting Jydral, this was the first chance they had to focus on nothing other than themselves and how much they missed each other.

"Never leave me again, Xicuz. I don't think I could bear it," Erabus said as he leaned down to press gentle kisses against his forehead and cheeks.

"Nothing but your rejection of me could ever tear us apart again," Xicuz swore as he pulled Erabus down to him and pressed his lips against his before he could respond. Knowing there was nothing that could ever make him reject Xicuz, or the love they shared, Erabus ignored his words for now; there would be plenty of time to answer his concern later. And at that moment, it was rather impossible for him to focus on anything other than his touch.

Apparently, not expecting or waiting for an answer from him, Xicuz flipped them over without warning, and Erabus squeaked in surprise before moaning a mere moment later when Xicuz's strong, gentle hands trailed across his chest. Everywhere Xicuz touched, Erabus's skin seemed to burn in the most amazing way, and he groaned out Xicuz's name. He felt Xicuz smirk against his skin as he trailed a path of featherlight kisses down Erabus's neck and to his chest.

"Xicuz," Erabus purred as his fingers found their way into his thick, silky hair on their own accord. In response, Xicuz nibbled on his shoulder and Erabus shuddered beneath him. "I want more," he moaned even as Xicuz licked and nibbled his way down to his stomach. As much as Erabus enjoyed every touch Xicuz gave him, all he could think was that he wanted more; that he wanted it all.

Xicuz smirked against him before quickening his pace as he made his way down to his waist. Cupping him from outside his pants, Xicuz kneaded his manhood, causing Erabus to arch off the bed as he moaned out an unintelligible attempt at his name. Taking advantage of his rising hips, Xicuz pulled his pants down in one easy swoop.

They landed on the floor before Erabus even realized what happened. Had he been able to focus, Erabus would have laughed but a moment before he could react, Xicuz's hot, wet mouth closed around the tip of his manhood and he sucked in air between his teeth instead. "Xicuz," Erabus hissed, his name seeming to have more syllables than usual. It appeared to be all he could say now.

Xicuz didn't seem to mind as he took more of his member into his mouth and ran his lips from tip to base, only to do it again a moment later. As Xicuz increased his speed and pressure, Erabus's eyes rolled back into his head and all thoughts vanished from his mind. All that existed at that moment in time was the feel of Xicuz's mouth around him and the suction his lips created.

Soon Erabus felt himself drawing closer to completion and tried to warn Xicuz, with what amounted to an inarticulate grunt, and instead of stopping, he increased his pressure once more. A moment later, as Xicuz's warm hand wrapped around his shaft, Erabus cried out in pleasure and felt Xicuz licking up any spilled seed from his tip. "I had forgotten how divine you tasted," Xicuz purred in his ear after he kissed and licked his way back up to his neck.

Growling in a raspy and lustful tone, Erabus pushed Xicuz off him and climbed on top of him before he could question the sudden movement. He slithered down his body, leaving a trail of saliva as he licked his way from one beaded nipple to the other before heading to his waist. Tossing the top of his loincloth aside, Erabus took hold of his manhood and brought the tip to his lips, dragging his tongue across it as he raised his eyes to Xicuz's.

"Erabus," Xicuz warned, his tone turning dark and husky in a way that excited Erabus even further. Without breaking eye contact, Erabus licked the shaft from base to tip and circled the top with his tongue once more. The husky growl that escaped Xicuz's lips had Erabus both smirking and growing hard again. Lowering his lips down the shaft, he began a firm but slow pace that soon had Xicuz bucking his hips unconsciously to get him to go faster.

For a moment, Erabus silently debated teasing him for a little while longer, but soon decided that in doing so, he would be making himself wait as well. Wrapping his warm hand around the base, Erabus moved in time with his mouth as he picked up the pace, and pressure, and worked the entire length of his shaft. Soon Xicuz moaned beneath him, trying in vain to keep himself still, and his reactions spurred Erabus on further.

Even as he applied more pressure and increased his speed again, Erabus knew it would not be long before Xicuz joined him in his completion. "Erabus," Xicuz groaned, and he brought him to his release as he pressed his lips tighter against him. The resounding moan that escaped his lips did not resemble any actual word, though Erabus knew that it was meant to be his name.

What else but his name could be on his mind at that precise moment. Licking away any trace of his release that remained, Erabus kissed and nipped his way back up until he was lying comfortably on his chest. Xicuz continued to pant for a moment before finally tilting his head up to him and placing a rather subdued kiss upon him. As much as he would have preferred a much more passionate embrace at that moment, Erabus knew Xicuz still needed to come down from his release.

Xicuz pulled him in to his arms and held him tightly against his chest. "I have missed you, my love. Far more than I would have imagined possible. I missed the sound of your voice and the way your eyes light up when they turn to me," Xicuz said, speaking into his hair as he pulled him impossibly tight against him. "Even with you in the same bed as me, it was never anywhere near enough for me.

"I do not know what I will do when you leave me again." The last bit Xicuz spoke so softly Erabus wasn't certain he meant to speak the words out loud. Either way, they had him wondering what in the world he spoke of. *When I leave him again*? It wasn't even spoken as a possibility but as a foregone conclusion. Erabus couldn't imagine why in the world Xicuz not only thought but seemed certain, he would ever leave him again.

"Hear me, my love," Erabus began as he rolled over to straddle Xicuz's hips and leaned as close as possible without touching his face, resting his weight on his hands that were placed on either side of him. "There is nothing in this world that would ever make me leave your side again. And I would not recommend that anything try. As you have said before, only your rejection could force me away.

"No matter what our future brings, it will be just that—*ours*. You are mine as I am yours, now and for every day and every night that is to come. If you worry because of who I am, who I am to become the moment I step back in Edith, let me assure you now that is something you need never worry about. I would abdicate my throne before I would let it steal you away from me.

"But that is not what our future holds, my love, of that I can assure you. As long as you stand by my side, nothing can ever tear you away from it." Though Xicuz smiled at him in response, Erabus saw he was not convinced things would go as he insisted they would. Unsure of what else to do to convince him, or at least take his mind off his worries at that moment, Erabus grinded against him, causing Xicuz's eyes to open wide in surprise.

Giving him no chance to react, Erabus grabbed on to a fistful of Xicuz's beard and pulled him closer, pressing their lips together. His kiss was hard and unyielding, more desperate than passionate, but Xicuz didn't seem to mind as he returned it with the same fervor. A moment later, Erabus felt Xicuz's hands gliding across his back and was flipped over once again.

Laughing at the sudden movement, Erabus grabbed the back of Xicuz's head and pulled him closer to continue their rough, lust-filled kiss. As Xicuz licked and kissed down his neck, Erabus wanted to tell him to hurry up, that he wanted nothing more than to feel Xicuz inside him, for him to take him in a rough and feverish way as though they were transformed into animals by their overwhelming desire for each other, but all he could manage were gasps and moans as Xicuz sucked on the pulse at his neck.

Yet, somehow, Xicuz seemed to be able to read the desire in his mind, and he chuckled even as he reached down between them. As the soft, dark hairs on his arm brushed against his inner thigh, Erabus knew he held his own member even if he couldn't see it from his current position. "Breathe, my love," Xicuz warned a moment before Erabus felt the tip pressing up against him.

Unconcerned by any momentary pain he might feel, knowing it would quickly give way to highly anticipated pleasure, Erabus grabbed him by the horns and drew his lips down to his once more. The moment they touched, Erabus felt Xicuz pressing in. His manhood stretched Erabus to accommodate his girth. Far too slowly Xicuz pushed forward until he was buried all the way to his base, but still he did not move.

"Take me, Xicuz. Now," Erabus demanded, or begged, he wasn't quite sure which, as he pushed back against Xicuz's head so he could see the certainty and desire in his eyes. As Xicuz pulled himself out to the tip once more, Erabus's eyes rolled back as the pleasure of what he felt overshadowed the pain. Before Erabus could tell him to keep going, as he paused for a moment when he removed nearly all of himself, Xicuz shot his hips as far forward as he could, sheathing himself to the base once again.

Erabus's moan turned to a scream of pleasure, which had yet to ebb out when Xicuz repeated the action. Faster and faster he thrust into him as Erabus tried to raise his hips to meet his pace, but realized it proved rather difficult in his current position. Xicuz buried himself completely once more before moving Erabus's legs over to one side and reaching under him to grip his waist.

A hand on each of his hips, Xicuz flipped him over faster than Erabus could realize what was happening and thrust into him again before he could even regain his balance. "Xi—" Erabus began, his voice cut off as Xicuz drew back slowly, "cuz...!" he finished, his name turning into a scream as he buried himself to the hilt once more.

Moving his hips back to meet Xicuz's in the next thrust, Erabus cried out in pleasure; the sound having no chance to finish before they were meeting again. Meeting him thrust for thrust Erabus panted and moaned in increasing volume; each sound seeming to arouse Xicuz further until he moved too fast and too hard for Erabus to keep up the pace.

Allowing himself to fall to his forearms, Erabus soon gave up trying to keep up with Xicuz and let him do all the work. Judging by his grunts of pleasure, Xicuz didn't seem to mind in the least. As Xicuz continued to keep up the impossible pace, Erabus was barely able to even breathe when one of Xicuz's large hands wrapped around his member and stroked it at the same pace as his thrusting. "Xicuz," Erabus moaned out before biting his bottom lip as his name tapered off into another moan.

"I know, my love. Me too," Xicuz grunted in his ear, each word punctuated by a thrust of his hips. As soon as he finished speaking he increased the pace once more, but it hardly mattered as the very next moment, Erabus found his release. Two thrusts later, Xicuz collapsed on top of him before rolling over on to his side and pulling Erabus with him. Curled in Xicuz's arms, his pounding heart beating against Erabus's back as he lay flush against his chest, Erabus felt himself being lulled to sleep.

They would need to rise soon and clean up, but at that moment, nothing in the world was going to get him out of

Xicuz's warm, comforting arms. Behind him, Erabus soon heard the only sound he heard from Xicuz in all the weeks since the curse first activated; the peaceful, deep breathing that signified he was asleep. Smiling to himself, Erabus debated going to sleep himself but knew he would regret that decision when they awoke and had to deal with the mess.

Sighing in defeat, Erabus untangled himself from Xicuz's arms and slipped out of the bed, glancing over his shoulder to make sure he didn't wake him. Erabus cleaned himself up well as he could and threw his pants back on and turned his attention to Xicuz and the bed. Once finished, he added another log to the fire and scribbled a quick *getting water* on the floor with a stick from the hearth and made his way down to the river.

Stripping once more when he reached the shore, wondering why he even bothered to put his pants back on in the first place, Erabus stepped into the cold water, washing away anything he might have missed back at home. Though he originally intended on heading back as quickly as possible, Erabus was distracted by the reflection of the moon on the mostly still water around him.

Sighing softly at the sight, Erabus realized for the first time how much he missed it. He watched it shimmer in the water for a few more moments before letting his hair down and sinking down into the reflection on the water. Running his fingers through the fiery strains, Erabus rose to the surface once more. As he stood his full height, the excess water cascading down him and he ran his fingers through his hair once more to remove the rest.

Glancing toward the shore, about to make his way back to his clothing, Erabus found Xicuz standing beside where he left them. As Erabus watched in stunned silence, Xicuz slipped off his loincloth, leaving himself standing there in nothing but his horns and hooves, and Erabus's breath caught in his throat. Biting his lower lip to keep himself from moaning at the sight alone, Erabus glanced up to find himself staring into hungry silver eyes that seemed to glow in the pale moonlight.

Raising his hand, palm up, Erabus gestured with his finger for Xicuz to join him, growing hard as Xicuz rushed toward him without a moment's hesitation.

Chapter Sixteen

It seemed strange to Erabus, waking up in his childhood bed after so long, especially since he was alone. Even when Erabus woke up in Ebrein, he was never alone. Xicuz, or Veom, were always there beside him. It wouldn't be for long, but it unnerved him for the time he did have to deal with it. Once crowned, Erabus would be switching rooms, though he had no idea where he would be sleeping after this.

He was supposed to move to his father's room, as Jydral undoubtedly did during his short reign, but without ever stepping into the room after the day his father died, Erabus already knew that such a thing was impossible. The room would forever be King Tribion's chambers and to move into it would be seen as nothing more than trespassing to him, even if it were him who resided in it.

Or perhaps even more so if it was him. Erabus failed his father and allowed Jydral to murder, not only him, but all the humans and satyrs who did not make it back from the preventable war between them. If Erabus saw what Jydral was up to sooner, if he did what needed to be done once the truth was known, or took him out after the first time his father got sick instead of idiotically assuming his recovered health meant he hadn't been poisoned in the first place...

If Erabus had only done any number of things that could have prevented his brother from doing all the hateful, despicable things Jydral did, perhaps then when it came his natural time to take over the throne, he might have felt more comfortable in taking his father's rooms. Alas Erabus had not and so he found himself with his current dilemma—where to sleep after being crowned king. It was a pity his current room was far too small, or he would remain there as originally intended when Jydral was set to become king.

His sleeping arrangements weren't the most important thing for him to worry about at that moment, but the more Erabus concentrated on it, the longer he could avoid dealing with the real issues at hand. By all rights with Jydral dead, no heir named to take his place, Erabus was the rightful king, even without considering that Jydral hadn't been a true heir of Tribion.

And while Erabus figured the majority of his people would accept him without issue, as they had known him and the kind of man he was long before any of this mess started, there would be some who saw him as a usurper and not the rightful heir of Tribion. Jydral's most devout men fell during the battle, but surely that could not have been all of those he corrupted to his side.

The ones Erabus knew for certain were loyal to none but Jydral he either saw fall, felled them himself, or saw their bodies buried, including Aothorn, Elovonos, Dlivion, and Azemar, but like with most threats, it was the ones you did not know of that were the most dangerous. As much as he tried not to, Erabus couldn't help but wonder if each man who walked past him were hiding a grudge or blade.

Would the guard standing outside his door plunge a knife into his back the moment Erabus turned it on him? Would the man who passed out the ale at dinner slip poison into his cup as Jydral had done to his father? Had the women gathering up his sheets to wash, lost husbands during the battle, at his own hand even, and lay the blame solely on him instead of on Jydral where it belonged? Every sound Erabus heard, be it a squeak of a floorboard, the opening of a door in the dark, or a boot tapping along down the hallway, was it his would-be assassin coming for his head?

He couldn't think this way—the paranoia would drive him past the brink, but no matter how many times Erabus reminded himself those who were left were the good and decent people, men who surrendered or had given up after being wounded, and women who remained back in Edith, he could not help but see the darkened shadows around them. It would be better after his coronation as Erabus would never be alone again after that moment, but until he knew who could be trusted within his own village walls, he would not be breathing easy.

Thankfully, that would be today. Now all Erabus needed to do was get up, get dressed and stand in front of his entire clan and hope none of them made a scene about him now being their king. If they did, if they refused to accept him or give any indication that he or his people were anything other than safe in their presence, Erabus would have no choice but to deal with them. And there had been far too much killing already. He wasn't sure his people, or Edith, could handle another death in such a short time.

And, of course, Erabus couldn't banish them either as that came with the added risk of them returning later to attack. Shaking his head to clear such thoughts, for the moment, at least, Erabus rolled over on the bed and looked sadly at the empty spot beside him for a moment before throwing back the covers and finally rising. He could put things off no longer; it was time to face whatever the day had to throw at him.

Once crowned, and the party was underway, Erabus could spend his time with the only one he wanted at his side at that moment: Xicuz. Of course, he couldn't be there with him now as Xicuz had his own fallen to deal with back at Ebrein and he needed to be with them to mourn their loss. King Heoltos wanted his help leading the rite of passage for their fallen warriors, and no matter how much he may have wanted Xicuz at his side, Erabus would never have even imagined trying to keep him away from his people who needed him more.

Rising out of the bed, ignoring the cold wood beneath his feet, Erabus made his way over to his dying hearth and rebuilt the fire as he stared into the embers. Behind him he heard his door opening and forced himself to turn around slowly. Even if Erabus didn't trust everyone around him, it didn't mean they could see him scared. If they did have anything nefarious planned, his fear might give them the opening they were waiting for.

If they didn't, they still might lose faith in him as a king and neither would help his case any. Erabus glanced over his shoulder and found a young woman standing in the open doorway, staring at him in confusion. "I'm here to rebuild the fire," she explained, even as her eyes flashed to the obviously already tended to hearth. Apparently confused by her already completed task, she continued to stand there staring at him in silence.

"Perhaps you could bring me something hot to drink and some bread to nibble on instead. After that, you may continue on with whatever other responsibilities you have or return to your superior for further instructions." Once Erabus finished speaking, he turned his back to deal with the fire. Though he felt her watching him for a few more moments in silence, Erabus soon heard the door closing behind her and dismissed her odd behavior.

Edith had seen three kings in a few short months, and he couldn't help but doubt Jydral ever did anything for himself. If she had been the one to tend to his hearth too, it was only natural she be confused by the sudden and undoubtedly drastic changes. Dismissing her from his mind, Erabus made his way over to the clothing set out for today's festivities.

The long silky tunic and pants weren't his usual style, but at least it would only be for today, and any other time Erabus was required to dress fancy. His daily garments would also change, just not quite as drastically as those he was expected to wear today. Instead of his usual open vest and buckskin pants, it would be a long sleeved, V-cut shirt and looser fitting pants. Along with his crown, Erabus would be adorned with ceremonious armor including wrist cuffs, thick-soled boots, a chest plate, and heavy shoulder guards that held his cloak in place.

It was a ridiculous ensemble, especially considering the amount of time Erabus would spend within the walls of Edith, but that was how they dressed human kings. Or, at least, it would be until he started making changes. And changes he would make. Starting with him having to constantly be in armor, always flanked by guards even when in the throne room tending to his own people's needs.

There were other things, of course, other things in desperate need of being changed, but they would have to wait until Erabus could assure his people, and himself, that he was worthy of being their leader and not having his decisions questioned. When Erabus had their confidence, then he would hit them with the big things. Turning his thoughts to the more immediate future, he changed into his coronation clothing.

Not long after Erabus finished, there was a knock at his door, and he called out for them to enter. The woman from before came in carrying a tray filled with a steaming pot, cups, and judging by the mouthwatering aroma that filled the air the moment she stepped through the door, bread that only just now finished baking. "You can leave it there," Erabus instructed before turning back to his reflection in the distorted, arched mirror and adjusted his garments as he scrunched his nose at his appearance.

Hearing the door close once more behind him, Erabus glanced back and found that he was alone again. How strange that something he was used to for most of his life, as Erabus tended to keep to himself rather than risk annoying Jydral, became such a foreign concept after such a short time of being with someone else. Sitting down in reach of the tray, Erabus moved to grab the first piece of bread when a sudden thought stopped him cold. Had anyone tampered with his food? Would there be any way for him to even know if they had?

Had King Tribion ever felt like this, as though he needed to watch for those who meant him harm around every corner, or was Erabus merely feeling that way after what happened to his father? Did he truly have anything to worry about with the woman, or anyone else who might have contact with his food, or had his father's death made him ridiculously paranoid? Unfortunately, Erabus knew the only way to find out for certain would also mean it was too late to do anything about it.

Taking an experimental sniff of the bread before him, Erabus sighed as he could not chance it. As good as it smelled and as hungry as he was, Erabus could not risk someone poisoning him, especially before he could fix all the things that were wrong with Edith and her people. Of course, that also meant Erabus would soon starve to death if he didn't figure out who he could trust and fast. At least later today it wouldn't be an issue as there would be plenty to eat at the feast that was served to all.

Erabus left the tray untouched and straightened out his clothing once more before making his way toward his door and stepping into the brightly lit hallway. Taken back by the sudden and drastic change from his room, which was only illuminated by the fire and the small amount of sunlight that managed to seep in through his lone window, Erabus blinked a few times to help his eyes adjust.

Once he could see who else was in the hallway with him, Erabus wasn't in the least bit surprised to see four guards waiting for him outside his doorway. Even without having to ask, Erabus knew they would be following him everywhere for the rest of the day. Then they would be relieved by another set who would guard his door all night, as they had been ever since he returned from Ebrein. As Erabus began walking toward the throne room, two guards leading and two flanking him, Erabus couldn't help but wonder two things with equal curiosity.

How did they know where he was going, and could Erabus trust any of them? He recognized all four, at least from the day group. There wasn't a chance to meet the overnight guards as he had been asleep for most of their shift, but Erabus heard them talking throughout the night when it was time to do hallway inspections. Turning his thoughts away from the men he planned to get to know before they were set to start their next shift that night, Erabus focused on the four currently surrounding him.

The man in front on the right was a bit older than the others, closer to Tribion's age than Erabus's. Named Cenhelm, he served his father as a guard, but had been in the service of Jydral as well. He was loyal to the crown and not the man and would be dutiful to him too for as long as Erabus remained the king. If any were to come to usurp him from the throne, as Jydral did with his father, Cenhelm would stand by their side the moment their coronation ended.

The man beside him, as well as the man directly behind him on his left, were faces Erabus recognized as men who surrendered during the battle, Hector and Emerick. They were either smart enough to know when it was better to give up or they were forced to fight for a cause they did not believe in and took their first opportunity to get out before the battle claimed their lives. Either way, Erabus wasn't certain where they stood as people or in regard to what they thought about him.

The fourth and final daytime guard he was most concerned about—Destrian. Though he didn't see him during the battle, Erabus recognized him from when they were younger. Destrian was the same age as Jydral and Erabus saw them together many times, though not for many years now. Apparently, they stopped traveling in the same circles, but until he found out why, there was no way for Erabus to know how it would affect his behavior with him.

Realizing they arrived at the throne room, Erabus allowed the guards to lead him in. Except for a path that led to the throne, the entire room was packed full of people; to the point there was barely any room to move around in. Though he could not see them from his current position, Erabus knew that King Heoltos or, at least, his delegates had accepted his invitation and were there. One of which was, hopefully, Xicuz.

Truth be told, Xicuz was the only person Erabus wanted to be there, but there were customs to follow. As they stepped into the room and hundreds of eyes turned toward them, his two leading guards began walking a little in front of Erabus and he knew, without having to look, the flanking guards would wait a few beats before following him. It was one of the many things that had not made sense when Cenhelm explained it to him over the last few days.

Whenever they were walking the halls, as they had just done, the guards would be extremely close even though there was no one else around. Yet, now when they were surrounded by countless others in such a small space, they spread out away from him because it was the coronation. *Well,* Erabus decided as he made his way down the aisle, *if you are hated enough to be killed during your coronation, they probably wouldn't want to lose their lives protecting you.*

Keeping his eyes straight ahead, Erabus focused on the throne before him, as they warned him that looking at the large crowd of people might cause him to trip over his own feet. According to Cenhelm, it happened before. As he got to the midway point, Erabus had to force himself not to turn his head when he felt his eyes on him. Xicuz stood off to his left, buried in the crowd. He felt the love and respect his gaze showered him with.

He might not have been able to look at him at that moment, but Erabus knew Xicuz came to support him, and he wanted, more than anything, to make sure Xicuz knew his presence was felt and appreciated. As he walked by, his gaze still focused on the throne, Erabus smiled as an image of Xicuz appeared in his mind and felt Xicuz smile back at him in return.

As he made his way down the rest of the aisle, Erabus wondered what went through the minds of those who were watching him. Xicuz, he already knew the answer to; the same thing that always seemed to be going through his mind when they were together. And it was identical to what was always on Erabus's mind, how much he loved and wanted him.

Everyone else, on the other hand, Erabus hadn't a clue. Best case, they were thinking about how boring a coronation was. At worst, they were already plotting his death. He reminded himself that thinking like that wouldn't do him any good. Erabus shook his mind free and climbed the three steps to the platform that the throne rested on. As he moved to take his position, the four guards split up and took up their own positions around the platform.

Standing before him now was an elderly man who had been in his position from the time of Erabus's grandfather. The Eminence of Virtue, Terrick. He was not only in charge of presiding over their coronations but also their weddings. "Kneel, my child," Terrick instructed and Erabus did as bid, even as he wondered if he resided over Jydral's coronation or if his brother refused any connection to King Tribion.

The Eminence still lived, and seemed to be unharmed, so Erabus could only assume Jydral used his services. Undoubtedly, Jydral would not have wanted to draw unnecessary questions to him or his becoming king. Pushing thoughts of his brother from his mind, Erabus turned his full attention back to him as Terrick spoke once more. "As with all your fathers before you and all your sons after, each life within Edith lives in peace and harmony or dies in pain and suffering by your actions.

"The hopes and prosperity of the people are within the king's control. If you are wise and true, your people will flourish, but if you are cruel and unjust, your people will suffer." As he spoke to him, Erabus wondered what Terrick thought about him, or about Jydral, as he uttered the words. "The king of Edith must be strong and brave to protect their people from enemies from without our borders.

"Or within," Terrick continued as he held up a large, crystal orb and placed it in his left hand. "The king must be intelligent and innovative to lead our great city into our future." In his right hand Terrick placed a staff whose shaft was carved with intricate designs depicting the symbols for medicine, art, and diplomacy. The last one Erabus assumed his father added, though he was a bit surprised that Jydral didn't scrape it off after his coronation.

As he stepped back, Erabus touched the tip of the staff to the orb and bowed his head before them. "For this, and all my days to come, I vow to guard and protect the people of Edith, from all manner of harm. I will guide them, teach them, and honor them for all the days of my life. Never shall I perform an act that would give my people cause to fear or doubt me as their king. I shall hold myself to the same high and unwavering standards and loyalty as my fathers before me and my sons after."

As he finished speaking, Erabus bowed his head to the staff and orb once more and rose to his feet. Crossing his arms in front of his chest, he turned back to the crowd, forcing his eyes to scan over all his people in attendance before letting them finally rest on Xicuz. In his eyes, Erabus saw nothing but pride and love shining back at him. Giving him a slight smile, Erabus turned his attention to King Heoltos and the other delegates who were standing around him, giving them a slight nod before continuing on.

All around them, countless faces stared back at him as he tried to judge their reactions to his coronation, but Erabus saw nothing that would give any indication either way. Turning his eyes back to Xicuz once more, he held his gaze for a moment before turning around and making his way toward the throne. Sitting down wasn't the easiest thing, especially since his hands were still required to be crossed in front of him, but Erabus managed to back into the seat without too much issue.

The Eminence of Virtue stepped in front of him and raised his arms as he glanced out at the crowd. "Long live King Erabus and long may he reign!" Though there were a few who seemed delayed by a moment or two, most of the crowd mimicked his call. After a few shouts, they calmed down and Terrick retrieved the orb and staff from him before stepping off the platform. Watching the crowd for a moment, Erabus couldn't help but wonder how they would react to the next part.

Though Erabus did it because it was what he wanted, it would also be a great way to determine how people would react. If they were able to handle this unexpected announcement, they would be able to handle anything Erabus threw at them. Though something at the back of his mind warned him that this could end badly, the voice of his father echoed in his ears to trust their people.

To have faith in them. Erabus rose from his seat and walked toward the front of the platform once more and raised his hands to silence the crowd. It only took them a few seconds to comply. "While I am well aware that it is customary for such things to be decided upon by a group of elders who sift through the candidates and pick the best one for Edith, I wanted to make this announcement first thing so said elders will not waste their time.

"I have already chosen my consort," Erabus informed them. The crowd whispered amongst themselves. Ignoring their questions for now, as they were about to get worse, Erabus turned and locked eyes on Xicuz. Apparently confused by what was happening, he could only stand there and stare at him in stunned silence.

Smiling to him, realizing he never did get around to explaining things to him as they had not seen each other since the morning after the battle ended, Erabus made his way down off the platform and into the crowd. The masses parted, everyone simultaneously knowing their king was not referring to them and wondering to whom he was. Erabus made his way deep into the crowd until he stood before Xicuz.

"You can't, Erabus. Your people would not accept me. They will revolt," Xicuz warned in a harsh whisper as he kept his hands clenched in fists at his side. As much as he longed to reach out for him, Xicuz had to make the decision for himself. Erabus may have been putting him on the spot by doing it so publicly, as it was the only way that would prevent the elders from trying to stop him, but he would never pressure Xicuz into it.

It only mattered if it was something Xicuz wanted as well. "Have faith, Xicuz. In my people. In me. Nothing but your rejection would stop me," Erabus said, using his own assurances on him. And as much as it would have broken his heart, he spoke the truth. If Xicuz had said no, refused to give his hand, Erabus would have walked away and never brought it up again. Thankfully that future never came to pass as Xicuz watched him in silence for a moment longer before finally raising his hand and offering it to Erabus.

Erabus took his hand and gave him a reassuring squeeze before turning and making his way back out of the crowd, pulling Xicuz along with him. Even before they climbed the steps to the platform, Erabus could tell as each section saw who he brought with him as their gasps and whispered questions reached his ears. Gently rubbing his thumb over Xicuz's hand when he felt him tense at the voices, undoubtedly able to hear even more, Erabus brought them to the front.

He turned to face the crowd once more. "May I present to you, good people of Edith, my chosen consort—Xicuz of the satyr clan," Erabus called out watching for any sign of a revolt or rejection. Instead, all he saw was a lot of confused faces staring back at him even as they whispered amongst themselves again. After what seemed like forever, Terrick came forward once more, standing at the bottoms of the stairs.

"Forgive me, my king, but how will you produce an heir with your consort?" *That was it?* Out of everything they could have complained about, every objection they could have raised, that was the problem? Not that Xicuz was a man? Not that he was a satyr? Only that they couldn't reproduce? Fighting the urge to shake his head and smile at such an innocent and legitimate question, Erabus turned toward him to address his concerns.

"I would not be the first of my family to rule without producing an heir. This kingdom survived it then and we will do so again. But fear not, as before I die, many years from now, I will name my heir to the public. Until then, they shall remain unnamed so they cannot be corrupted by outside forces." Terrick's expression showed that he didn't quite understand or believe him, but Erabus couldn't tell him, and the majority of Edith, that he did not know who the next king would be because Ith'tar hadn't told him a name yet and wouldn't for many years down the road.

Though he looked like he still had many questions left to ask him and would undoubtedly voice them later when they had more privacy, Terrick watched them for a few moments before turning to face the crowd. "Long live the king consort!" Terrick called out; his voice as unwavering as it was when he called out the same for Erabus. The most amazing thing happened at that moment and Erabus could only stand there staring in wonder.

The moment Terrick finished, the entire crowd cried out in unison, "Long live the king consort! Long live King Erabus!" Turning toward Xicuz, Erabus found the same stunned wonder that reflected in his eyes. Their unexpected acceptance was more than either of them could handle at the moment, so instead of responding to the still shouting crowd, Erabus squeezed his hand tighter before sending him a loving smile.

*

Xicuz could not believe everything that happened, even though he saw it all with his own eyes. Erabus claimed him, much as he had with him, in front of his own people. Erabus called him his consort and pulled him to the platform so all could see who, and what, Xicuz was. And far more surprising and impossible than that, his people accepted him. They saw him as a man, as a satyr, and they did not care.

Perhaps Xicuz expected the worst of them because he assumed more of them were like Jydral, but it seemed the opposite was true; they were more like Erabus. They were kind, and open, and welcoming. Perhaps there were those who did not approve and chose to keep their objections silent for the moment, but most of them hadn't been bothered by it in the least.

You could see it in their eyes. There was no hate, no disgust. Only confusion and, surprisingly, wonder. There would be talk for a long time to come, gossip and whispers spreading throughout the village, and a constant barrage of questions aimed at Erabus, and perhaps even himself when they become more accustomed to speaking with him, but it was to be expected after dropping something like that on everyone.

Of course, Erabus's people, Xicuz supposed he should call them his people now, wouldn't be the only ones with questions for their new king. He would have more than his own share to ask, and he would have plenty of time alone with him to voice them. Starting with, what is a king consort, and what does being one entail? It was made, rather, obvious by the Terrick's question about heirs that it was his version of a chosen and had Erabus been anyone else, Xicuz wouldn't have been so confused.

Certainly, a king's consort had to be different from one of the average person's. Were they even called the same? What was expected of him now? Realizing the crowd began to disperse, no doubt heading for the area outside they were setting up when he arrived that morning with King Heoltos, Qom, Xaaxex, and the others who were left at the border, Xicuz turned his attention back to Erabus and found him making his way toward the satyr king.

"You honor me with your presence here, King Heoltos. Edith is grateful for your continued friendship and I am pleased our two clans are forever joined by our union," Erabus said with a deep bow, probably more so than a king was ever supposed to bow to another, before righting himself with a smile. Even before Heoltos could answer him, Xicuz smirked at what Erabus said without realizing it.

Of course, how could he? It wasn't as if I ever explained things to him. Not intentionally, it honestly never came up. "More so than you even know, King Erabus. Xicuz is my younger brother; we share the same father. Not only have our clans joined, but so have our houses. Though, I must say, I do appreciate you conferring with me before naming him your consort. They were not needed, but I did feel more secure having extra guards at the forest line in case things went sour."

Glancing back and forth between the two kings, Xicuz couldn't decide who he should question first, or what he should ask. That was why Heoltos brought extra guards? Erabus asked for Heoltos' permission? Heoltos knew what would happen during the coronation and didn't warn him? How had the two of them spoken? If Erabus came to Ebrein Xicuz would have known, but who would he have trusted with a message like that?

And how had he not noticed a messenger? Too many questions vied for priority and Xicuz eventually gave up with a sigh as he turned his attention back to them and found Heoltos smirking at him with a twinkle in his eyes and Erabus gazing at him in question. "Does that mean King Zhul was your father?" Erabus wondered after a moment as he glanced back and forth between the two brothers.

"No, our crowns are not inherited, but earned. Any satyr may challenge the current king in combat for the crown. If the king has passed or is too weak to participate, then he names a champion or another who wishes for the crown can fight. We have ancestors who were kings, but only because they too won the combat," Heoltos explained and Xicuz watched in amusement as Erabus nodded, though his expression showed that he remained a bit confused.

Not that he could blame him. Xicuz himself found it odd the humans just gave the crown to their offspring. Doing so often resulted in men like Jydral becoming king and having to fight against another for the crown would have prevented that from becoming a reality. Jydral was a coward who used poison and attacked from the shadows; the satyrs would never have accepted such a king.

"It seems, there is still much we can learn about each other's clans, and I very much look forward to it. But for today, let us join the endless feast and celebration that should be starting up outside. You are all more than welcome to partake in today's festivities as are your men still out in the forest," Erabus told them with a smile before turning his attention back to Xicuz. He wasn't sure why, but for some reason having his eyes on him caused a blush to rise up on his cheeks.

He could tell by the twinkle in his eyes that Heoltos noticed, but he was polite enough not to mention it and instead nodded to Erabus before heading out of the hall with the other satyrs trailing behind him. "My love," Erabus called out to him, drawing his attention back now that they were alone. Before he even realized his feet were moving, Xicuz closed the distance between them and crashed his lips down on his startled king.

It only took Erabus a moment to respond with the same passion and as soon as he had, Xicuz pushed him back against the platform without ever breaking contact or slowing down. Slipping his hand behind his neck, Xicuz pulled him even closer as his free hand slipped underneath the hem of his tunic and traced circles over his ribs. Erabus shivered against his touch and moaned into the kiss.

"Erabus," Xicuz moaned before nibbling on his bottom lip and slipping his tongue into his warm mouth when Erabus opened it to gasp. His touch became frenzied as he lifted Erabus up, so he sat on the platform and wrapped his legs around his waist. Erabus moaned, the sound vibrating against his lips, and Xicuz hardened in anticipation. Running his hands up his thighs, he felt that Erabus was in the same position and moved to close his hand around his manhood through his pants when someone cleared their voice behind him.

Growling in annoyance at the interruption, not missing the moan that escaped Erabus as the sound turned him on even more, Xicuz broke the kiss as he turned to glare over his shoulder. Standing in the doorway leading out of the throne room was the four guards who led Erabus into the room for the coronation. *Have they been there the whole time?* Xicuz wondered, but soon decided it didn't matter; it wasn't as though their relationship remained a secret anymore.

"Forgive me for the interruption, King Erabus, but the Eminence of Virtue is already making his way back down the hall, looking for you, and I did not think you would wish for him to walk in on you," one of the guards pointed out and Xicuz fought the urge to point out that it didn't make a difference who interrupted them as it ended the same either way. Holding Erabus's gaze with hungry eyes, his promise of what was to come shining in his silver orbs, Xicuz planted one last chaste kiss on his lips before stepping back.

"We should go," Erabus agreed, his voice a tad huskier than usual, before drawing a deep breath and hopping down from the platform. "We have nothing but time, my love," he promised as his fingertip caressed his cheek before Erabus took his hand once more and began leading him toward the guards. As much as he wanted to have him all to himself right that minute, Xicuz reluctantly agreed to share him for now. Tonight, however, Xicuz pitied anyone foolish enough to get between them.

*

There was already so much going on when they stepped out into the sunlight from the dimly lit hallway and all eyes turned toward their new king; every man, woman, and child bowed at different degrees, and Xicuz wondered if there were a reason for that. If the depth of their bows signifies their loyalty to their king, or if it was what each of them were comfortable with.

Making a mental note to ask Erabus about it later, Xicuz turned his attention back to him and found he could not take his eyes off him, even for a moment. He seemed to radiate a warm, enchanting light that caused his breath to hitch and his heart to beat faster. To anyone else, it was obvious the bright sunlight caused a halo around him, but to Xicuz it was so much more.

As though a light guided him, telling him that this was it. This was what Xicuz was meant to do, who he was meant to be with. That he would stand beside this man until his last day, would love him until his very last breath and even though, by right, Xicuz should have been frightened by such a strong and sudden feeling, all Xicuz felt was a welcome warmth spreading through his entire body.

Realizing Erabus stared at him in silence, holding out his hand for him, Xicuz shook his head in embarrassment before accepting his hand and allowing him to guide them around the festivities. There was all manner of ways to celebrate the coronation that day, including no less than three long banquet tables filled with far more food than Xicuz could name, let alone eat. A group off to one side danced as men played instruments he had never seen.

One looked like an impossibly large bow and its player plucked away at many strings that ran along its length. Another was two different sized, elongated barrels covered in animal hides on both ends, that a man beat on while they rested between his legs. They reminded Xicuz of the drums they had back in Ebrein, but the satyrs were much larger and required a padded stick to bang on them. A third appeared to be a set of sticks that had notches carved out of them and the hands that held them pulled them back and forth against each other, making a haunting sound.

The final musician had, what seemed to be, a flat disk that he shook in his hand and each time it moved, there was a soft, *tching* sound as what was inside it made a melodic rattling. Whatever it was filled with, Xicuz figured it must have been something small and light to make such a sound. Making another note to ask Erabus about them later, Xicuz turned his attention to the next section and found another group of dancers, only instead of dancing with female partners as the first were, they seemed to be dancing with their swords.

A few yards away from them were several pairs of men sparring with swords and spears, their expressions concentrated, but not violent or aggressive. After them, far enough away to prevent accidents, was one of the three tables of food, and just past it a makeshift stage that had a group reenacting the battle between the satyrs and the humans. Erabus tensed in his hand before releasing his grip as he stomped his way over to them.

Noticing the look of fury that Xicuz knew was on his face, even if he couldn't see it himself at that angle, the group of performers stopped and turned their full attention to their king. "Find something else to perform or disperse. You will not make light of the death of so many innocent people, satyrs and human alike. I catch anyone doing something like this again and they will spend a week in the dungeon. Do I make myself clear?" Erabus demanded harshly and was answered by five nodding heads.

As he turned back, his face softened once more, and Xicuz held out his hand as Erabus had done a few minutes before. With a smile, Erabus took it and Xicuz turned his attention to their surroundings again. Past the stage, where the performers were whispering loudly to one another, trying to come up with something else to do, as they gestured toward their costumes and props, there was the second banquet table.

After the table was a group of women doing a dance Xicuz recognized as the women who became the chosen of the satyrs would often perform it after they were joined with their chosen in their own ceremony. As he smiled at the thought of a handfasting with Erabus, Xicuz couldn't help but wonder what the humans' version was. Surely there had to be more than claiming him in front of the others, but none of the women ever requested to perform their own ceremony before joining.

Or, if they had, Xicuz wasn't privileged to it. Two more notes to add to his ever-growing list of things to ask Erabus later. The dance itself comprised of slow, gentle movements that seemed to take their entire body at once to perform and it was not meant to entice their chosen, though he supposed it was possible to do so anyway with such a beautiful a dance, but to bless their union.

Though Xicuz saw it numerous times before, it had always been one woman at a time, but now there were a good six or seven dancing in perfect harmony and Xicuz couldn't help but be mesmerized by their movements, wondering if this was how the other satyrs usually felt upon seeing them dance. Then he wondered what it would look like if Erabus performed the dance, and what the chances of him being willing to were.

Past the dancers was some sort of strength competition that had men lifting rocks of increasing size over their heads and dropping them back to the ground after the man, who seemed to be in charge, counted to five. As much as he hated the idea of letting go of his hand for even a moment, Xicuz had to admit it might be a good way to get more of them to like him, as opposed to just tolerating him.

Giving Erabus's hand a quick kiss, Xicuz bowed his head to him before releasing him and making his way over to the smallest rock, which was about the size of his fist. "May anyone join?" Xicuz inquired of the man in charge, who seemed to stare at him in confusion for a moment before enthusiastically nodding and gesturing for him to lift the first rock.

"You must hold it above your head for five seconds and make sure not to drop it on your toes...err hooves," the man corrected, looking more than a little embarrassed, "when you are finished." Smiling at him in reassurance that he didn't take offense to the slip, Xicuz picked up the first rock and held it above his head as though it weighed nothing.

After counting, he gestured toward the next rock and Xicuz tossed the first back to the ground. As he went through the same motions with the second, this one the size of his two fists together, Xicuz saw the man before him having issues lifting the second to last rock, or boulder was more accurate. He got it about midway with a lot of grunting and straining, but eventually gave up and let it drop back to the ground, jumping back so it wouldn't land on his foot.

Glancing at the man from the corner of his eye as he lifted the second rock, he could tell that strength, or lack thereof, had not been his problem. He was well built and muscular. The rock must have been even heavier than it looked, which was already a lot. It appeared to be the same size as a man in a curled position and apparently more than the weight of one.

Turning to the third rock, Xicuz lifted that one even as he questioned, "Has anyone lifted the last rock?" The man in front of him faltered in his counting for a moment, startled by his question, before shaking his head and informing him that he could drop the one he held now.

"No one has ever lifted the second to last to even get to the final challenge. We have done this challenge many times and never a winner. Think you have what it takes to change that?" the man prompted, raising his voice with more confidence than shown before. It only took Xicuz a moment to realize the reason why; a crowd gathered around them. Smirking, he tossed his current rock down, this one the size of a large rabbit, though a bit heavier than one, and moved on to the next.

After that one, there was only two left. His next rock, the fourth in line, appeared to be about the same size as a boar, and Xicuz wasn't surprised to find it weighed about the same. This one took a little effort, but he still easily raised it above his head and tossed it back to the ground after the required five seconds passed. "If you can lift this one, you will be our winner today, though if you are strong enough to lift the final challenge, there will be a special prize for you as well," he informed Xicuz. He wondered if it were something he could give to Erabus in honor of their union.

If Erabus gave him some kind of warning, Xicuz could have hunted the elusive buck near their home and presented it to him. Turning back to the rock before him, Xicuz crouched down and grunted as he slowly lifted the rock. It was even heavier than anticipated.

Digging his hooves into the dirt, Xicuz grunted as he forced his arms above his head and held them outstretched and shaky as the man counted the lengthiest five seconds he ever witnessed. The instant he hit five, Xicuz tossed the rock back down and jumped back to prevent it from landing on his hooves as the man warned.

The crowd that gathered erupted into cheers, including the man who was only able to lift the rock to his waist, and Xicuz wanted to join in the celebration, but his arms were too weak and tired from the exertion.

"Well done, King Consort. I hereby crown you today's champion!" the game master called out even as he waved another man over. Turning his attention to him, Xicuz realized that he carried a large, open basket in his hands, filled with an assortment of goodies. A bit of silky looking fabric, a whetting stone shaped like a sheath—though from there Xicuz could not tell if it was hollow like one— small, glossy baked goods that were in a smaller basket, and a bit of dark fur, probably enough to fashion a pair of boots.

"Each time we host this challenge, we add another prize. The rock you just lifted takes at least two men to carry it out," he explained, and though Xicuz wasn't surprised to learn that, his mind was preoccupied wondering about the final rock to register what he said. "If you are able to lift this one," he continued as he gestured toward the impossibly large rock, standing nearly as tall as Xicuz was, "you will win your own crown and get to be king for a day."

Curious, Xicuz turned back to Erabus who nodded at him with a smile. "It is a tradition. Or at least it would be if anyone ever got this far. Though there are certain rules to follow, such as no changing any laws, the one who beats the final challenge will be able to sit in my throne and rule over Edith for a full twenty-four hours. So, I guess that would make me King Consort for a day," Erabus teased with a flirty smirk and Xicuz decided to rise to the challenge.

Turning back to the rock, Xicuz walked around it for a moment, debating if he would be able to at least try without hurting himself. Judging by the shape and size, Xicuz estimated it weighed about three times as much as the previous rock. Perhaps if it were only twice as much, he would be able to lift it all the way into the air, but Xicuz figured he would be lucky to even lift it off the ground.

But Xicuz couldn't give up without even trying. *You only fail if you do not try*, he reminded himself, using the same quote his father often used on Heoltos and him when they were younger and starting to learn how to hunt and fight. Raising his arms up above his head, Xicuz turned his attention to the crowd gathered around him and soon had them worked up into a cheering frenzy.

Turning his attention back to the impossible task before him, Xicuz took a deep breath, glanced over his shoulder at Erabus for a moment and then crouched down beside the boulder. Wrapping his arms around it as best as he could, as it stood much longer than his actual wingspan, Xicuz dug his hands under the base and drew one more deep breath. All around him the crowd went silent, and he smirked to himself.

Perhaps the extra bit of confidence their attention gave him would be able to give him a little more strength. Exhaling, Xicuz grunted as he used every last ounce of strength, to lift the boulder off the ground and sent it flying over his shoulder as it raised without any resistance. Startled and confused, Xicuz could only glance around at the others as they realized what happened and started laughing.

"All hail King Xicuz!" Erabus called out cheerfully, and Xicuz spun around to find him hidden behind the large boulder he held as if it weighed nothing. Which it pretty much did. His mouth gaping like a fish, he could only stand there trying in vain to question what happened and Erabus dropped the boulder before laughing at his expression.

"It's a hollow, man-made, 'boulder' made from cloth and a sticky paste of water and flour. We have been waiting for a long time to prank someone with it, but no one ever got this far before. Only my father, Herveus here, and I knew the truth. Next time we have a festival, we will have to find something else to add the end to the challenge since everyone now knows the truth." Xicuz rolled his eyes at Erabus's gleeful expression and turned his attention back to the practically weightless boulder.

Lifting it effortlessly, as he had with the first rock, Xicuz turned it around in his hands a bit. Though it was hard to maneuver due to its size, Xicuz doubted his arms would ever grow tired no matter how long he held it. Or, at least, he would become bored before they grew tired. "So, where's my crown?" Xicuz joked as he turned toward Herveus, who was already instructing others to set the rocks back up in case anyone else wanted to try even though the prize had already been won.

"It will be brought to you first thing in the morning as your twenty-four hours starts then. It gives us the chance to set up anything we need to prepare for you, such as foods you might want or activities you might want to see or do." Nodding in understanding, Xicuz turned back to Erabus and found him holding out his hand to him. Bidding Herveus a good day, Xicuz took Erabus's offered hand and allowed him to lead him around the festivities again.

"I don't know about you, but I worked up quite the appetite watching you lift all those rocks," Erabus admitted so casually that Xicuz could only stare at him in shocked silence as he tried to determine if he realized how his words sounded. After a few moments, Xicuz decided either he hadn't, or Erabus had become quite adept at hiding what he was thinking. Eventually he decided it didn't really matter as he was going to make sure Erabus knew exactly what his words brought to Xicuz's mind. .

"So did I, though, unfortunately, they are not serving what I wish to devour," Xicuz teased, his voice taking on a huskier, deeper tone than usual. Erabus stopped short and tensed in his hand, though judging by the blush that rose to his cheeks, he could tell it was a good kind of tensing. Taking advantage of their momentary pause, Xicuz leaned down to whisper beside his ear, "The moment we are alone, I shall devour you, my king. Over and over until your throat is hoarse from screaming out your pleasure and you are too weak to stand.

"Then tomorrow, my first act as king will be to embrace my consort in a bout of lovemaking that is so passionate you will never wish to leave my bed again." Xicuz felt Erabus's hand start to sweat at his words, felt his pulse beating faster and faster. His eyes closed and his face flared bright red and Xicuz smirked even as others looked at them, trying to figure out what was going on.

"You have no idea what you do to me," Erabus whispered without opening his eyes, his voice higher than usual. Smirking once more to himself, Xicuz leaned so close to his ear Erabus would feel his hot breath fanning over the sensitive appendage with each word he whispered.

"But I do, as it is the same as you do to me, my love. I do know what I do to you." Xicuz paused to run his tongue ever so lightly across the edge of his ear, knowing his own head blocked everyone's view of what he was doing, smirking in satisfaction at his sudden inhale, the noise sounding like a hiss. "And I know what I am going to do to you." Xicuz felt the shiver of anticipation that coursed through Erabus's entire body and stepped back before he could respond.

"But you are right, my king, we should load up on energy. We'll need it."

"Xicuz," Erabus warned and Xicuz loved how husky his voice sounded at that moment, as though all the lust and arousal he felt transferred to his voice. Smirking at him, Xicuz turned away and began making his way over to the first table of food. Everything looked rather appetizing, though he didn't know what most of it was.

There were many types of meat, but with the way they were cooked up, many dishes with white and green vegetables, covered in a rather dark broth or a creamy, brown gravy, it was impossible to tell what was what. They did, however, smell delicious, whatever they were. Besides the meat dishes, there were plate after plate piled high with vegetables of every imaginable color.

Some looked as though they were intentionally placed directly in the flames while cooking. Others were sliced thinly and drenched in something that looked like honey. Still others were steamy, brothy soups with large chunks peeking over the top of the liquid. Beside the meat and vegetable platters were a few baskets of different types of bread. They were the one constant Xicuz saw on all the tables when he wandered around before.

Bread. There was bread, cut up into thin slices and spread out in intricate patterns, along with the seemingly endless supply of fruits and cheeses on the table to their left. The fruits Xicuz could at least tell what they were and recognized many of them from the forest that separated their villages. On the table to their right, there were many types of sweet bread, covered in honey or delicate pink flowers.

Others were sprinkled with a dark brown spice he didn't recognize. Along with those, the table was covered entirely with every imaginable sweet and sticky baked goods he could imagine. Xicuz couldn't wait to try as many of the new dishes as he possibly could, but first, he would need to store up some energy for the long night to come. Smiling to himself, Xicuz grabbed a wooden plate and began piling on the meat.

*

Though it was already sometime in the early evening, the party showed no signs of slowing down. Xicuz, however, grew tired of having to share Erabus with the entire village of Edith and decided, now that it grew dark, they had had enough of their new king. Now it was his turn to be with his chosen, whether they liked it or not.

The thought of any of them protesting brought a slight smile to his lips as Xicuz would love to see anyone foolish enough to get between them after he waited all day long to be with him when his fingers had been itching to touch every inch of his flesh ever since he saw him walk into the throne room that morning. Longer in fact. Xicuz had been counting the seconds before he could hold him again since they woke up in their home for the last time and made their way back to their respective villages.

Now, however, Xicuz was done being polite. Now Erabus was his, as he was Erabus's. He knew his chosen felt the same way he had all night; he saw the looks Erabus sent him out of the corner of his eye. Xicuz felt his hand on his thigh, the unconscious action sending a shiver of anticipation through his entire body and causing him to bite his lip to prevent himself from moaning out loud at the thought of how close his hand was to the junction between his thighs.

As they made their rounds once again, Xicuz had long lost count of how many times Erabus walked the length of the village to check in with his people, Xicuz decided it was now or possibly not at all that night. If he allowed Erabus to get distracted again with one mundane conversation or another, it could be hours before Xicuz got the chance to get him away from the crowd again.

Making their way through the outside of the party area, Erabus stopping to shake hands or share a few words with any, and everyone, who came up to him, Xicuz couldn't help but notice they were getting rather close to the building he knew Erabus's chamber was in. Glancing around and finding a slight ebb in those seeking his attention, Xicuz smiled to himself as he tightened his grip on Erabus's hand and pulled him through the door as they were passing it.

Slamming the door behind him, grinning at Erabus's startled gasp, Xicuz pushed him up against the closed door before leaning in to breathe in the enticing scent he missed for far too long. "What are you doing, Xicuz?" Erabus questioned, a tremble in his voice as Xicuz rubbed his nose against the pulse at his neck. Instead of answering, Xicuz stared into his eyes for a brief pause before licking his lips and crashing them down on Erabus's.

As Erabus moaned into the kiss and responded with the same passion as Xicuz, he nibbled on his lip before releasing him with a cocky smirk. Keeping his eyes trained on Erabus's curious green ones, Xicuz dropped to his knees and cupped his manhood through his pants before he knew what was about to happen. The groan that came from Erabus's clenched teeth spurred him on and Xicuz licked his lips once more in anticipation for what was to come.

Giving him one more gentle squeeze, Xicuz released his hold to loosen his pants, allowing them to drop to his ankles. "Xicuz," Erabus moaned from above him even as Xicuz reached his hand out once more and ran the pad of his thumb across the tip, causing a bead of his nectar to seep from his already hardening member. Watching Erabus worry his bottom lip, half tempted to rise once more so he could be the one to do so, Xicuz dragged his tongue across the tip, licking him clean.

As Erabus hissed through his teeth, fisting handfuls of Xicuz's hair as he tried to keep himself steady, Xicuz wasted no time in slipping his mouth around him and sheathing him to the base. Erabus groaned out something that sounded like his name before it was drawn out into a louder moan when Xicuz moved his mouth against him. Wrapping his fingers around the base, he moved his hand in time with his lips, causing Erabus to lean back against the door for support as he moaned out unintelligible sounds.

Grinning around his shaft, Xicuz picked up his pace and pressure, loving the way his fingers felt gliding along the silky skin and the moans coming from the man above him. Using his free hand, he caressed his way up his thigh and to his ass, kneading the flesh as his own manhood bucked in anticipation of what would come next.

"Xicuz," Erabus moaned above him, his tone clearly warning he grew close and Xicuz couldn't help but smirk to himself at how easily he could bring him to completion. Undoubtedly it meant Erabus had not touched himself in their time apart. He saved himself for this moment and Xicuz wasn't going to disappoint his patience. Increasing his pressure once more, he pulled him over the edge.

*

Banging his head back against the door behind him, Erabus moaned loud enough for the people outside to hear him as he found his release. His hands were still fisted in Xicuz's hair; his fingers clenched tighter as he rode the wave of pleasure that washed through his entire body. It took every ounce of willpower not to collapse into a pile on the floor. Growling at him, Erabus reached down and grabbed a hold of his beard, pulling him back up with it.

Continuing to pull him until Xicuz was level with him, Erabus attacked his lips even as he pushed him backward down the hall, kicking off his pants. As they moved, Xicuz returned the kiss with the same passion, their rhythm uninterrupted by their bumping into the walls. Realizing they were near his bedroom door, Erabus pushed Xicuz against the wall behind him, breaking their connection.

Licking his lips as he stepped back to survey the man in front of him, Erabus bit his lower lip and panted. "Do you have any idea how much I want you right now?" Erabus demanded, growling when Xicuz responded with that arrogant smirk of his and his knees grew weak at the sight of it. Before he had the chance to point out that it wasn't an answer, Xicuz lifted him into his arms and flipped them around so Erabus was pinned against the wall instead of him.

"I know exactly how much you want me, my love, for it is the same as I want you. But no more talk. There are far more enjoyable things we can be doing with those lips of yours," Xicuz teased and Erabus laughed before squeaking in surprise a moment later when he rushed them to the bedroom door and opened it without releasing him. Erabus closed the door behind them and attacked his neck with his lips, his teeth, and his tongue, causing him to moan beneath him.

Erabus reached his hand down between them and kneaded his manhood causing Xicuz's step to falter. Erabus tapped his arm to let Xicuz know to release him. As he kissed and nibbled his way down his chest, Erabus never paused his ministrations, even as he turned Xicuz so he faced away from his bed. It wasn't until Xicuz stood right where he wanted him that Erabus finally released his hold and pushed him onto the bed before he could realize what was happening.

Erabus climbed up beside him and pushed his loincloth out of the way and licked his shaft from base to tip, causing Xicuz to moan low and deep. The sound had him hardening again, and Erabus licked his tongue across the tip of his member a few times before sucking the head into his mouth, rolling his tongue around it as he caught Xicuz's gaze. His silver eyes were beginning to roll back in his head even as he fought to retain the contact.

Allowing more of him into his mouth, Erabus created a hard suction before pulling back out so he could tease the tip more. "Erabus," Xicuz moaned, his hands fisting in the sheets as he repeated his actions, moving slowly to drive him crazy. Deciding he suffered enough when his member pulsed and seemed to heat up in his hand, Erabus picked up the tempo and soon Xicuz was writhing beneath him.

Digging his nails gently into his inner thigh with his free hand, Erabus soon sent him over the edge and felt him release into his mouth as Xicuz groaned out his name once more. Licking his lips clean, Erabus turned back to Xicuz and found him staring at him with heated silver eyes that seemed to glow in the dim light. Laughing as Xicuz growled and pulled him down onto the bed beside him, Erabus could only stare up at him as his heart pounded in his chest.

There was something about the way Xicuz looked at him, the animalistic way his need and want of him reflected in his eyes. Lifting his legs up onto his hips, Erabus nodded ever so gently to Xicuz, who seemed to be waiting for his permission, and sucked on his bottom lip as he slowly pushed his tip inside him. Xicuz buried himself to the base and waited until Erabus wiggled beneath him, his sign to continue, before doing so.

He pulled out, to the tip, dragging a long, husky moan from Erabus's lips before thrusting into him again. Meeting him thrust for thrust, as best as he could in that position, Erabus grabbed a hold of his beard once more and pulled him down to his lips. Soon he moaned into the kiss as Xicuz moved faster, each thrust reaching deeper within him until Erabus had to give up on trying to keep up and just enjoyed the ride.

"Pleasure yourself, my king," Xicuz whispered in a deeper voice than usual, his lips beside Erabus's ear, before he licked his way down to his neck. Shivering as the trail left gooseflesh in his wake, Erabus ran his fingers down Xicuz's stomach as he reached his hand between their hot, sweaty bodies and wrapped them around his hardening member. Beginning to stroke himself from base to tip, Erabus fell into pace with Xicuz's thrusts and soon alternated between moaning and biting his bottom lip to prevent himself from doing so.

Feeling himself drawing closer to release once more, Erabus pulled Xicuz down for another kiss. Before it could go on for long, Erabus threw his head back and screamed out his pleasure. A few more thrusts and Xicuz joined him in his release, collapsing onto the bed beside him as he came down from his high. As Erabus panted, his entire body seeming to tingle in the aftermath, Xicuz rolled over and drew him into his arms, burying his nose in Erabus's neck.

Though tempted to ask Xicuz if he was smelling him, wondering if he had an advanced sense of smell along with his hearing, Erabus decided the answer wasn't worth breaking the peace that fell over them. Xicuz was comfortable, and he refused to interrupt them for such an unimportant question.

After a few minutes passed, Xicuz drew a deep breath before rising to rest his head on his hand, propping himself up with his elbow, to gaze down at him. He placed a gentle kiss on his brow and returned to his propped-up position. "Promise me, my love, that we will be together forever. I could not live without you by my side," Xicuz admitted as he stared down at him with love and perhaps, a bit of sorrow in his voice.

Rolling over and pushing Xicuz onto the bed so he could lay across his chest, Erabus cupped his cheeks as he closed his eyes and pressed his forehead against his. "There is not a man alive, my dearest Xicuz, who could ever keep us apart," Erabus swore with conviction before opening his eyes as he leaned back to gaze into his endless silver orbs. "And any who were foolish enough to try, would soon find themselves regretting that decision. I shall be by your side forever, my love. This I vow."

Epilogue

The day Erabus had been dreading for most of his life finally arrived, but he discovered, after waking that morning and finding Xicuz's still, lifeless body beside him in the bed they shared for more years than he could count, losing him didn't devastate him in the way he always expected it to. Erabus was in pain, felt as though he could barely breathe, but his death didn't kill him as anticipated.

Certain it was due to two factors, that they shared a lifetime of love and passion and that he would be joining him soon, Erabus found the strength to smile down at the man he knew for far longer than he had been without him and kissed his lips, whispering his final goodbye to the love of his life. "I will join you soon, my love, my life," Erabus promised before laying his head upon his chest, listening for a heartbeat he would never hear again.

Somehow, Erabus managed to go on with the day, dealing with everything that needed to be done after a member of the royal family passed. Xicuz was buried in the royal tomb as members from both clans came to pay their respects and say their final farewells. To comment on how amazing he had been, but Erabus didn't need them to tell him that. He had known the depth of his heart and his soul for over seventy years.

Their wonderful journey together was not dimmed by his passing, their bond not weakened by his death, as it was only another beginning. Erabus would find him again in his next life, of this he would make certain no matter what obstacle tried to get in their way. Theirs was not a love meant to be confined to one lifetime, but an endless cycle of rebirth to find each other and love each other over and over until the end of time.

He knew that the day of the coronation and each passing year only convinced him even more so of their truth; they were meant to be together forever just as they promised. And they would be one day. Hopefully soon. Making his way back into their room, even as the celebration of his life continued outside, Erabus crawled onto his side of the bed and wept into his pillow.

Erabus hadn't realized he had fallen asleep until he felt a presence behind him and was jolted awake by its sudden arrival. Wiping the sleep and tear tracks from his face, Erabus sat up and turned his attention to the man standing at the edge of the bed. At first, he thought Xicuz had returned to him, young as he was when they first met, but as Erabus blinked his eyes in disbelief, the appearance of the man in front of him became clearer.

He had long, midnight black hair and stood well over six feet tall. His muscular form was clothed in a loincloth and a bear fur vest that was clasped down the front with bone fasteners. "Ith'tar," Erabus whispered in realization before climbing down off the bed and stepping toward him in unveiled fascination. Ith'tar looked exactly as he had the last time Erabus saw him, many decades ago.

He supposed it made sense, though Erabus never thought about it before then, that the devils didn't age. After all, how could they be around to collect on all their bargains if they aged like those they made the deals with. "I knew you would be here soon," he greeted with a soft sigh, smiling to himself despite the situation. "I cannot live without Xicuz. My death is imminent, isn't it?"

There was no fear or sorrow in his voice, just acceptance of what was to come. His next life with Xicuz couldn't begin, anyway, until this one had run its course. "You are correct, Erabus. I am here to collect your end of the bargain," Ith'tar confirmed as he stepped closer until there was only a foot or two separating them. As with every other time they met, Erabus did not fear the devil standing before him.

He allowed him to save the love of his life and even if they had been cursed for the rest of their days to never see each other again, it would have been worth it. All that ever mattered was keeping Xicuz safe and because of the bargain Erabus struck with Ith'tar, and the curse being broken once Jydral died, he was able to spend a very long life loved and in love with the greatest man he had ever known.

"If I may ask, Ith'tar, who do you plan to make king in my stead?" Erabus couldn't help but wonder, a question at the back of his mind since he first made the deal with him, and which the elders repeatedly asked him about throughout the years. Who would be king after Erabus passed on? With Erabus never having any children his direct family line would end with him, but he did not want to leave this life without at least knowing who would be taking up the torch after him.

"You," Ith'tar informed him, causing Erabus to nearly take a step back in his confusion. How could he possibly be the next king? Erabus couldn't understand, he was dying, rather soon if his presence was any indication. "In this life, Erabus, yes you are dying, but you will be reborn soon to become king once more."

"I do not want to be born to be king again, Ith'tar. I want to be free to search for him in our next life. Please do not make me go through a long life without him by my side," Erabus pleaded, not wanting to break his word, but also unable to imagine a world that did not have Xicuz in it. Instead of answering his plea, Ith'tar stepped closer to him, causing him to back up until his knees hit the bed behind him.

Leaning forward, he stared deep into his eyes, so far that Erabus saw not only his own reflection, but something else even deeper than that. It wasn't an image staring back at him, more of a feeling, a presence he sensed hidden deep within Ith'tar. "You're Xicuz," Erabus mumbled in disbelief, half thinking his grief played tricks on his mind, but also convinced it was his presence he felt while staring deep into his eyes.

"Xicuz was one of my reincarnations," Ith'tar "explained" in a way that gave Erabus more questions than answers.

"How is it possible for you to have a reincarnation when you are still alive?" Erabus inquired, deciding that was the most pertinent question to start with.

Ith'tar held his confused gaze for a few moments before finally giving him the briefest of smiles. "What makes you sure that I am?" The silence hung heavy between them and Erabus wondered if Ith'tar wanted a response, but eventually he spoke again, answering his question and giving him so many more. "Many centuries ago, when I was but a young man, I met the love of my life—your first incarnation.

"We were happy, as you and Xicuz were, but we were not graced with the long, blessed life that you two shared. You were able to save your love from death, but I was not.

In my grief, I called out to a bargaining devil, pleaded with him to bring my love back to me, but alas, even we cannot raise the dead. So, I did, instead, what you are wishing to do now, Erabus; I made a deal for us to be together in each and every life from that day forward.

"In payment, the devil requested the use of my soul as a bargaining devil. He took but a small piece, just enough to keep this body animated long after I should have been dead, and the rest is reborn in my reincarnations, such as Xicuz. I do not know if the devil did so intentionally, or if it was how things were always meant to play out between our two souls, or perhaps if it is because my reincarnations are missing a piece of my soul, but in each of our rebirths, you end up needing to make a deal with me to save you both.

"It is why Jydral could not use your life as payment, you are fated to ask me in every life for a deal and you could not die before then. Though, I must admit, this was the first time anyone else's deal interfered with your lives. It was why I had to curse you. I could not undo Jydral's deal, but I knew if you two survived long enough things could get back on track for the lives you were meant to have with each other and did." As Ith'tar fell silent, Erabus tried in vain to wrap his mind around everything he told him.

Erabus doubted he would ever understand it, even if he had years left to process it. "Is it guaranteed that I will meet him in the next life, in each life?"

"You are fated to, my love," Ith'tar said, his voice sounding so much like Xicuz in that moment it sent a shiver down his spine. Reaching up to caress his cheek, the devil sighed deeply, a sudden sadness to his eyes that Erabus had not expected to see, though in truth he probably should have with the story Ith'tar told him. "I am the only one destined to be without you.

"Only this small sliver of a soul is left in the cold as my reincarnations are the ones who get to be with you." Waving his hand over Erabus's face before he could respond to his words, not that he had the foggiest idea of what to say to a confession like that, he felt his body tingle all over. In the mirror behind Ith'tar, Erabus saw the face of a much younger man staring back at him.

It was not the face from his youth, not exactly, but it was close enough that Erabus knew whose eyes were staring back at him, even if he didn't have a name for them. Even as he realized it was his first incarnation staring back at him with the same deep, green eyes, Ith'tar pressed his lips against his in a soft, unhurried kiss. He responded to the kiss, but it was no longer Erabus in control of his body.

He felt as though he watched his body from above as another kissed Ith'tar as passionately as Erabus kissed Xicuz and smiled down at their reunion, no matter how short it would prove to be. As Ith'tar pulled back, breaking the connection between them, he saw the devastation in his eyes and knew their time was up. "Until our next life, my eternal," Ith'tar whispered as he leaned forward, catching Erabus as he felt himself slipping away; ready to find the love of his life once again.

I'm coming, my love.

About the Author

Hairann is the author of the Outlaw Seven series and Damned if you don't. She is an out and proud Pan who lives with her amazing family in Montreal. She's worked as a ghost-writer on Fiverr since 2018 and has ghost-written over fifty stories. She has an Associates degree in Early Childhood Education. She invites you to follow @AuthorHairann on Twitter.

Email: Hairanntheauthor@hotmail.com

Facebook: www.facebook.com/HairannTheAuthor

Twitter: @AuthorHairann

Other NineStar books by this author

The Midnight Twelve

Also Available from NineStar Press

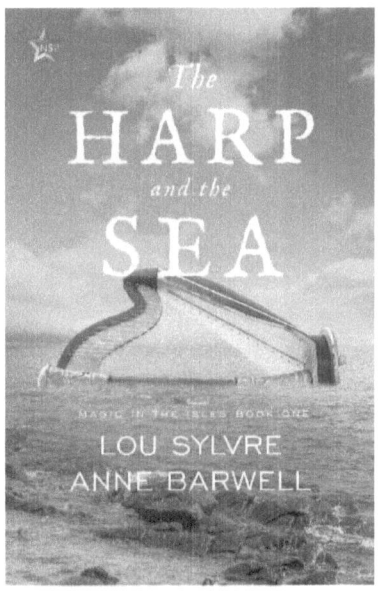

Connect with NineStar Press

www.ninestarpress.com

www.facebook.com/ninestarpress

www.facebook.com/groups/NineStarNiche

www.twitter.com/ninestarpress